W9-AEG-570

PRAISE FOR TERRI BLACKSTOCK

"Crisp dialogue and unexpected twists make this compulsive reading, and a final chapter cliffhanger leaves things poised for a sequel."

—*Publishers Weekly* on *If I Run*

"A fast-paced, thoroughly mesmerizing thriller, *If I Run* offers distinct Christian undertones. Though not preachy, this layering adds to the complexity of this suspenseful novel. An enthralling read with an entirely unexpected conclusion makes the reader question if a sequel could be in the works."

—*NY Journal of Books*

"Few writers do mystery/suspense better than Terri Blackstock, so I leaped at the opportunity to read her latest *If I Run* . . . Needless to say, when Book Two comes out, there will be no 'if' about it. I'll run to get in line."

—*Love & Faith in Fiction*

"*If I Run* is a gripping suspense novel. Both of the central characters are very appealing, engaging the reader . . . The tension is palpable throughout and doesn't let up until the very end . . . highly recommended."

—*Mysterious Reviews*

"Blackstock's newest novel, *If I Run*, is the best suspense novel I've read in decades. Boiling with secrets, nail-biting suspense, and exquisitely developed characters, it's a story that grabs hold and never lets go. Read this one. Run to get it! It's that good."

—Colleen Coble, *USA Today* bestselling author of *Mermaid Moon* and the Hope Beach series

"The exciting and heart-pounding conclusion to Blackstock's Moonlighters trilogy is quite a thrill ride. The intrigue and danger come to a dramatic culmination as the villain gets backed into a corner."

—*Romantic Times* on *Twisted Innocence*

"Blackstock fans will be drawn to this third novel in the Moonlighters series with its themes of forgiveness and second chances. While being able to be read as standalone fiction, readers will enjoy a richer character understanding having read the previous books."

"The second book in Blackstock's Moonlighters series starts off with a frightening incident and is filled with action from that point forward. A multilayered story of deception, greed, and secrets unravels at a perfect pace to keep readers interested and entertained."

"Blackstock has such a way with characters that they can get away with almost anything—like being part of a family with an unreasonably high body count—and still manage to be believable. Distortion is a good suspense novel but more than that it brings up a number of attitudes and actions that will have readers examining their own thought patterns and values."

"Crisp prose, an engaging story, and brisk pacing make this thriller another home run for Blackstock. Recommend it to readers who enjoy material by Lynette Eason and Erin Healy."

"A story rich with texture and suspense, this family murder mystery unfolds with fast pacing, a creepy clown murder suspect, and threatening blog visitor to boot."

"The Restoration series comes to a dramatic end. Blackstock is absolutely masterful at bringing spiritual dilemmas to the surface and allowing readers to wrestle with them alongside her characters. This is a fitting conclusion to this unique series."

"Good writing, well-honed descriptive details, compelling characters, and a conclusion that doesn't succumb to pat answers keep the pages turning, making this an engaging novel for fans of Christian nail-biters."

"Blackstock's superior writing will keep readers turning pages late into the night to discover the identity of the culprit in this amazing mystery. The unique setting and peek into the Nashville music scene are fascinating. Suspense lovers are in for a delightful treat."

—*RT Book Reviews*, 4¹/2-star review, TOP PICK! on *Double Minds*, 2009 Nomination for Best Inspirational Novel

"Drawn in from the first line, my heart ached for Kara, Lizzie, and their moving story. The satisfying end didn't stop the lingering sadness, as there's so much more to this novel than just the life of two little girls and the wounds that should never have been. Ms. Blackstock tactfully and skillfully deals with the undesirable traits of her characters (promiscuity and subsequent abortion, which are briefly mentioned). The book is so well written it is hard to believe it's just fiction!"

—*RT Book Reviews*, 4-star review of *Covenant Child*

"In a departure from her usual heart-stopping mysteries, Blackstock delves into the world of a con man who meets his match. This fast-paced novel doesn't provide any astounding twists, but the story is incredibly well told and will keep the reader fascinated until the last page."

—*RT Book Reviews*, 4-star review of *Shadow in Serenity*

IF I'M
FOUND

BOOKS BY TERRI BLACKSTOCK

IF I RUN SERIES
1 *If I Run*
2 *If I'm Found*
3 *If I Live* (coming March 2018)

THE MOONLIGHTERS SERIES
1 *Truth Stained Lies*
2 *Distortion*
3 *Twisted Innocence*

THE RESTORATION SERIES
1 *Last Light*
2 *Night Light*
3 *True Light*
4 *Dawn's Light*

THE INTERVENTION SERIES
1 *Intervention*
2 *Vicious Cycle*
3 *Downfall*

THE CAPE REFUGE SERIES
1 *Cape Refuge*
2 *Southern Storm*
3 *River's Edge*
4 *Breaker's Reef*

NEWPOINTE 911
1 *Private Justice*
2 *Shadow of Doubt*
3 *Word of Honor*
4 *Trial by Fire*
5 *Line of Duty*

THE SUN COAST CHRONICLES
1 *Evidence of Mercy*

2 *Justifiable Means*
3 *Ulterior Motives*
4 *Presumption of Guilt*

SECOND CHANCES
1 *Never Again Good-bye*
2 *When Dreams Cross*
3 *Blind Trust*
4 *Broken Wings*

WITH BEVERLY LaHAYE
1 *Seasons Under Heaven*
2 *Showers in Season*
3 *Times and Seasons*
4 *Season of Blessing*

NOVELLAS
Seaside
The Listener (formerly
The Heart Reader)
The Heart Reader of Franklin High
The Gifted
The Gifted Sophomores

OTHER BOOKS
Shadow in Serenity
Predator
Double Minds
*Soul Restoration: Hope
for the Weary*
Emerald Windows
Miracles (The Listener / The Gifted)
Covenant Child
Sweet Delights
Chance of Loving You

IF I'M FOUND

TERRI BLACKSTOCK

New York Times Bestselling Author

 ZONDERVAN®

ZONDERVAN

If I'm Found
Copyright © 2017 by Terri Blackstock

This title is also available as a Zondervan e-book. Visit www.zondervan.com.

Requests for information should be addressed to:
Zondervan, *Grand Rapids, Michigan 49546*

Library of Congress Cataloging-in-Publication Data

Names: Blackstock, Terri, 1957- author.
Title: If I'm found / Terri Blackstock.
Description: Grand Rapids, Michigan : Zondervan, [2017] | Series: If I run ; 2
Identifiers: LCCN 2016042867 | ISBN 9780310332497 (hardback)
Subjects: | GSAFD: Suspense fiction. | Mystery fiction.
Classification: LCC PS3552.L34285 I35 2017 | DDC 813/.54--dc23 LC record available at
https://lccn.loc.gov/2016042867.

All Scripture quotations, unless otherwise indicated, are taken from the New American
Standard Bible®. Copyright © 1960, 1962, 1963, 1968, 1971, 1972, 1973, 1975, 1977, 1995 by The
Lockman Foundation. Used by permission. (www.Lockman.org)

Any Internet addresses (websites, blogs, etc.) and telephone numbers in this book are offered
as a resource. They are not intended in any way to be or imply an endorsement by Zondervan,
nor does Zondervan vouch for the content of these sites and numbers for the life of this book.

Publisher's Note: This novel is a work of fiction. Names, characters, places, and incidents are
either products of the author's imagination or used fictitiously. All characters are fictional, and
any similarity to people living or dead is purely coincidental.

Interior design: Lori Lynch

Printed in the United States of America

17 18 19 20 21 22 / RRD / 20 19 18 17 16 15 14 13 12 11 10 9 8 7 6 5 4 3 2 1

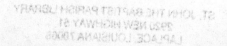

This book is lovingly dedicated to the Nazarene.

1

CASEY

The police lights in my rearview mirror almost destroy me. Only ten miles out of Shady Grove, police race through traffic behind me, sirens cycling and blaring, those blue bulbs painting terror inside my rain-drenched car. There's no place to pull over—the traffic ahead is jammed and the sides of the road drop off into ditches.

My heart fists and slams, and I break out in sweat.

But there's also the tiniest relief. Soon it will all be over— this running and hiding, this pretending to be someone else, this detachment from real life, because relationships can be so painful when you have to rip them off like wax. But as quickly as that relief comes, reality banishes it. It's my life that will be over, as soon as they turn me over to my tormentor. And then they'll start on my family.

I glance at myself in the rearview mirror. They'll identify me right away because of my injuries. My jaw is bruising and swollen, and my hand is sticky with blood. Under my torn jeans, my legs feel bruised and bloody. They won't care that I fought for my life tonight, and for someone else's. It won't matter what good I've done, because my best friend's murder scene was covered with my DNA. In their minds, I'm a cold-blooded killer. They'll say I deserve whatever happens.

As the police cars weave through traffic and move up behind me, I pull into a movie theater parking lot, knowing they'll fly in behind me and surround me, weapons drawn.

Instead, they stay on the slick road and hurry past the parking lot. Holding my breath, I turn around in my seat, staring out the wet back window, amazed, watching as they reach their destination a half mile up the road. It's a two-car wreck, and the team of police cruisers barricade it, stopping traffic.

I let out my breath as tears overtake me. So it's not over. It goes on. I'll keep running.

I wipe my eyes on my wet shirtsleeve and gather myself enough to pull my car around to the dark side of the theater. I reach for my purse and the duffel bag I stashed on the floor-board behind my seat days ago. I dig into my purse and find a concealer stick and a lipstick. I wish I had shadow and base, but they're in the apartment I can never return to.

I turn on my mirror light, smear concealer over my bruising cheek and just above my lip. I use lipstick to color my cheekbones, to try to make them look more normal.

It's not perfect, but at least it isn't immediately apparent that I've been beaten up tonight. I zip open my duffel bag and pull out my plain black baseball cap, tie up my hair in a ponytail, and pull it through the back of the cap.

I dig into my car's ashtray and find a nickel that I hope will work as a screwdriver. I slip out and walk back to the front parking lot. It's late and the last movie is over, but a handful of cars are scattered around. A rusty Buick with two flat tires is closest, so I kneel behind it—rain soaking me—and unscrew the license plate.

Then I hurry back to my car and switch mine out. Soon they'll be broadening the search for my Kia. I'll have to ditch it somewhere, but until I can get far enough out of town, this will have to do.

I find a side street and pull onto it, heading away from the traffic and the wreck. I follow the back roads, trying to head west. After an hour or so, I no longer expect to hear sirens every minute. I don't know where I am, but when you have no destination, it doesn't really matter if you get lost.

⌒

———

Hours later, I pass the Mississippi line, putting Alabama and Georgia behind me. I have to get rid of this car soon.

My jaw aches, along with my knee and my bloody shin, and fatigue pulls at me like elastic tethers. I have to get somewhere and clean myself up.

An hour or so later, I enter a seedy little town where men loiter on the corners. I detour to a different street, but nothing looks any safer. Up ahead is a motel that would struggle to get a one-star rating, but they're more likely to accept cash and not demand to see my driver's license.

The office behind a dirty glass window is thick with smoke. A man with piercings in his lip greets me.

"I need a room," I say. "I'm paying cash."

His hair hangs greasy over his sleepy eyes. He doesn't ask me anything else, just takes my money and gives me a room key.

"Are the sheets clean?" I ask.

His eyes flash to life. "Changed them this morning," he says, clearly insulted that I would ask such a thing.

I want to ask how many hourly tenants have checked in since then, but I sigh and take the key down to the room he's given me. At least it's the last room at the end, so I don't have anyone on one side of me. Maybe the other side is vacant. My car is at the other end of the parking lot, and that's where I leave it.

The room smells of cigarettes and an array of rank scents I can't name. I go in and pull back the thin bedspread. The sheets look rumpled, but they do seem clean. I slip into bed, fully clothed, trying not to think about bedbugs or mice . . . or a SWAT team with rifles.

I find the sticky remote and turn on the TV. It just has basic cable, so I flip to a news channel and watch for an hour or so to see if the national news has picked up anything about me. I don't see anything. Maybe it'll only make the news in Shady Grove.

I imagine what the media will say about me tomorrow. Will they focus on the girl who was missing and is now reunited with her family?

"Fugitive Rescues Kidnapped Girl"—that's the sensational headline Brent would have given it, to make AP and Reuters pick it up. It heralds a story no one could resist reading.

I wonder if the Shreveport police will hold Dylan accountable for my escape. He was hired to find me. Why would he let me walk away like that?

There's no other explanation but God, whom I called out to more than once in the last few days. I barely know him, but I think he must know me. As I close my eyes, I whisper, "Thank you," before I drift off to sleep.

2

DYLAN

I don't mind admitting that Casey Cox is the bravest person I've ever met, and I've known guys who've thrown themselves over grenades to protect their brothers. But I can't say that to Gordon Keegan or Sy Rollins, the police detectives who have a bull's-eye on Casey's back. To them she's a ticking bomb that has to be defused, before she blows their illegally padded lives to kingdom come.

Detective Keegan sits in my passenger seat as I drive him back to his plane—the one he probably bought with blood money—and I can feel the tension pulsing through the car. "I can't believe you let her walk away," he says.

My jaws ache as I lock down on my molars. "I was distracted by the screaming girl Cox was trying to rescue and the violent man trying to kill her and her baby. It was simple triage. I tended to the most dangerous situation first."

"But you knew it was Casey." His lips are tight, compressed, and his words are clipped. "It wasn't one or the other. You could have gotten the girl and baby out and still arrested Casey."

"In the heat of battle, things don't always go as they should."

He shoots a bullet of a look at me. "Don't give me that heat of battle dreck. I fought in Desert Storm, but I was on the front lines, not hiding behind a badge."

He knows nothing about what I did as a criminal investigator in the army, so I don't answer.

"Back then we didn't coddle our soldiers with some over-inflated excuse for putting their lives in neutral. When our guys came home, they had to work and make something of themselves."

Really? I think. There was no PTSD in Desert Storm, or Vietnam? In Korea? In the World Wars? It all started with the war on terror?

Keegan is an even bigger fool than I thought. I wonder what excuse he uses to justify his extortion and murder. Will he use those defenses in his trial, when I finally nail him for all his sins?

"I'll find her," I say. "Don't worry. I tracked her down here, didn't I? I'm starting to understand her patterns and her thought process. Every minute I spend with you is time I'm not going after her."

I get to the small airport and pull into the parking lot in front of the building. Keegan shakes his head. "Just drive out onto the tarmac. I'll show you which plane I'm in." As I pull around the building to the concrete pad, he grabs his duffel bag out of the backseat.

"Plane yours?" I ask him, scanning the twenty or so planes lined up.

He hesitates half a second, which I'm realizing is a tell. What follows is usually a lie. "Belongs to a buddy. He lets me take it now and then."

I've known lots of pilots, and those who own their own planes don't loan them out like Weed Eaters. The insurance costs a mint and doesn't extend to occasional pilots, and logging extra hours results in more expensive maintenance. But I don't call him on it.

"You ever thought of learning to fly, Dylan?"

"Took lessons when I was in college," I say. "Got my license, but I haven't flown in a few years."

He looks disappointed. I want to tell him not to take it so hard, but I stay quiet as he points the way to his Cessna 182.

As he loads his stuff into the cargo bay of the single-engine plane, I write down his tail number. He comes back to my car, leans in. "So what are you gonna do now?"

"Go after her. Keep looking."

"Naw," he says. "Just come home. I don't know if we're gonna keep you on the case. Besides, we have the attention of all the police departments in a five-state area now. National news will jump all over this, probably make her identifiable anywhere she goes. We don't need you."

I don't bother to tell him that Casey isn't stupid, that she'll change her identity again. She probably already has. "I don't work for you," I say, keeping the edge from my voice. "I work for the Paces." Brent's parents, who hired me as a PI to find the girl they're certain murdered their son, won't be any happier than Keegan that I let her get away. But if anyone's going to fire me, it'll have to be them.

"We'll see about that. Come home. Time to regroup and reevaluate."

I nod. At least if I'm meeting him in Shreveport, that's precious time that will allow Casey to get farther away. "All right. I'll start home right now. You want to meet tomorrow?"

"Yeah. Come to the department at one. That'll give me time to talk to the chief and the Paces and see where we are."

That'll give me time to talk to them too. We shake hands, because if I don't, he'll know I'm on to him. As I turn my car around, he starts his preflight checklist before the flight home.

I'll be in the car most of the night, driving back home. But as I drive, I pray for Casey, that she'll have time to get well hidden before Keegan goes after her.

It's the wee hours by the time I get home, and my apartment feels stale. The smell I noticed when I first moved in is apparent again. I guess when you're away from something for a few days, your olfactory senses sharpen and are easily offended again when you come back.

I check my fridge and my garbage disposal drain to make sure nothing is rotting there. I squirt a dollop of dishwashing soap down the drain and run the disposal for a minute, and the smell clears up, but the scent of previous tenants doesn't go away. I figure my brain will filter it out again in the next day or so.

I open the doors to my tiny balcony and step out to the rusted railing. Leaning out, I can see the parking lot where a young couple is arguing through a car window. She's threatening to leave, and he's yelling at her. When she pulls away, he curses after her. Then he storms into a downstairs apartment and slams the door.

Quiet again.

I lower into the folding lawn chair that collects pollen, and put my feet up on the plastic bin I've turned upside down to use as an ottoman. That old familiar dread thickens the air, making it hard for me to breathe. My shrink calls it depression and wants to dig deep into it.

I've told her how disappointed I am in myself, that I feel lazy and useless since coming back stateside, that I have no purpose. Funny how chasing Casey made me forget all that. I did have purpose. I was trying to find the suspected killer of my childhood friend.

Now I have another purpose.

I drop my feet and plant my elbows on my knees. Why does the thought of keeping that secret deepen the dread? I'll have to hide what I know until I can make a case that can't be ignored or swept under a rug. I don't like lying to the Paces, who've been through enough and who trust me, not only as a PI but as their longtime family friend. They expect me to bring their son's killer to justice.

I will do that. It's just that the person they're paying me to find is not his killer.

I also don't like what this will do to the Shreveport Police Department, where I hope to work someday. I admire and respect cops, always have. There are good people in law enforcement who have made a difference in my life. There are men and women who run toward gunfire and screams and explosions, when everyone else runs from them. The corrupt ones make it tough for those with courage and integrity.

I don't want to lower the Shreveport cops' morale or paint them with a broad brush. I want my approach to be surgical, taking out the men who deserve to be in prison, the ones who give cops a bad name, the ones who are dangerous. I want the force to be rid of these, and make them an example to any others who use their badges to terrorize and extort. And I want them to pay for every one of Brent's stab wounds, every lie they staged to cover up his murder, every moment that ticks by as they star in their own fiction.

But who am I to do all that? I'm damaged goods. I can't even depend fully on my brain these days.

Still, I can't back down now. Casey's life depends on it.

As my eyes close, I see her eyes, when we stood face-to-face under a streetlamp. They were miles deep, filled with words that she didn't utter, words I would have loved to hear. I would have liked to tend to her injuries, stare into that pretty face, and bask in the peace that came over me just by being close to her. I think of those words she wrote me in an email from an account she'd set up just for that purpose, written to an inbox I'd set up for the same reason.

There is real evil in this world. I've seen it up close. Hiding for the rest of my life would be an acceptable cost for avoiding that evil. If only it weren't everywhere . . .

Then she nailed me with a challenge.

Do you have the courage to go after the evil that plagues me, even if it means that the job you've been hired to do is an extension of that evil?

Here are the names. Keegan, Sy Rollins, for sure. Don't trust their close friends or Keegan's son. Keegan and Rollins are not just dirty, they are brutal. Evil sits in the Major Crimes unit, making proclamations on people like me.

———

I go back into my apartment and pull my computer out of my bag. I open it and go to that inbox, checking to see if she's contacted me again. There's nothing new, so I read back over the ones she's already written.

It pains me that Casey doesn't have God to turn to. I want that for her. Loneliness is too crushing a weight to bear alone. Jesus never promised to erase his believers' burdens, but he did vow to help carry them.

I lie down on the couch, staring up at the stained ceiling tiles, and pray for her. She doesn't have to be a follower to have God watch over her. As I pray, I feel his fondness for her. He sees in her what I see.

I wonder if she's still driving. I hope she's ditched the car by now, before Keegan's BOLO gets her pulled over. Maybe she's found a safe place to sleep. I hope she's still got cash to get her through.

I know I will find her again, and hopefully when I do, I can make it safe for her to come back and confront her accusers.

3

CASEY

knew this time would come, so for the last several weeks I've carried a bag in my trunk with some things I would need when I had to make a fast getaway. I have hair color in three shades—black, red, and platinum blonde—along with scissors, a couple of baseball caps, my cash, and some clothes. I knew when they came for me I wouldn't be able to go home. I would have to just drive away with whatever I had.

Thank God I had warning that they were closing in. I never returned to my apartment after that.

The motel bathroom is missing tiles over the tub, where

moldy Sheetrock peeks through. The vinyl flooring peels up around the base of the commode, showing more mold on the floor beneath it.

I stand in front of the mirror, trying to decide who I will be this time. My natural color is blonde. For the last few weeks I've been a brunette.

I cut my bangs first. I'll figure out the rest of it later. I'd already cut my hair to my jawline for Shady Grove, and I'm sure they have pictures of me with brown hair now. I could hack it off shorter, but that might be too predictable, and once I cut it all off there's nowhere to go from there. I leave my bangs long enough to hang in my eyes, which I know will take some getting used to. My eyes are the hardest part of me to disguise, mainly because they're almond-shaped and bigger than average. In Shady Grove I didn't wear eye makeup, because in the pictures of me that the police are circulating, I had on a little eyeliner. I don't know what to do this time. The change has to be significant—I can't just look like version one or two of me. I didn't let anyone take a picture of me in Shady Grove but, even so, they'll have security video from places I've been. Chances are, no one has a clear enough picture of me as a brunette for the media to use. They'll keep using the blonde photo.

I color my hair black, then shower and rinse it out. I don't like the look. I have the skin of a blonde, but it is what it is. By the time I have it dried, I look like a different person. Doing my eyes with a smoky, dark look, rounding my eyeliner so my eyes don't look so almond, might change my look entirely. If I can get the swelling to go down in my jaw and cover the bruising with makeup, I might not draw a second look.

I flush the clippings, then blow my hair dry and cut a little more.

Tears spring to my eyes as I work on the style, angling it slightly shorter in the back, teasing it messily at the roots. I don't know why I would cry over lost hair when I endure my lost life, but I can't seem to help myself.

When I've done all I can to change my look, I set the clock next to the bed to wake me in two hours. I'll need to get rid of my car before daybreak. I dry my tears and fall quickly into a deep sleep.

I dream of a man kicking and swinging at me, smashing pain . . . then it morphs into Brent's dead body . . . then my dad's. . . .

When the alarm goes off I fly up, terrified. Where am I? I'm shaking and my skin shines with sweat, but I remember I'm in a motel. I force myself out of bed, brush my teeth, shower again, and muss my hair a little more. I make up the bed, leaving it the way I found it, and steal quietly out to my car. I drive away without being seen, at least as far as I can tell.

Around five a.m. I find a truck stop open. Sweeping my bangs over my eyes, I go in and buy some chips and a drink and a pay-go smartphone in a plastic container, along with a card to put minutes on it. I activate it quickly and get it working. It already has a charge.

Once it's working, I use the GPS to find the closest bus

station, twenty miles away. I follow the directions there. I find it easily just as the sun begins to come up.

Should I leave my car in the parking lot here—a dead give-away that I took a bus somewhere—or park it somewhere else? I drive around the area for a while until I find a bank's parking garage. You don't have to pay until you exit the place, which I have no intention of doing. I leave my car there, hoping it will be a long time before it's sighted, then I walk back to the bus station wearing a white baseball cap, my bangs pulled low over my eyes.

The sun is up now as I get a schedule to see what's going out. I need to get back to Durant, Oklahoma, where I know I can get another driver's license and fake name. It's possible I could find a place here to get one, but the fewer people I involve, the better. Besides, I'm scared of the people I would have to encounter to get to the lawless underground in a place like this. Though the man at Pedro's Place in Durant breaks the law, he seems to have a modicum of decency. I'm not afraid of him.

It looks like I can take a bus to Dallas, then transfer to a route that goes up to Durant. I think for a moment before buying the ticket. Did Dylan find out I got a driver's license there before? Will he think of me doing that again? Will Keegan?

I don't think so. They know I went to Durant, but it's doubtful that they know everything I did there.

I think about my look. I don't like the black hair, but it's not like there are fifty colors of hair to choose from. I do a quick Google search for wigs and find several local places. As I find directions to the closest one, it occurs to me that I can't walk into any of them. Too risky. There are people—like cancer victims—who would seem natural buying a wig, but not someone like me. It might raise red flags.

I look on Google again and find an online store based in New York. The synthetic wigs look pretty good in the pictures, but again, if I wear a wig that's obviously a wig, I'll call attention to myself. I'll have to pay more for real hair.

I scroll through their product images and find long wigs with bangs in both blonde and brunette. I click Add to Cart for both of them, then go back and find a short, clean cut in strawberry blonde. I add that one too. The total comes to over a thousand dollars. How am I going to pay for it? I have the cash, but no credit card.

I call the customer service number and ask if I can send them a money order. They tell me I can, so I place the order. When they ask where I want it mailed, I hesitate again. I'm heading for Durant, so maybe they should ship it there. But I don't know which motel.

I put the phone on speaker, then thumb-navigate my way back to Google and put in "Pedro's Place, Durant, OK." Up comes the restaurant where I got my fake ID a few months ago. I give them Pedro's address. Then I tell them I want it FedExed to him as soon as they receive the payment. I'll add the cost to my money order.

I go to the post office, wearing my baseball cap and keeping my head down to avoid security cameras, and purchase a money order. Then I find a FedEx store and pay cash to overnight the money to the wig store.

Everything has to be so complicated. I have to think ahead, plan it all out, imagine what could go wrong. But I'm tired. Part of me just wants to let them find me if they're going to.

No, that's stupid. I have to hide. I can't let Keegan and his demons murder me.

I take a taxi back to the bus station. The bus is leaving at nine a.m., so I sit in the bathroom in the wheelchair stall until closer to time. I'm so tired that I can't even cry.

Finally, I get on the bus and sit near the back, right in front of the bathroom. I take the aisle seat, hoping no one will want to sit with me. I plug my earbuds into my new phone, but then I realize I don't have music on it. As the bus is boarding, I download a Pandora app, create a free account under a fake name, and find a station I like. I wish I could transfer my listening preferences from my own account. What's the point in all those thumbs-ups if I can't use them? I guess I'm destined to be someone who has her music chosen for her.

The music lulls me to sleep before the bus even takes off, and I sleep for several hours. When I wake, my soul feels blanched at the reality that the last twenty-four hours—or the last few weeks—can't be erased by waking up.

4

DYLAN

I don't understand how that girl is being credited with heroism."
Jim Pace's words come with the rasp of deep grief. "She's a
cold-blooded killer, and they're sensationalizing it and making
it sound like she saved that girl."

He backs up the video and replays the Fox News coverage of what happened in Shady Grove. Keegan and Rollins
sit across from him and Elise at Jim's square conference room
table, and the chief, the captain, and I sit at the end opposite the
TV. "That girl broke into that house," Keegan says, "not once,
but twice. She's a thief, not a savior."

I stay silent, rigid, looking down at my hands. If I defend her now, it'll all be over. They'll take me off the case and I'll have no chance of protecting her.

"Dylan, you were there," Elise says, teary-eyed. "Can't you tell the media what a horrible person she is? Can't you explain to them what she did to our boy?"

I draw in a deep, ragged breath. "I don't know that my going on TV is going to help us find her," I say. "I need to stay under the radar. If people recognize me, she could be tipped off when I get close."

"What is she, a spy?" Jim demands. "How could she evade the law this long? It's like she's been trained by the CIA or something. I don't get it. She was living there in plain sight. Going to work every day, talking to people."

"Her dad was a cop," I say. "She must've picked up a few things."

"Jim, the media in those areas weren't showing what they were showing here," Chief Gates says. "But trust me, now that it's gotten national attention, she's going to be recognized wherever she goes. Someone will turn her in."

"I don't know about that," I say. "She'll change her appearance. Probably has already."

"Still," Elise says. "She's recognizable with those eyes. That's why they're making her the story of the week. Because of how she looks."

I look at my hands again.

The chief looks like he hasn't slept in days. He rubs his

eyes. "Jim, Elise, I know it's disappointing that we were so close and she got away, but I assure you that we're going to find her."

Keegan points to me with a thumb. "*He's* the one who let her walk away. Let's face it, we don't need a PI to find her. Let Sy and me work on it. If you're willing to pay travel expenses for him, pay them for us instead and we can bring her back."

Captain Swayze, who hasn't been in the meetings until now, speaks up. "We can free them up for a few days, Chief. I say let them go."

I hold my breath, waiting to be fired.

But the chief bristles. "No. We don't have the manpower or the budget. Too many open cases here. I can't take two of my Major Crimes detectives out of the rotation."

Jim clears his throat and looks at me. I brace myself. "Truth is, Dylan found her," he says. "Nobody else did."

I seize that. "I'll find her again, and I promise you that I'll get justice for Brent."

Keegan hasn't given up. "Look, with all due respect, this guy has problems. I'm sorry to say this, Dylan, but I think what happened is that the situation triggered your PTSD."

"My PTSD is under control," I say, though I only wish that were true.

"Right. That's why the army discharged you."

That slices into me. "Honorably," I say, though I know everyone knows that.

Keegan takes another tack. "You understand, don't you,

that she stabbed your son five times in places sure to kill him? She had to plan that, research it. Even *one* of those wounds would have—"

"Stop," I cut in. Elise's face is white, and I know that each image he paints in her mind is like a lethal wound to her.

"Detective," Jim says, "you don't have to remind us what that girl did."

"I'm sorry," Keegan says, "but I want to underscore how urgent this is. For all we know, the Cox girl was working with that kidnapper in Shady Grove. She has to have help or she wouldn't be hidden so well. They're making her look like some kind of hero, but you're telling me she just stumbled onto a girl who'd been kidnapped for two years? Sounds fishy to me. Something's not adding up."

"There's no evidence that she knows him," I say quickly. "The Shady Grove police have confirmed the kidnapped girl's story. When Casey was arrested for breaking in the first time, she explained how she learned the girl was with him. They didn't take it seriously enough. Remember, I was there. Casey broke in to get the girl out. She'd been trying to get her out for days."

"You defending her?" Captain Swayze accuses.

"Of course I'm not, but you can't change the facts just because they don't serve us. She's calculating, yes, but she doesn't fit the profile of a psychopath. She risked exposure to save that girl."

Everyone protests at once, but I raise my voice over theirs.

"It's important that we profile her with a clear head. That's how I was trained. She is what she is."

Keegan cuts in before anyone else can. "He's right."

Stunned, I turn to him.

"She probably isn't a psychopath. Maybe she has some deep, obsessive sense of justice. Maybe she thought Brent was doing something unjust, so she was obsessively righting a wrong."

Everyone takes that in. I stay quiet, suspicious.

"Her mother has OCD off the charts. It probably runs in the family."

"A genetic link to OCD isn't settled science," I clip out, since I've already researched that. "Experts disagree on that. And her friends and family didn't see any signs of mental illness in her."

"Do you hear this?" Sy asks the chief, speaking for the first time. "He sounds like her defense lawyer. Whose side are you on, Dylan?"

I shake my head. "Not a defense attorney. I sound like an investigator helping you prepare the case you'll turn over to the DA. Do you want a solid case or not?"

"You weren't hired to help us prepare our case," Keegan says. "You were hired to bring her back. That's it."

The veins in my temple are pulsing. "I'm not a bounty hunter. I'm a cop."

"You're neither," Keegan shouts over me.

"Shut up!" the chief says, and we all turn to him. "Dylan's perfectly within his charge to investigate and record evidence in this case while he searches for her, and frankly, detectives, I hope you're more informed than you appear right now. So get off this guy's back. Dylan got closer to her than you did. Jim, I agree that we need to let him keep working on it, and I appreciate your providing the resources to do that."

Jim stares at me with those tired eyes. "Dylan, I trust you," he says. "I want you to stay on."

"Thank you," I say. "I won't let you down."

Keegan leans back hard in his chair. "Already did."

"That's enough," the chief snaps. "It's decided. Dylan, let us know what you need. Stay in touch with Keegan and Rollins—share whatever evidence you come across—and if you need anything beyond that, you know how to reach me. This case is a priority to me, and I'll do whatever I can. Let's get this done."

We all say cordial goodbyes. Jim asks me to hang back when they leave so he can pay me and give me more money for my travel expenses. I wait outside Jim's office while he finishes talking to Gates. When he comes out, he hands me a check.

"I'm glad you're staying on, Dylan," he says. "I don't mind telling you, Keegan rubs me the wrong way. Rollins, he may be a decent guy, but he doesn't say much. Sometimes I think I smell alcohol on his breath. But Detective Keegan . . . Has he been hard to work with?"

"He's got a bold personality," I evade. "But I can work with anybody. It'll be all right. I think he has a personal stake in finding her."

He clearly thinks I'm talking about his ego. If he only knew what the real stake is.

"I want you to have everything you need," he says. "Charter a plane again if you need to. Call me if you need to get a flight. The second you locate her, get there as fast as you can."

I assure him I will. As I walk out, I wonder again if I should have told Jim the whole truth. Would he believe me? No, of course not. There's nothing right now that will convince them that the girl whose DNA was at the scene of their son's murder isn't a killer. Why would they sympathize with her? And you can't go making accusations about cops without having a lot of evidence to back them up. I can't get that evidence unless things stay as they are for now.

As I walk out to my car, I see Keegan pulling out of the parking lot. He gives me a look out his window, and a chill runs down my spine. I shove on my sunglasses and pretend I didn't see it.

5

_____

DYLAN

The look Keegan gave me as he left Jim Pace's parking lot gives me a sick feeling. He's a dangerous man, and if he senses that I'm not on his side or that I don't buy his story, I'll be as dead as Brent. When I'm a couple of miles away from the Pace house, I pull over at a Burger King and open my laptop. I sign on to their Wi-Fi and copy the files I've compiled about Brent onto the thumb drive Casey sent me weeks ago, the one with all of Brent's research. Then I delete the files from my email account and hard drive.

I copy the files from that thumb drive onto another. Then I

drive to my bank, rent a safe deposit box, and leave the original thumb drive there. I take the key with me, trying to decide who to give it to. Who can be trusted?

My shrink? I could tell her that if I wind up dead, I want her to get the evidence to the FBI or the state police. But that sounds a little paranoid, like that Mel Gibson character in *Conspiracy Theory*. I don't want her thinking my PTSD has escalated to a whole new level.

I could give the key to Hannah, Casey's sister, but I feel like she already has the evidence. I know she's sent Casey a package already. It was probably this very drive.

I could give it to the Paces, but I don't know that they would be able to keep themselves from going to see what's in there.

There's no one I can trust enough.

The thought dips me back into depression, but I force myself out. I can't go there. I have to act. I'll figure out what to do with the key at some point, but I can't let it hang me up now.

Department resources or not, Keegan and Rollins are going after her. They have their own resources, which is part of the problem.

At some point, I need to email Casey again so we can compare notes. If I can make her trust me, maybe she'll tell me where she is.

Yeah, and pigs fly. I know I'm fantasizing now.

My phone chimes as I get to my apartment. I look at the

readout and groan. My mother. I consider not picking up, but before the fourth ring, I click Accept. "Hey, Mom." I know my voice sounds flat.

"You haven't called me in weeks. I wanted to see if you're dead."

"No, Mom, I'm not dead."

"You would think you'd be in touch more often after being gone for so long. It's not like you're busy."

"Actually, I am," I say. "I've been working."

"Working? Who hired you?"

I don't want to go into it. "I'm contracted to help the police department on a case. I've been out of town a lot."

"Do they know about your problem?"

I hate the way she says that word, as though it has quotations around it.

"Yes, Mom. So how are you?"

"I'm fine. Just curious why you can take time to go out of town but not come here."

I bristle. "You threw me out."

"I did not throw you out. It was a little fight, that's all." Her words are slurred. "I didn't mean you could never come back."

I breathe a quiet, bitter laugh. "It was time for me to move on anyway." I can only think of one reason she would call. She's made it clear she doesn't care much about seeing me, and when she does, it disturbs her that I'm not the version of myself that she expects.

"Do you need money, Mom? Is that why you're calling?"

"No," she grunts. "I really wanted to know if you'd heard about Brent Pace. Got himself murdered."

I don't want to talk to her about Brent even more than I don't want to talk about myself. "Of course I heard. It happened months ago."

"All that attention those people paid to that boy, and this happens. Brent must've been involved in something shady."

"He wasn't."

"You don't know. And all those years, judging me, like that kind of thing would only happen to my kid because I'm such a terrible mother. Never them."

My face gets hot. "Serves them right, huh?"

"I didn't say that, but now that *you* have . . ." Her voice trails off, as though she knows deep down that's a deplorable thing to say. I hope there's still that much conscience left inside her.

"So your uncle is coming home with his family next weekend. I told him you'd be here if you could drag yourself out of bed."

I wet my lips, wondering why my mouth feels so dry. "I probably can't make it. I'm about to leave town again."

"What's he gonna think if you're not here?"

Stomach acid is burning a hole in my gut. "That I had a breakdown and I'm in a straitjacket somewhere?"

"He doesn't think that."

"The last phone call I had with him, he told me to snap out

of it. Said I was embarrassing the family, that it was time to grow up."

"He just has high standards."

My mother's little brother has never spent a day in service to his country, but he has lots of opinions about those of us who have. "I have high standards too, Mom." I clear my throat. "I'm sorry, but you shouldn't have told him I'd be there without asking me. I can't come."

I don't tell her that my shrink has warned me to keep some space between them and me for a while. People who don't understand PTSD—or any other normal vulnerability— shouldn't have the power to reverse my progress.

My skin is thick enough to tolerate that ignorance in most people, but it's harder to stand it in people who are supposed to care.

"What will I tell your dad?"

"Tell him I've gotten out of bed."

"He spent his whole check at the slots. I don't know how we'll pay the light bill."

There it is. I knew it. "How much?"

"One-fifty."

"Give me the account number. I'll call Southwestern and pay it."

"I don't have it memorized. Just send it to me. I'll pay it."

I know better. My parents are both alcoholics. My dad has cirrhosis so bad he vomits blood. They drink away every disability check before bills come due. I could say no, I won't send it, but then she'd get mean, and I'd spend the next few days obsessing about it instead of thinking about Casey. I finally agree so I can get off the phone.

Sometimes family is a live minefield.

6

_____

DYLAN

'm benching 250 now even though I've lost weight since I was discharged, mainly because my shrink thinks I need to focus on every area of health. I didn't feel like working out at first. I wanted to stay in bed and count ceiling tiles—there are 196 in my bedroom, by the way—but my buddy Dex sort of shamed me into going to the gym with him. Dex is another of the survivors of the IED attack that killed five of the guys with us in the convoy that day. He's as stubborn as a goat, and he hated the idea of me checking out when I had so much going for me.

It's hard to argue with a double-amputee, nagging you about using the body that was spared.

So I go to the gym when I can, and he pretty much acts as my personal trainer, forcing me to go ten more reps, to go up ten pounds, to sweat more. And I have to admit, it does help clear my head, and it calms the anxiety.

Dex has been diagnosed with PTSD, too, but it seems like he's up to the challenge. His attitude dwarfs mine.

After we shower up, he asks me what he always asks. "So you want to go get a beer?"

"We can get coffee," I say, as I always do.

"A beer now and then might actually help you, you know."

"I'm sure both of my parents said that at one point."

"One beer does not an alcoholic make."

"No, but one beer and a bunch of painkillers and anti-depressants and anti-psychotics . . ."

"You don't take any of that."

"No, I don't. Not going to. But everybody thinks I should."

"So do you sleep?"

"Not much. You?"

He shrugs. "My arm and leg hurt when I try."

I glance at his remaining leg. "Probably from carrying all the weight."

"No, not that one. This one." He kicks up his prosthesis. "Phantom pain. What in blazes are you supposed to do with *that*?"

"Painkillers, of course."

"Yeah, those doctors need to be schooled about addiction."

"I think they are schooled about it," I say. "But it seems to them like the easiest and least time-consuming treatment. All in the name of compassion."

I know Dex agrees. He has avoided pills, too, since he got out of the hospital. "But hey, you know what?" he says. "I heard about this new thing they have, this patch. They put it on your forehead, and it's supposed to interrupt your brain waves or some such thing. Supposed to help with the nightmares. Dr. Coggins wants me to try it."

"Do you have to wear it all the time?"

"I don't think so. I don't know much about it, but I'll let you know."

"Be careful. Sounds a little like a lobotomy."

He grins. "Yeah, I'll be sure to avoid that. So coffee. No beer. You want to or not?"

We wind up at Starbucks, and after we get our drinks, I tell him a little about the case I'm working on. Dex wasn't in Criminal Investigations; he was a medic. But before he joined up he worked as an EMT here in Shreveport and spent a lot of time with cops.

"So I'm impressed, dude. No wonder you seem like you're doing better."

"Yeah, it's gotten my mind off myself."

"And you might get a real job out of it."

I'm quiet when he says that.

"What? You don't think so? When you bring that girl back?"

I sip on my coffee for a minute. "The thing is, the more I dig into this case, the more I think they're barking up the wrong tree. Just between you and me, man, I don't think she did it."

Of course, there's no thinking to it. I know for a fact that she didn't, but I can't just blurt that out.

"You know, that crossed my mind, too, when the news broke about her rescuing that girl. I didn't know you were on that case, but I thought something didn't add up about the story. So if she didn't do it, do you know who did?"

I sip again, letting the liquid burn my throat.

"You gonna tell me?" he asks after a moment. "Or is this one of those things where you'd have to kill me?"

I don't answer. I glance up at the cash register and consider another cup.

"Okay, dude," he says finally. "Don't tell me. But hey, listen, if you need any help with your new gig, don't forget that I have nothing but time on my hands."

I give him a long look. I haven't considered that, but the moment he says it, I realize that I could put him on watching Keegan. Keegan doesn't know him, might not notice him. I could even pay him some of what the Paces are paying me. He needs the cash. Military disability isn't going far toward supporting his family.

If I weren't following Keegan or Rollins, I could look into

some of the other cops who were around at the time of Casey's father's supposed suicide. Maybe some of them quit or retired. I could find them, see what they could tell me about Andy Cox. The ideas come to me even as I'm sitting here with him. Maybe I don't need more coffee after all.

"You know, that sounds like a great idea. I could use a little help. You feel like doing some PI work?"

"Long as I don't have to chase anybody on foot. Sign me up."

～⌒

After I give Dex as much info as he needs to follow Keegan and record his activities, I buy a couple boxes of donuts and bring them to the personnel office at the police department. The sergeant at the desk, who probably wouldn't have given me the time of day before, suddenly has respect for me. It's funny how manipulative food can be. "Hey," I say. "Thought you guys could use some breakfast." I open one of the boxes and hand it to him.

"Whoa," he says. "There goes my low-carb diet. Don't tell my wife." As he takes one and bites into it, I introduce myself.

"I'm Dylan Roberts. I'm a PI, working with some of the detectives upstairs on a local homicide case."

"Yeah?" the man asks, chewing.

"I was wondering if you could help me. I'm looking to hire a few retired cops for my PI business. Do you happen to have a list of people who've retired or just quit the force in the last fifteen years or so? I'm mostly looking to hire former cops or ex-military."

The sergeant shrugs. "I could probably pull up a list of retirees. You got an email address?"

I give it to him. I wish I'd come up with a better story so I could get a list of the deceased officers too. That might give me insight about other cops who were targeted by Keegan and his henchmen. I don't think I can ask this sergeant for it without looking suspicious. I call Dex and ask him to meet me. I need him to make a phone call.

A half hour later, I sit with him as he calls the public relations department of the Shreveport PD. He gives them his real name, tells them he's writing an article for *North Louisiana Magazine.* "I'm working on an article about fallen heroes," he says. "I wondered if I could get a list of all the cops from the department who've died in the last twenty years. I'd like to talk to some of their families, maybe feature some of them."

I can hear the PR guy's voice in the background. I recognize it from TV interviews on the news. "Are you asking for those who've died in the line of duty?"

"No, just any cause of death. I'll locate their families, see if they have good stories to tell. Might get a few articles out of it."

"Yeah, I can get you that list, no problem."

Dex gives him his email address, then hangs up and high-fives me.

"Give the man an Oscar," I say. "You're good at this."

7

CASEY

To give the wig store time to get the wigs to Pedro's Place, I get off at a bus stop along the way and spend the night in another dive. Then I get a bus that'll take me all the way to Durant. I spend another night there before going to the restaurant.

Pedro's Place hasn't changed that much since I was here a few months ago. I go in and stand at the cash register, looking around. There are twenty or so diners. I shouldn't have come at lunchtime.

One of the waitresses comes over to me. "How many?" she asks.

I shake my head. "Actually, I need to speak to the manager."

"My father's in the back," she says. "What's this about?"

"I'd like to apply for a job," I say.

"We're not hiring, but I can get you an application in case something opens."

I sigh as she goes away, waits on one of her tables, then disappears into the back. If she comes back with an application, I don't know what I'm going to do. What name will I use to fill it out? I guess I can make something up. If I just sit around here long enough to fill it out, maybe Pedro will come out.

It occurs to me as I sit here that the people who work here all know what Pedro does in the back room. I study the face of the other girl who waits the tables. She could be family. She does look a little like him.

I'm relieved when he comes back with the waitress who went for him, holding an application in his hand. He glances at me without seeing, then does a double take.

"Hi," I say. "I liked it so much here I thought I'd give it an encore." I don't know if he will understand the term "encore." He seems like he's Mexican and, though he speaks English, his accent is heavy. "I'm trying to find myself again." The code words I used the first time change his expression, and it dawns on him who I am and what I'm doing. He clears his throat. "Come back to my office," he says.

His daughter heads off to take care of her customers, and I follow Pedro back to the room where I had my picture made before.

When we're back there, he turns to me. "What you doing here?" he asks, his voice accusatory.

"I need another ID," I tell him. "I have to change my identity again."

He steps back into the doorway, looks into the dining room. I imagine he's searching the faces of all the customers, making sure ICE or the FBI aren't sitting there waiting to pounce.

"I promise I'm alone," I say. "No one's following me. I took a couple of buses and got off when we stopped in Durant to gas up. I don't think they'll trace me here."

He stares at me as if wondering what he's gotten himself into.

"Please," I say. "I can't use the one you gave me anymore, and it's not because I did anything wrong. It's just that my cover was blown. I have money."

"You told no one?"

"No, I promise. Did anyone come talk to you?"

"No."

"They would have if they'd known." I look around the room, and my eye settles on the FedEx box on the floor next to his desk. "That box. Have you opened it?"

He frowns. "The wigs."

"They're for me," I say. "I had them sent here."

His face flushes crimson. "That safe for you, not safe for me! If Immigration watches me, if they know, that would be dead giveaway!"

I realize now that having the wigs sent here wasn't such a

good idea. "I'm sorry. I didn't think about that. I was only trying to figure out my situation."

He opens the box and thrusts the wigs at me. "I give customers identities so that they can work, not so they can commit crimes."

I don't point out that giving them identities *is* committing a crime. But I know what he's saying. He thinks I'm worse than anyone else he's dealt with. Maybe I am.

"I didn't do what they think I did. I'm just trying to stay alive."

I almost expect him to throw me out, but he crosses his arms and stares at me for a moment. "Can you not find someone else to do this?"

"Probably," I say. "Look, if you do it for me one more time, I'll buy two. I have the wigs now. You won't have to see me again. I can pay cash."

He seems to consider it. Finally, he shakes his head, then he goes to a cabinet. He sits down at his desk and pulls up a shelf, revealing a safe tucked under it. He unlocks it. It must be where he keeps the info about the identities. He sifts through it. "How old you are again?"

"Twenty-five," I say.

He pulls one out. "This girl was thirty year old. Two others thirty-five. You don't look thirty-five, but I don't have any other young as you. Most are old."

"Maybe I can pass," I say. "I'll take the two youngest women."

He goes into a closet and gets a case, from which he gets his camera and tripod. He sets it up, then unrolls the backdrop he uses. I wait quietly. "Stand there," he says, pointing to the backdrop.

I fluff my hair, then stand there, waiting for him to snap my picture. "What did they die of?"

He stops focusing and drops his hands. "Why you always ask that? Do you want, or no?"

"I just want to make sure I'm not stealing a live person's identity."

"I do dead people." He snaps the picture, looks at it disapprovingly, then snaps it again. "That'll be twenty-five hundred dollars," he says.

It's a big hunk out of my stash, but I know I'll be hiding for a long time. Maybe the rest of my life. "Half now, half tomorrow?" I ask.

He nods his head.

"And that includes social security cards?"

"Yes," he says. "Like last time."

I start out the back door, and as I open it, I hear his voice behind me.

"Car accident," he says as he breaks down the camera.

I turn back. "What?"

"Obituary not always tell how. These two die of car accidents."

I'm quiet for a second. I picture the funeral, where their parents must have stood in shock, nodding to the mourners whose words all blurred together. I swallow hard. "Okay," I say. "Can you give me their names yet?"

"Miranda Henley . . . Liana Winter . . . ," he says, pronouncing them slightly wrong.

"Okay," I say. "I'll be back tomorrow. Seven thirty?"

"Yes. Don't be late."

I check into the Hampton Inn under the name of Miranda Henley, telling them my usual story—that I have to pay cash because I was robbed of my wallet and don't have any ID. They take payment in advance for one night.

When I get to my room, I sleep deeply, and I wake the next morning refreshed. I get up at five thirty, grab some breakfast downstairs, then pack and check out. I walk back to Pedro's Place a few minutes early and knock on the back door. He doesn't answer, so I wait, checking my watch. At exactly seven thirty, he opens the door.

I step inside.

He doesn't speak, just hands me an envelope. I check and see my picture on Miranda Henley's driver's license, and a counterfeit social security card. Same for Liana Winter, which I hope I won't need. "Great." I dig the envelope out of my pocket with the rest of his money in it.

He holds up his hand, stopping me. "No. I give you money back." He pulls out the cash I gave him yesterday, rolls it up, and thrusts it at me.

I don't take it. "Why? Didn't you say $2,500?"

He wipes his thick mustache. "I look you up on Internet," he says. "Under name I give you before."

My heart jolts. "Oh."

"I see what you did. Why you have to run. The girl and baby."

I just look at him with dread. Now he knows my real name and the story I didn't want him to know. "I didn't kill my friend."

"On the house. You go now."

I suck in a breath. "On the house? No, I couldn't. Please, let me—"

He puts his hand over mine, forces me to take the roll of money. "You did right thing," he says. "I do right thing too."

Tears rim my eyes. "Thank you, Pedro."

He doesn't say anything else, just opens the door and lets me out. When I'm back outside, I stand there a moment, considering that kindness. I wipe my eyes and walk back to the hotel. I call a cab and wait, sitting on the curb. Where will I go now?

When my cab arrives, I still haven't decided my next destination. Maybe I need to just take a day or two and figure things out. I have the driver take me to another motel across town. I check in under Miranda Henley, paying cash and a big required deposit in case I trash the place or something. Then I try to regroup and make a plan.

8

CASEY

I hate depression. It isn't a normal state for me, despite the truths that have haunted me for years. My mind tries to shake it off and find something to smile about, but this time the mood latches onto me and holds me hostage. My eyes are raw and I want to stay in bed and sleep until my nightmare ends, but when I try I sink into terrors about finding Brent, and I wake up shivering and damp with sweat, wondering if I cried out in my sleep and if anyone heard me through the wall. Then I lie awake, turning onto my side, my stomach, my back, pulling my knees up, straightening them, working so hard to find some comfort even though my head hurts and my mind races.

I try to concentrate on normal tasks—adding up the money I've spent and how much I have left, making lists of things I'll need to buy. But it all feels so useless. I wonder if I'll ever pull out of this, and if you can die from it.

Then my thoughts go to the morbid—me dead in my hotel bed, no one looking for me at all until someone forces their way inside to get another day's payment. Since they don't know my real name, they wouldn't be able to notify anyone or give me a proper burial. My family will never know what happened to me.

I get up, put on my shoes, and go outside for a jog. I'm not particularly fit, since I don't normally run, but I do it anyway, running way faster than a jogger normally does, focusing on the feel of my feet hitting pavement and my breathing in and out. After several blocks, I stop, out of breath with a stitch in my side, and drop to a curb to catch my wind. Those tears assault me again, and grief pulls at my face until I wish I'd brought my sunglasses. Cars drive by, but no one glances at me.

I have to talk to somebody, so I go back to my hotel room and use my new phone to get on the Internet. I navigate to the website where my secret email account resides, with the name "NotGoingDown." I look to see if Dylan has contacted me. He has.

Let me know when and how we can talk. I have a lot to tell you.

I want to answer, but I think better of it. I've come this far, hidden this long. If I call him, how will I know he isn't sitting next to Detective Keegan, sharing the call?

Then I remember his concerned eyes as he helped me out of Dotson's house, as he pulled me to safety from that terrifying basement, as he let me walk away.

Maybe I can trust him, at least to some degree. If I'm careful . . .

I type, Yes, we can talk. Give me a safe number.

I wait for half an hour or so, refreshing often to see if he's responded. I force myself to focus on TV, not certain what I'm watching. Finally, two hours later, when I refresh I see a message.

It's a phone number, then the words, Please call. It's safe.

My throat constricts and I swallow hard, wondering if I'm risking my life by doing this. But a peace falls over me—the first peace I've felt in weeks. I pick up my burner phone and punch in the number. My heart races as I wait for it to connect. It rings once, twice . . .

"Hello?"

I'm silent for a few seconds, then I say, "Why did you let me go?"

"Because you're innocent."

Tears push over again, and I can't say if they're tears of relief or deeper grief. "How do you know?"

"I've been digging, investigating. I believe the things that you sent me—the things that were in Brent's file. They're true.

I'm going to take down Keegan and Rollins and everyone else involved. But I can't do it until I have indisputable evidence. I'm building a case. They won't get away with this."

I sniff and wipe the tears on my sleeve. "Are you still looking for me?"

"Yes," he says. "I'm trying to find you before they do. You're not safe from them. Tell me where you are."

"No," I say quickly. "I don't trust you that much."

He's quiet for a few seconds. "Casey, are you all right? Dotson beat you pretty badly. Have you had medical attention?"

"No," I say. "I'm fine."

"You have amazing courage."

I interrupt him, irritated. "No, I don't. I ran." I squeeze my eyes shut and pull my knees up to my chest. "I'm a fugitive!"

"But you were framed."

"So what do you want me to do? Come back? Is that your solution?"

"No. I want you to stay where you are, or go wherever you'll be safe. Even if I don't know where it is."

I open my eyes again and wipe my face.

"If I can't find you, then probably Keegan can't either. I'm pretty good, actually."

I laugh, and it surprises me. "Yeah, you are."

"You are too. The average person couldn't stay off the grid for as long as you have."

"It's kind of important."

"Yes, it is." A soft moment stretches between us. "Casey,

I've told you I have PTSD. It helps to see someone. If you got a counselor, they would have to keep it confidential."

"Not if they think I've committed murder."

"Then go to a church. You need help. You can't endure the things you've been through and handle it on your own. I know."

I look toward the TV, but I only see Dylan's face, that one time I saw him. "Why do you have it?"

"PTSD? I was a criminal investigator for the army, and I was deployed three times, once to Iraq and twice to Afghanistan. I wasn't in combat, but I was caught in mortar attacks a few times. Worst thing that happened was the second time I was in a convoy and we hit an IED. I lost . . . people."

I hear the pain in his voice, the way he's clipping the words.

"I know I should be happy I survived, but I can't always control my thoughts."

His voice trails off, and I know he won't say more about that. I don't know how to respond. Anything I think to say sounds trite and overused.

"You've had trauma, too, more than once," he goes on. "You were twelve when you found your dad. Did you ever talk to anyone about that?"

"I talked to some other cops who sounded like they cared, but then they quit and I didn't hear from them again. And I talked to Brent." I cover my face again, as though he can see me. "Dylan, if you want to help me, protect my family. Protect Hannah and her husband and baby. Protect my mom . . . She's not well."

"I'm on that," he says, but not very emphatically. I know he can't keep Keegan from getting to them. "Hannah's doing well, embracing the suicide story about your dad, going along with the police's version of it. Not being a threat to them. I know she doesn't believe any of that, but as long as she convinces Keegan, she'll be safe. He can't afford to have another murder to cover up if he can avoid it."

"He doesn't care. He's bloodthirsty. Who will stop him?"

"I will."

"After the fact. After it's too late for the people I love."

"Casey, you need to focus on yourself. Too many eyes are on Hannah right now anyway. The press are camped out at her and your mother's houses, trying to get statements. I don't think anything can happen to her right now."

I get to my feet. "Really? They're hounding them? Why?"

"Because of what you did in Shady Grove. It's fascinating to the press. Imagine the questions. Are you a killer or a saint?"

"I'm neither."

He's silent for a moment. "Sainthood isn't what people think. You should check out the Bible's definition."

"I don't know much about the Bible," I say.

"That can be fixed. You might like it." I like the gentle sound of his voice. "I really believe God is on this. I'm on your side because of him."

Tears again. I rub them away.

"Casey, I want you to see where he's working. Keep looking for it. Start with me."

I think about that, and if he's not lying, if he's really on my side, his very existence in my life today is something of a miracle. I think about my escape from Shady Grove, when he showed up at the most crucial moment, even if it was just to arrest me. But he didn't.

"I can see," I whisper, balling the end of my sleeve in my fist and wiping my cheeks, my nose.

"Good."

I don't know why this moment with Dylan is a comfort to me. I wish I could see him face-to-face. I wish I could touch his hand.

I wish I didn't have to break the connection, but it's possible that he could be tracing the call. If so, I'm probably already sunk, but I don't think I should drag it out longer. "I have to go now," I say in a soft voice.

"I'm glad you called. Call back. If I can't answer right away, I'll return it."

I don't know if I'll ever call him again. Just in case, I say, "Thank you, Dylan."

"Be safe," he says. "I'm praying for you."

I click the phone off, astonished at the kindness in that statement. That someone, anyone, would be praying for me. It gives me strength, and I don't feel so weak any longer.

Tonight I will sleep, and tomorrow I'll do something other than grieve.

9

CASEY

Sunday morning I take a cab to Armstrong, just outside of Durant, and stay there that night. Monday morning, I try to think what my next step should be. I need to contact my sister, but I don't dare call her on the cell phone I sent her when I was living in Shady Grove. Now that they can trace my steps in Georgia and know the name I was using there, they have probably wiretapped that phone.

I can't send her a new phone through her in-laws again. They'll get suspicious.

Afraid to stay in one place too long, I call a cab. While I

wait for it, I look in the Dumpster for a box. I find one with an Amazon logo, big enough to hold a toy for my niece. If I send a phone in that, anyone watching the house will think it's something Hannah ordered herself from Amazon.

By now the cab is pulling up, so I tell the driver to take me to the nearest Walmart. He drives me a couple of miles away, where I find a stuffed animal that plays an annoying song. I find the sound box tucked inside a flap in the back. If I can cut that out, there's room to hide the new phone there. Then I can close the Velcro flap back over it.

I buy that and two new burner phones and cards to activate them, along with packing tape and scissors. There's a restaurant with a Wi-Fi signal nearby, so I walk over to have breakfast. While I'm waiting for my food, I put the toy on my lap, partially under the table, and cut the electronic guts out of the stuffed bunny. I stick the phone and charger into the pocket, close the Velcro flap, and examine my work. It looks perfect. I hope Hannah tries to turn it on and realizes that something's not right. I pack the toy into the box, tape it up, and get it ready to send via FedEx.

"Here you go." The waitress sets my plate on the table, but before I can thank her, she retreats and runs back across the dining room.

I stare after her, wondering if she's recognized me. I'm just about to grab my stuff and leave, when the other waitress says, "Sue'll be right back, hon. She's got a little morning sickness."

Relieved, I start to eat. Sue comes back in a few minutes

with a coffeepot. "I'm sorry about that," she says. "I wasn't feeling well."

"She told me," I say, nodding toward the other server. "Morning sickness?"

"Yeah. I used to like my job, but now every plate kind of brings it on."

"Maybe you could get someone else to deliver the food to the tables."

She fills my cup. "That would be helpful, but nobody in the back is willing to do that. It'll be okay when this first trimester is over, they tell me."

She looks pretty young, so I ask, "Your first?"

"Yeah." She doesn't look that happy about it. Maybe she's getting sick again.

I eat as she disappears again. When she comes back, I hear the other waitress telling her she's leaving for a meeting at her kids' school. Sue will be handling things alone. I feel bad for her.

A couple of people sit at one of the tables near me, and they ask her for more coffee, but she's dashing to the bathroom again. "Just one second," she says, and vanishes.

The diners look disgruntled, so I get up and find the coffeepot sitting on a burner near the kitchen. I fill their cups, and they thank me like I'm one of the restaurant employees. Sue comes back out as I'm putting the pot back on the burner.

"I got their coffee," I say. "You all right?"

"I think so. Thank you. Really. Your food is on the house."

"No, I couldn't do that. I didn't do anything but get them coffee. All I want is to be able to work on my computer for a little while. I'll keep ordering things if I need to."

"No, stay as long as you want," she says. "We're slow today, thank goodness."

I go back to my table and spend the next couple of hours going through the files Brent sent me on a thumb drive the morning he died. I've been over them all before, and most of them are no longer mysteries. But there's one that baffles me.

The file is called "Candace Price." When I open it, it only says, "Dallas, TX." There's nothing else there. I can't imagine why he would name a folder that and have nothing in it. Maybe he was working on it on the day of his murder. But who is she? What did he know about her?

I do a Google search of "Candace Price Dallas Texas," and after I sort through the people searcher sites trying to make me give them my credit card, I count three Candace Prices. I click through each of them, but nothing about any of them is remarkable. I can't tell which one Brent was interested in.

I almost give up, thinking he accidentally put a random file on the thumb drive, but Brent never did things randomly. He must have had a reason.

I try Googling "Candace Price Dallas Shreveport." If Brent was linking a woman in Dallas to the events regarding my father's murder, then this woman must have some connection.

Up comes only one of the Candace Prices. She's a real estate agent in Dallas. I look through the rest of the search results and see a .pdf file of her résumé. She used to be a teacher in Shreveport, until five years ago.

Brent was on to something. I find her Facebook profile, which isn't open to everyone, so I quickly create a fake profile, make it private so she can't see how many "friends" I have, and send her a Friend Request. I refresh every few minutes as I eat, then suddenly, she accepts.

I'm always baffled by how easily people accept Facebook friend requests, especially when they've marked their pages private. For all she knows I could be a predator . . . or a fugitive . . .

I quickly go to her profile. She's proud of her good looks and posts pictures several times a day, mostly selfies, so there could be a lot of material here. I scan through the images, one after another, until I've seen dozens, hundreds. I'm clicking them too fast, not sure I'm seeing whatever is there.

Then something stops me.

I spread my fingers on my track pad to enlarge the picture. There he is, posted four years ago, right there next to her at a baseball game, grinning into her selfie. Gordon Keegan.

I go back to more recent ones, clicking more slowly, studying every face in every picture. I find him in the background two more times. In one, they're wearing leis and floral shirts, and the caption reads, "Chilling in Hawaii. Tough duty, but somebody's gotta do it."

And then I know what Brent would have told me. Candace Price from Dallas, Texas, is Gordon Keegan's mistress.

Suddenly things snap into place. I know where I'll go next.

I pay my tab, then grab my duffel bag and call another cab. After I have it take me to FedEx, where I leave the package, I have the driver take me to the train station.

I get to the ticket window, my heart pounding with my decision. "I'd like the next train to Dallas, Texas," I say.

10

KEEGAN

Casey Cox could be dead by now, but instead she's a burr abscessing into my skin, reminding me every single minute that it's there. She's out there ticking, ticking, ticking like a bomb, ready to go off when I least expect it.

"We have to take action," I tell Sy, my partner, as he piddles around like an old man in his dated kitchen. "The press she's getting is turning her into a hero. It's a nightmare. We have to stop that."

Sy's frown ripples like scored leather on his face. The

alcohol is aging him. "We should give the press some of the photos of Brent Pace's body," he says.

"Too risky," I say. "Chief won't like that. He'll say we've compromised the investigation."

"We could leak it, then rant and rave that it got out. If we're the ones who are livid, Chief won't think we did it. We can blame Dylan Roberts."

I think about that for a minute, taking his suggestion to its logical conclusion in my mind. So the TV news anchors who are so intrigued with the murder suspect who saved a girl and her baby—and would love to break the story that she's not really a killer—would get a taste of the bloody crime she's wanted for. It could work to reverse public sympathy for her.

"We both know it wouldn't compromise anything," Sy adds. "The evidence is what we wanted it to be."

I grin. "They'd have to go back to talking about how dangerous she is." I let out a heavy breath and kick the chair in front of me. "He should have gotten her in Shady Grove. This could all be over."

"I don't know." Sy gets up and walks across the kitchen, his house shaking with his boot steps. He pours three fingers of whiskey into a glass, throws it back with a grimace. "Gotta hand it to that girl. She's got instincts. And if we go trashing Dylan to Chief Gates, he's just going to dig in. The Paces helped the chief get his job. If they want Dylan to keep looking for her, Chief's going to stand by his decision." He lifts the bottle and offers it to me. "Want some?"

———

"No," I say. "Need to keep my head clear. So do you. We can't be making mistakes."

Sy puts the bottle down hard, and the liquid sloshes against the sides.

"Okay," I say, "here's our strategy. First, we leak the pictures to the press, along with a list of the evidence—her DNA left at the scene, the knife in her car . . . Then we go ballistic all over the department, threatening anybody who had access to the pictures. Indignant, we're-gonna-get-to-the-bottom-of-this kind of rant."

"You'll get it to the press?"

"Yeah, I'll do that. But then we'll plant stories about Dylan to the chief. Can't be blatant. We just put some more bugs in his ear about Dylan's incompetence. Like he's had some crazy PTSD episodes that we tried to overlook."

"That didn't get any traction when you tried it in Chief's office. Dylan seems too competent. I think we have to be more subtle."

"We still have to plant doubts."

"But what about looking for her?" Sy grabs the bottle again, drops into his recliner, levers the footstool up. "We have to find her. I can't sleep nights knowing she's out there, on to us. She could expose us anytime. I wouldn't fare well in prison."

"Shut up, you're not going to prison. And how do you know she's on to us? She's running from prosecution. That's all. It doesn't mean she knows anything. We've gotten this far, haven't we?"

When Sy drinks out of the bottle, I get up and go to him. I grab his face, give it a light slap, then tilt his chin up. "Haven't I made you rich? Haven't I? Don't tell me it hasn't been a blast. All the garbage we have to put up with, we *should* be living like kings. We put our lives on the line every mind-numbing day, and most of us don't make enough money to drive a new car. They owe us this, and we had the backbone to go after it. We got what was ours."

Sy jerks his face out of my grip. "Maybe we went too far, Gordon. The Andy Cox thing got us in over our heads . . . and then Brent . . ."

"Every single time you get drunk you start wailing about Cox. It was thirteen years ago. We *did* get away with it." I grip his face again and set my jaw as I stare into his eyes. "Are we in over our heads? Have we been caught? Has anything happened to us, ever?"

Sy jerks his face away.

"No," I say, "we're still living the good life, and Casey Cox is just some kid out there trying to keep her head down. She's not talking to anybody. We'll find her soon enough, and when we do, we end it. That's all. She can join her Honest Abe of a dad in the grave he's rotting in."

"But even if he finds her, or if *we* do, if *anything* happens to her, the press will be all over it. It's got their attention now."

"If we leak the right things, none of that will matter." I slap the top of his head, point my finger at him. "You keep your head straight, you hear me? That whiskey is making a coward out of you. *We* control this story, and nobody else. You've trusted me this far, and I haven't let you down. Everything we've done is because we had to. We've done good, Sy."

"Okay, Gordon. I get it."

"No, you don't. Look at me." I tip his face up again. His eyes are bloodshot. "Look at me, Sy. Do you trust me?"

"Things get out of control, Gordon."

"Do you trust me?" I say louder.

He jerks away from me again and wipes his mouth with the back of his arm. "Yes, I trust you!"

"Then we do it this way, and we keep our heads clear, and we follow our strategy. And when Casey Cox is dead, we're home free."

"What about Dylan?"

"Dylan's head's so twisted that he'll move on too. Especially if we get him a job at the department. That's what he really wants. He'll be fine."

When I finally get Sy under control, I drive home, my mind racing with the strategy. Adrenaline pumps through my veins as I think of the steps involved in ruining what's left of Casey Cox's name. I'm good at this. I've done it for years. I even like it.

Unlike Sy, I sleep fine at night.

11

DYLAN

I have another restless night, my attempts at sleep broken up by times on the Internet. Finally, I give up and make coffee, then turn on the TV. The local news is on, and when they flash Brent Pace's picture on the screen, I step toward the TV.

Local authorities are still trying to find Pace's alleged killer, who surfaced in Georgia after rescuing a girl and her baby from kidnapping. Today, an anonymous source gave us pictures of the Brent Pace crime scene, which puts this crime back into perspective. The brutal murder happened months ago . . .

As the anchor reads off the story, they show the picture that even I wasn't allowed to have, of Brent's bloody body at the foot of his stairs.

The pictures are not shown for very long and a lot is pixelated, but the anchor says that if you want to see more you can go to their website. I dash to my computer and open it, go to that site. The unpixelated pictures are right there, gory and brutal.

I feel the heat in my ears, burning in the back of my throat, my heart racing as I think of Brent's mother seeing these pictures, feeling violated as all of her friends discuss them over lunch. Without a doubt, I know why they were released. It is Keegan's way of reminding the public that Casey Cox is not a hero, but a killer. And I know who will be blamed for the leak.

I leave the TV running and storm out of my apartment, race down the stairs to my car. My hands are shaking as I drive to the department.

When I get there I speed walk across the lawn and up the steps into the building. I start to go to the detectives' floor, to confront Keegan myself, but then I change my mind. It's useless confronting him and Rollins. Instead, I go to Chief Gates's office at the back corner of the building, hoping he's there. His secretary is on the phone and another line is ringing, and in his office I can hear him talking.

He's already heard about the pictures and he's talking his way out of it. I slide my shaking fists into my pockets. "I need to see him," I tell the secretary. "Tell him it's Dylan Roberts." She looks alarmed at the sound of my name and puts her call on hold, then goes to his door. "It's him," she says. "Dylan Roberts."

"Dylan, get in here!" he yells, and she motions for me to go in. As I walk in I see that Chief Gates is just as livid as I am. He's standing, pacing behind his chair, holding the phone to his ear as he rants on. "No, I don't know what he was thinking, but I'm about to find out. Let me call you back."

He slams the phone down and leans over the desk. "There are a couple of very dear people who are grief-stricken all over again because they had to see their son's bloody body plastered on the TV screen and going viral across the Internet. What do you know about this, Dylan?"

"That's why I'm here," I say. "I want to know the same thing. Who leaked those photos?"

"Keegan says it was you. Sit down!"

I can't sit down. "Keegan knows full well that I wasn't given those photos." My hand is still shaking as I pull out my phone and go to my photos. I swipe through until I get to the first of the pictures that I took that day, pictures of evidence markers and none of Brent's body. I hand him the phone and watch as he swipes through.

He finally thrusts the phone back. "This doesn't prove anything, Dylan. For all I know you deleted them on your way here."

"Why would I come straight here when I saw it?" I ask. "Brent was *my* friend. I don't want people gawking at him like this. This has Detective Keegan written all over it."

He grunts. "Why would you even say that?"

"He doesn't like the PR that Casey Cox is getting," I say. "He wants to change the narrative."

"So did I," Chief Gates says. "You probably did too. But this—"

I finally sink down into the chair and rub my face. "Has Brent's mother seen it?"

"I was just on the phone with Jim," he says. "She was in Best Buy when she saw it flashed on ten big screens. She's going to have to be sedated. She's devastated all over again. It's like it just happened."

It takes me a minute to get my emotions in check. I rub my mouth, stretching it into submission. "In my whole history of detective work, I have never leaked anything," I say. "I wouldn't do that, especially when my friend's family is involved. Is there any way we can get an injunction against the television station? Something to make them cease and desist?"

"It's too late," the chief says. "The pictures are out there. People are taking screenshots of them, passing them along to their friends."

I let out a deep breath. "People are sick."

"Because it's spectacular. It's scandalous. It's horrible and people like blood." His hand swings across his desk, and he knocks over a bottle of water and a coffee cup. The mug breaks into pieces on the floor, splashing its brown contents onto the baseboards.

His secretary runs in. "Sir, are you all right?"

"No, I'm not," he snaps. "Get Keegan and Rollins in here right now. Wherever they are, tell them I want to see them. And call the DA back. I can't avoid him any longer. Get him in here if he'll come."

I hope the fact that he's calling the detectives in means he believes me. The secretary gets the DA on the phone and I give the chief a minute, walking out into the hallway, checking my phone to see where else the photos have been posted. Suddenly I hear cursing from the end of the hall and look up. It's Jim Pace coming toward me, his eyes red, his stride purposeful. "Dylan, tell me you didn't do this!"

The fact that he even questions me makes my eyes burn even more. I step toward him. "Jim, why would I want those pictures plastered on TV like that? Why would I want people passing them around and Elise looking at them? I can't think of anything worse."

Jim's mouth trembles and he loses his hold on his emotions. He covers his face and turns his back to me. "I can't believe this is happening," he chokes out. "His mother . . ."

"I can't believe it either," I whisper.

He swings back to me. "Who had those photos?"

"The CSIs who took them in the first place," I say, "then they would have given them to the detectives. But the detectives wouldn't release them to me, for this very reason. There is a very distinct chain of custody for those pictures. It's all for the sole purpose of keeping the family from having to go through this kind of thing."

Suddenly there is a commotion down the hall, and I hear Keegan's voice as he comes toward me, Rollins following a few steps behind. Keegan looks angry, his chin pressed in the air, looking down his nose at me like he's about to punch me out. I stand straighter and step toward him.

Then Keegan sees Jim and his demeanor changes. He reaches out his hand. "Jim, I'm so sorry about this. We're going to get to the bottom of it, and when we find out who did this . . ." He lets go and points his finger at me, thrusting with each syllable. "When we find out . . ."

Chief Gates hears us and calls for us to come in. Keegan is on the offensive as he goes in first. "Chief, this is what happens when we contract outside help. He's a rookie—an *amateur!*— and he has no business working on a homicide case."

"You know I didn't release those photos," I bite out.

"Oh yeah? How do I know that?"

"Because I asked for them and you said no!" I turn to Rollins. "You were there. You heard him." Rollins looks like he just rolled out of bed, and he smells like alcohol. He doesn't say anything.

"You took pictures of the pictures," Keegan says.

"Not of the ones with his body! You were aware of every one I took. You sat right there and watched me. We talked about which ones I could have."

"And you apparently didn't listen!"

"Sit down!" the chief yells, kicking a chair as he passes it. Keegan and Rollins sit, but I stand with Brent's dad in the doorway. I need to tell Jim that he'll have to decide who he trusts—me or them—but I have to be careful.

Everyone's talking at once, trying to go louder than the others next to him, but I remain silent and lean against the wall.

Finally, Chief Gates drops into his chair. Everyone goes quiet. "Jim, I hope you believe me when I say that I didn't know this was going to happen, and I'm starting an investigation today to find out who released the pictures." He looks at me, then Keegan, then Rollins as he says those words. "Believe me, when I get to the bottom of this, heads are gonna roll."

He massages his temples and folds his hands in front of his face. "Jim, I'm calling the station and asking them to take them down, but it's not going to stop all of it. The other media have probably picked them up by now. It's the age of sharing and retweeting. We can't get those pictures back."

He leans back in his chair, rakes his fingers through his hair. "But if there's a bright side to this, at least it'll remind people that Casey Cox is not some female knight in shining armor. That she's a cold-blooded killer. Maybe it will make someone turn her in, wherever she is."

Jim turns his haunted gaze up to the chief. "That's not enough to get that image out of my wife's head."

"I know," Gates says.

"Do you?" Jim snaps back. "He wasn't your son. You didn't even know him. Do you really know?"

Chief Gates gets quiet now, and he seems meeker as he shrinks back into his chair. Keegan and Rollins sit looking at

---

the floor, not willing to make eye contact with anyone. I look at Jim, wishing I could take away the pain. He meets my eyes and I see that he trusts me. That's all I need.

These men sitting in the room with him are the ones who murdered his only son, and if it's the last thing I ever do in my life, I'm going to make sure they face justice for that. I would love nothing more than to let Jim know that Casey Cox is not the one we should lock up for this crime, but I know he's not ready for that news just yet.

Finally, Jim speaks again. "Dylan didn't do this. I want him left on the case."

I look down at the floor, thankful. I wish I weren't deceiving him.

"All right," Chief says. "But so help me, when I find out who leaked this, somebody's getting fired. I may even charge the person with obstruction of justice and tampering with a crime scene."

Keegan nods and shoots me a vicious look. Rollins never looks up.

"All right, the three of you get out of my office," Chief Gates says.

I walk out first, Keegan and Rollins shuffling behind me. As we reach the hall, Keegan grabs my arm. In reaction, I slam him against the wall. I'm sweating as I hold him there, my face inches from his. "Do not ever touch me," I say through my teeth.

My actions startle him—as they startle me—and when I

let him go, he takes a few steps away before turning back to me. "You're losing it, man! You're a hundred percent certifiable."

Rollins stands between us, and he tries to shut Keegan up. I can see that he fears what I might do next.

But Keegan has more to say. "And for the record, you ever touch *me* again and you'll see what I'm made of."

I want to tell him that I know what he's made of, and ask him if he intends to stab me to death like he did my friend. Ironic that he's just out of my reach as he threatens me. I've got to get out of here before I do something stupid. Shaking my head, I push past Rollins and roughly brush shoulders with Keegan, daring him to react. The coward takes another step back.

I take off down the hall.

12

CASEY

get to Dallas in the wee hours of the morning and check into a small independent motel as Miranda Henley. I sleep for three or four hours, then wake up and spend time on Facebook checking out Candace Price.

I scan down her Timeline and see that she loves shopping. She posts many of her purchases as if she were a fashion blogger. She seems to be in real estate and posts some of her listings. None of them is very high priced.

I open the pizza that I got on the way, and as I read the

screen and flick through her pictures, I take off the peppers and onions before biting into it.

Candace Price is clearly a partier. Every few days she posts selfies of where she was the night before, usually in a club or a bar with lots of people in the background.

I click through her photos as I eat, and there are many of them. Finally I click to one of her sitting in a stadium at a ball game, Gordon Keegan sitting next to her, staring at the field. This one was only taken last fall.

I recognize Keegan's profile, but would anyone else? I scroll my cursor over his face, but it's not tagged. Even so, I'm convinced now that Candace is a key person to help me take Keegan down. I get my legal pad and list everything I can figure out about her. I get her real estate office name and phone number from the signs in the yards of the listings she's posted. On those listings, I find her personal cell phone number. I scroll through her posts and find where she likes to shop, narrowing it down to an area of town. I see her car in another photo. It's a white Mercedes SUV, a high-ticket item. Her license plate is even visible, so I get her tag number.

Then I see pictures of her on a Viking cruise ship, floating past the Greek Islands, a picture of her at the Vatican, another of her in a bikini at the beach in Turks and Caicos. She gets around. It seems like she makes a lot of money for a Realtor with low-priced listings. I spend the next couple of hours writing down every fact I can find about her, every potential lead to follow. Then I do a search on the Internet and find her address. It isn't that hard.

I'll have to get a car today so I can follow her around. I'll need to stay in Dallas for a while. That makes me nervous, because it's only three hours from Shreveport, but I don't have any other choice if I want to expose Keegan and get my life back.

After I shower, I turn on the TV and watch an hour and a half of the news cycle, waiting for anything about myself.

After a couple of hours, Fox News's show *Outnumbered* comes on, and I'm in the fourth segment. As they show pictures of me as my former self and talk about what I did in Shady Grove, they play clips of Laura and her family reunited. Miss Lucy is sobbing as she embraces her granddaughter. It makes all I went through worth it. Sandra is holding her grandchild as if they've already bonded. They show pictures of their horrific captors.

Then they talk about me.

"This morning, a Shreveport TV station aired photographs of the Brent Pace crime scene. This is a grim reminder of what Casey Cox is alleged to have done to her close friend."

They flash a picture of Brent's body on the floor, just as I'd found him. His face is blurred out, along with the knife wounds, but the blood is visible. I can't even look.

"Casey Cox should be found and prosecuted for the brutal murder of Brent Pace, regardless of what happened in Shady

Grove. Mark my word, there is something sinister that explains why she was in that house and saw the kidnapped girl."

"I agree," one of the other leggy panelists says. "And the fact is, the Shady Grove events won't even be admissible in court. The jury won't be told what she did in Georgia."

"But you honestly think the jurors won't have heard about that? Let's face it, it's going to be hard to get objective jurors who haven't followed the news about her."

"They will be instructed not to consider anything except the evidence presented regarding Brent Pace. These pictures will be imprinted on their minds."

I feel sick, like the waitress in the diner. But the nausea just hovers in my chest, with no relief.

"Well, police have to find the girl first." The blonde who's been quiet stops the others with that comment. "I have to wonder if she really is the one who murdered Brent Pace. If she risked her own exposure to rescue the kidnapped girl, does she really have it in her to be a killer?"

"If she didn't do it, why did she run?" one of the other women says. "Police haven't been able to find her to interview her, so we don't know what she might have told them. And let's not forget all her DNA left at the scene, plus the knife found in her car, along with a blood trail."

It's almost like it's a game to them.

If only there were other journalists courageous enough to dig like Brent did, but then they'd just end up dead. When the segment is over, I turn off the TV and sit alone on the bed, hugging my knees. I want so badly to go home to see my little niece, breathe in the scent of her. I want to see her reach out to me, and teach her to call me Cay-Cay. I want to see my mom.

I think back to the things that Dylan said in the emails we exchanged with each other. He's been through a lot, too, and he leans on the Bible. Maybe I should give it a chance. I reach into the bed table drawer for the Gideon Bible that always seems to be there. There's a navy-blue book with the stamp of the Gideons at the bottom, but there's also another one there—a leather-bound Bible that looks well used. I pull it out and open the front. There is a name inside—Cole Whittington—and I see a folded paper sticking out of the top. I pull out that page, unfold it, and read:

Dear Daphne,
By the time you find this, I'll be dead.

I almost choke, then catch my breath and read on.

I didn't want to do it without saying goodbye, but I want you to know how much I love you. You have been a beautiful picture of God's love for me since the day I met you, and I cherish it. But these last few weeks have been a nightmare for all of us, and I want it to end. I love our children, and this threat hanging over our heads is too intense. I can't let them suffer while I'm dragged through the gutter. It has to end for the sake of everyone I love. Please remember me to the kids the way I was before the accusations, not after, and let them know that their daddy cherished them too.

He signs it *Cole*. My heart hammers as I look around the room for signs of blood or anything that indicates he killed himself right here. But if he's dead, they clearly didn't find the note or the Bible.

If he killed himself, then his wife needs to have this Bible.

I summon my strength and go down to the desk. A girl is working, busy over her computer, but she looks up at me and smiles. "May I help you?"

"Yes," I say. "I'm in room 138, and I was just wondering, has anything weird happened in that room?"

She frowns. "Anything weird? Like what do you mean?"

"Like maybe a death? A suicide, maybe?"

She doesn't bat an eye. She just grins and shakes her head. "No, ma'am. I'm sure I would know. I've worked here for five years. Why do you ask?"

"I don't know," I say. "I'm just getting a vibe."

"If the room's not acceptable, I could move you."

I think of telling her about the suicide note and the Bible I found, but then I'd have to hand it over for her to return it, and what if they just throw it in Lost and Found? No, someone's got to make sure his family gets it. "No, that's okay," I say. "I'm fine. Just . . . never mind."

I know she thinks I'm a kook, and now I wonder if I've

called too much attention to myself. "Could I get a Diet Coke?" I say, hoping to change the subject.

"Sure," she says and reaches into the little store next to the desk. She gets one out of the fridge, sets it on the counter. "You want to add this to your room?"

I pay cash right there, then ask, "And how late is the pool open?"

I hope these last questions will distract her from thinking I'm a wannabe medium. I take my Diet Coke and go back to my room. I read over the note again, extracting all the clues I can. I feel an intense sense of responsibility, as if this should trump all else in my life, but I know that's crazy.

I should just let it go and turn the Bible in at the desk. But what if he killed himself somewhere else, and his family members don't know there's a note? What if it could give his wife some comfort?

I can almost hear my sister's voice, telling me to mind my own business. Any departure from my plan puts me more at risk of being caught and killed. But the thought of that note plagues me.

I stuff the Bible into my bag. I'll decide what to do later. But first I need to do what I came here to do, and for that, I have to find a car.

I search Craigslist and find one that looks like it'll do, one that I can afford that is offered by an individual, so I call them and ask about it. They're willing to bring it to the Kroger parking lot a block down from my motel so I can test drive it. I leave the hotel and walk down.

It's a ten-year-old black Honda Accord with 100,000 miles and a scrape on the back left fender, but it drives fine. The person selling it is a seventy-year-old man, and he says it belonged to his deceased wife. I offer him cash, and he accepts it. He doesn't remember to take off the tag that's in his name, and I don't remind him. Armed with the title signed over to Miranda Henley, I drive back to my motel.

My main task will be following Candace Price in hopes of getting some sort of condemning evidence about Keegan. Even so, I can't get that suicide note out of my head. I decide to take a detour. I have to find Cole Whittington's family to see if he carried out his suicide plan somewhere else, and give them these last words from him. Once that's done, I'll be able to move on.

13

CASEY

Cole Whittington is listed in the Dallas phone book, with his address as clear as day. I jot it down, then check the local newspapers' obituaries to see if he went through with killing himself. There are several Whittingtons who've died over the last few years, but none of them is named Cole.

So maybe he's not dead. Maybe he just planned it, then changed his mind. Maybe he was just having a really bad day, and pulled himself together. Since he had his own Bible, I figure he must be a Christian. Miss Lucy was a Christian, and even though she'd had horrible things happen in her life,

I can't picture her ever committing suicide. But I guess even Christians can get clinically, brain-sick depressed.

The Bible is marked up, verses underlined and highlighted in color, notes in the margins, like he spent time studying it.

Maybe he just hasn't done it yet. There's not a date on the note, and it was probably left there recently, or it would have been discovered by now. That thought fills me with a sense of urgency. What if he's still making his plan, setting his affairs in order, preparing for the day when he actually carries it through?

I load my things into my car and check out, keeping the Bible with me, its note tucked between Genesis and Exodus. I drive by the address in the phone book and see a For Sale sign in the yard. There's a white Nissan SUV in the driveway, and there's a magnetic sign on the side that says UpDown Seat Company. There's an address, a phone number, and a website. I jot them all down.

I could go to his door right now and knock on it, hand the Bible to whoever answers, and walk away, never to look back. Or maybe they would just toss the Bible on the foyer table and forget about it until they're notified that he killed himself *after* I could have done something.

I fight the sense of responsibility that rises in me. This is the same kind of obsession I had in Shady Grove, when I had the overwhelming sense that I knew who'd kidnapped the missing girl. I felt like I was the one who had to save her, and in that case, I was right.

Hannah would tell me to stop this, that it's not my job, that

I have to stop playing God. She would tell me to move on and hide, to take care of myself. But I know myself well enough. I couldn't live with myself if I let this go. What if, later, I look the guy up on the Internet (which I know I would do) and learn he's killed himself? What if one of his kids finds him? What if they never get over it?

I check into another motel. By Monday morning, the obsession still hasn't left me. I drive back by Cole Whittington's house, and the white SUV is gone. So I drive over to the UpDown Seat Company. It's a small metal warehouse building with a sign on the outside. I pull into the parking lot and glance in the mirror. Do I look like myself? Will they recognize me from my pictures?

My hair is up in my baseball cap, and my eyeliner is smudged, my eye shadow smoky. I've lined my lips to be slightly bigger than my real lips, creating a fuller, rounder effect. Nobody will be fooled into thinking my lips are really that way, but I hope all this makeup will distract them. I certainly don't recognize myself, as hard as I look.

I grab the Bible and go to the door, where a Help Wanted sign is taped. There's an older woman sitting at the front desk behind a counter. She smiles and looks up at me. "Hey there. Can I help you, baby?"

"Yes," I say. "I wondered if I could see Cole Whittington. Does he work here?"

"Sure does, sweetheart. He's my son. He's in back. I'll go get him. Can I tell him what it's about?"

"I just wanted to return something of his I found."

She seems a little distracted, so she doesn't ask what. "Okay, sweetie. Wait right here."

While she's gone, I look around to see what kind of place this is. I glance at a framed ad on the wall across the room, featuring a seat that seems to be their main product. Apparently it moves somehow. Up and down, I'm guessing?

There's another Help Wanted sign on the counter.

The woman rustles back in. "He's on his way, hon."

"Thank you. What is it you make here?"

That smile pops back up to her face. "My son Blake invented this hydraulic seat that moves up and down from the floor to regular chair height with just a button. It's great for people with arthritis in their knees or hips, who can't garden or play with their grandbabies or do normal things, because if they're like me, they can get down but they can't get back up. We make it here. A hundred percent made in America. We have so many orders we can hardly fill them all."

Before I can respond, Cole steps into the office. He's a nice-looking man, probably about thirty-five, but he looks tired and pale. He seems a little apprehensive as he approaches me. "Can I help you?"

"Yes," I say, pulling his Bible out of my bag. I lower my voice and lean toward him. "I found this Bible, and it has your name in it. I just wanted to return it."

I see the recognition on his face. "Yeah, I've been looking for that. Thanks. Where'd you find it?"

"In a motel bed table," I say so low that his mother can't hear.

His pupils flicker, and I wonder if he's thinking about writing the note. He looks at me as if wondering what I know, but I just smile. "So . . . if it's yours . . ."

"I appreciate it." He reaches into his wallet and pulls out a twenty. "Here, take this for bringing it back."

I hold up a hand. "No, I can't take that. I just . . . wanted to get it back to you." I want to ask him if he still wants to take his own life, if he still sees things as hopeless.

Instead, I just stand there looking at him. His phone rings, and he grabs it out of his pocket and looks down at it. Without another word to me, he rushes out of the room.

"Thank you for bringing it back, hon," his mother says. "He's been real distracted lately. Maybe you helped restore his faith in humanity."

I think of telling her about the note, but then I decide that whatever is going on with him, I might make it worse if I do that. Not knowing what the right move is, I go back to my car.

14

CASEY

Hannah should have gotten the box by now, and I hope she's found the phone inside the stuffed bunny. I know she's desperate to hear from me and has been worried that I'm injured or dead. Hopefully this has put her mind at ease.

I know she often goes for a walk after supper, so I drive about thirty minutes outside of town and try her at six thirty. If she's followed the same instructions we had for the previous phone, she has it on silence all the time. Still, I call her. It rings to voice mail, which hasn't been set up. I hang up and hope she'll see the missed call soon, and that the phone is not still stuffed inside the toy.

I find a park at the edge of a lake, and I get out and walk as I wait for my phone to ring. After a few minutes, it does.

I click it on, my heart pounding. "Hey."

"Hey." Her voice is tight, high-pitched. I can tell she wants to say my name, to ask if I'm okay, to demand I tell her everything, but she's quiet. I hear the wind whooshing, and I know she's walking.

"Are you all right?" she asks.

"Yes, I'm fine. So you got the bunny?"

"Yes," she says, "but come on. I almost missed it."

"I knew you'd try to turn it on. Did Jeff see the box?" I ask.

"No, I was home by myself with Emma when it came. You know, you're really good at this. It's a little scary."

"It's in my DNA," I say.

"How come it's not in mine?"

"I hung out with Dad a lot."

She's quiet for a moment, then she says, "They're saying you're a hero. You saved that girl."

My hand is sweating, so I switch to the other ear as I walk out onto a public pier. "Almost got caught, but I got away."

Footsteps jar her voice. "The media is all over it. It's like dueling news stories. They released the crime scene pictures."

"I know."

"First they call you 'the homicidal hero,' then they're

debating whether you're a psychopath. I want to call them so bad and tell them you're not any of that."

"Don't!" I say. "Don't ever do that. Do you understand me?"

She sighs. "Yes, of course."

I lean over a rail and look around to see if anyone is within earshot. "No, I'm serious, Hannah. It's not just you. It's Emma, and Jeff, and Mom. You can't let your emotions lead you into doing something reckless."

"*Me*, reckless?" she says. "You're the one who risked everything for a girl you'd never even met. I have to let them just keep thinking those things about you. The media is crazy here, camping out on the front lawn, blocking our street. I had Jeff park my car on the street behind us and I snuck out the back way just so I could come to the walking park."

The word *sorry* seems so useless. "Don't throw the old phone away at home. They might go through your trash."

"Can they do that?"

"Yes. Once it's taken out to the curb it's fair game. In fact, have Jeff take your garbage to the dump. Don't leave any of it out for them to dig through. Remember? Dad used to go through trash when he was investigating crimes. The media can do it too." I draw in a long breath, let it out. "Are they camping out at Mom's too?"

"Yeah, some of them."

"How is she?"

"She keeps having these horrible thoughts that you're going to die. She has all sorts of new rituals. She checks the mailbox about seventy times a day, even though the media is there. I'm taking her to the doctor twice a week. They're adjusting her dose."

I squeeze my eyes shut and cover them. "What about the police? Are they harassing you?"

"They come by every so often to see if they can badger me into spilling my guts. I think I'm being followed."

"Who's come by? Keegan? Rollins?"

"Yes, they come together."

My head is starting to ache. "Have they threatened you?"

"Their very existence is a threat. I just keep acting like I'm mad at you, like I hope they find you so this will be over for all of us."

"Good. Hannah, just tell them whatever they want to hear. You can't let them think you're a threat."

"You've told me that over and over."

I feel the tears rising in my eyes, my throat constricting. "How is Emma? I miss her so much."

"She's trying to walk. So precious. I wish I could be like her and be oblivious to all this." Her voice catches. "I wish you could see her."

I swallow back the knot in my throat and press my tear ducts. Crying does no good. "I know you're a great mom. Take care of her."

"Just worry about you." She's quiet for a moment. "Casey, you have to figure out a way through this. I can't stand never seeing you again."

"I'm working on it."

"Really? So there's a possibility that this will end someday?"

I don't want to get her hopes up, but maybe hope is just what she needs. "I just have to get enough evidence against them that they can't squirm out of it. Once I do . . . Yeah, maybe there's a chance."

I hear her muffled crying on the other end. I hope she can't hear mine.

15

DYLAN

Though I've got a lot on my plate, I know I'm in a dark, dangerous place. My actions with Keegan were stupid. I should have kept my cool with him instead of lashing out. But it is what it is. Out of self-preservation, I take the time to go to my group meeting at ten o'clock, since I haven't been in the last couple of weeks. Until a few weeks ago my PTSD defined me, but since I've been chasing Casey Cox, it hasn't seemed so looming. The Keegan thing was a setback.

I go in and get a Styrofoam cup of coffee, made bitter by the brown industrial pot that is probably in need of a deep cleaning. I nod to a few people I know.

Dex, probably my best friend here, is already in his seat, his prosthetic leg stretched out in front of him like a trophy. Leo, who is also dealing with the loss of a leg, is clearly still unemployed or he wouldn't be here. Grayson, a kid who's barely nineteen, still has that distracted look in his eyes, as though the blast that killed his buddies was only thirty seconds ago. He's got a PTSD service dog that pants as it sits at attention next to him.

"Dylan, dude!" Dex says, lifting his hook for me to fist-bump. I'm not in a fist-bumping mood, but do it anyway as I drop into the seat next to him.

"You okay, man?"

"Yep," I say, sipping the sludgy coffee. "You?"

"Never better," he says, and I know it's a load of garbage, but it always makes me smile. "Just sent you an email. Got that list we were talking about."

My eyebrows shoot up. "Really?"

"Dylan, you're back." I turn to see Dr. Coggins making her way to the empty seat we all save for her, as if it has her name on it.

"Yeah," I say.

"Well, it's good to see you. Everybody ready to get started?"

My phone vibrates as she introduces the newcomers, and I check it. An email has come in from my donut contact at the police department, with a list of the cops who have retired or resigned from the force in the last decade and a half. Right behind it, I see the email from Dex, with the list of those who've died.

Suddenly I don't want to be here. I need to go home and get to work on these.

"So, Dylan, why don't you start? Tell us how you've been doing."

I look up, my thumb still on my screen. "What?"

"You've been gone a while. Are you doing okay?"

"Yeah, pretty good," I say. "I've been out of town, working."

"Working. That's great."

The other guys who know me nod, and someone spouts out, "Gainfully employed, brother!"

Across the circle, a girl named Rose, who's an army nurse, asks, "So, your friend who died . . . Have you been taking that okay?"

I don't remember telling them that, but I suppose Dex may have relayed that info. "Yeah . . . no, he's . . . he was . . ." My voice suddenly fails me, shredding into ten voices in different pitches. I clear my throat and try again. "A good friend."

"Want to talk about the triggers that pulled in you?" Dr. Coggins asks.

My leg is crossed over my knee, and I look at my foot, shaking like I'm amped up on something. "Uh . . . not really, no." I can't tell them that I'm working on his case, that I'm trying to nail the killer, that the person they all think did it isn't the one.

"So your job," someone asks. "What is it you're doing?"

"PI work," I say. "Routine stuff."

"Dylan was a cop in the army's Criminal Division," Dr. Coggins provides. She quickly deflects and turns to someone else. "So, Leo, did you have that talk with your wife that we discussed?"

Relieved that the spotlight is off me, I stop shaking my foot and drop it to the floor. I lean forward, listening to my buddy. After he talks, a new guy pipes in. He's just back from deployment and has no physical signs of injury. When she draws him out, he sounds just like me.

"I was looking forward to coming home, being with my wife, my kids. But my wife says she got back a stranger."

"Tell me," Dr. Coggins says. "What kinds of triggers are you having?"

"My kid's birthday the other day—number five—some genius brought firecrackers, and the minute the first one popped I knocked my daughter to the floor . . . trying to cover her."

"Oh no," one of the women whispers.

He leans back in his seat, rakes his fingers through his hair. "I scared her to death . . . My wife drags me up to get to our daughter, and I left the backyard then, trying to get it together. I heard her friends telling her I'm dangerous."

"You weren't dangerous, dude," Dex tells him. "You were protecting your little girl. What idiot would set off firecrackers around you?"

"They don't get it."

"We've all done that, man," I say, my voice suddenly clear. "The other day, my car backfired and I swerved into a ditch."

The room gets quiet, and I wonder why I said that. I wouldn't have told it when the spotlight was on me, but now . . .

"I went to a movie the other day with my girl," one of the new guys says. "Couldn't stand not being able to see behind me, and on the screen, there was gunfire . . . and the sound . . . Chest got tight, heart pounding, sweat covering me. I slipped out to go to the bathroom and just kept walking. Never went back. Now she won't return my calls."

Dr. Coggins's voice is soft but confident. "I can promise you that it'll get better if you just stay with us."

Another guy who hasn't been to group in a few months jumps in. "It hasn't gotten better for me."

Levi, three seats down, leans forward and says, "Well, you wouldn't know that since you stopped coming the minute your disability payments kicked in."

The first guy stiffens. "Are you accusing me of something?"

"No," Levi says. "It's just that we see this a lot. Guys coming here to check off boxes until they get their disability, but once they get it, they don't really *need* the group anymore. Just makes you wonder if you really had a problem in the first place. And if you're lying, it makes it harder for the rest of us. All the fraud in the system."

"We don't need to judge each other," Coggins says. "I'm sure Will had a good reason for not coming."

"It's not like I owe this guy an explanation," Will says. "I have diagnosed PTSD just like the rest of you, but if you don't want me in this group, I'll find another one."

"He wasn't even in combat," Levi says. "This guy had a desk job. He never took mortar fire. He never saw an IED explosion. He never had one minute's trauma other than missing his mommy, yet he said all the right things to get on disability, while most of us here can't get the help we need."

Will springs up, shoving his chair back.

"You want to come out and see how messed up I am?"

"No, we can do it here!" Levi says, coming to his feet, and before anyone can stop him, he punches Will in the jaw, knocking him off balance, and when Will goes down, Levi keeps going at him.

I jump up and grab Levi. Another guy restrains Will, and we drag them away from each other. Dr. Coggins is on her feet now, and she's yelling at them to stop.

Levi jerks away from me. "I'm not coming to this group with people like that here, Doc. You make a decision whether this group is for people who really need help or not." He storms out.

Will just stands there, his lip bleeding. "That dude is sick."

"That's why he's here," Coggins says.

"No, he's dangerous. He needs to be in an institution."

"The thing is," one of the women says, "he's right. We all think you're a fake."

Will shoots her a look like he could take her head off, but since she's female, he holds himself back.

———

Dr. Coggins steps between them. "Will, let's set up a private session. Just call me this afternoon. I'm sorry this happened."

He leaves, and I sit back down. I hope she's not going to tell us that Will's accusers are off base, because the woman is right—we've all thought he was a fake. There's no one who has less patience for a PTSD fraud than people who really do have it.

Instead, she just looks at each of us. Her hands are shaking. "Everyone here is in a lot of pain, and as they say, hurting people hurt people. Part of your recovery is learning how to manage your anger outbursts, and even if you think certain things, you can't say them, because what will follow is not what you want. Can we agree on that?"

A few people nod.

"Some sources say that twenty-two veterans a day kill themselves in the US—almost one per hour—and groups like this one are supposed to keep that from happening. We're all trying here. We can't get inside each other's heads. We can't judge. We have to be accepting of each other. If we can't do that, who will?"

After several comments on what she's just said, Dr. Coggins switches gears and asks us all how we're sleeping, what's working, what's not. She shows us the patch Dex mentioned to me earlier, says it's a promising new therapy that might help. I make a mental note to find out more when I have a chance.

When the meeting breaks up, I talk to a couple of people on my way out. The new guy who knocked his kid down stops me just outside the door. "Interesting meeting."

"Yeah, it wasn't boring," I say.

"Does it really ever go away?"

I drag in a deep breath. "For some, yeah."

"How long?"

"Let me know when you find out," I say. "But keep coming, man. I'm better than I was."

When I get back into my car, I say a prayer for that man and his family, that his issues won't paralyze him. Feeling guilty that I didn't say more to give him hope, I pull my phone back out. I can't wait to get home and get back to work.

16

DYLAN

I spend the night and much of the next day marking off the cops on the list who have died of natural causes—checking their ages and obits, making sure there was nothing off about their deaths. Then I figure out which ones transferred to other departments or agencies, like the state police or the FBI or ATF. Then I check the age-appropriate retirements and mark them off the list.

I'm left with thirty or so who just left the department for reasons not mentioned on this list. There's a cluster of five in the few months following Andy Cox's death. I circle all their names. I'll follow up on those first.

I do a search on each of them, find out where they're living now. One of them still lives in town, so I check out what he's doing now. I find that he's working in his father-in-law's business, so he probably just got a better deal.

When I check out the other four, I find that two are dead. My heartbeat ramps up, and I follow the trail to see what happened. One of the guys died a year after he resigned. He was thirty-two. Brakes failed, and his car crashed into a tree. No other vehicle involved. He had a wife and two small children.

The second one was in his fifties and died of cancer, so I cross him off.

There are two guys left who I need to find and talk to, plus the wife of the man whose brakes failed. I track down their addresses. One lives in Jackson, Mississippi, now, and one in Grand Rapids, Michigan. I try calling both of them, but their landlines have been disconnected, and they don't have cell phones in their names.

I pack a bag and throw it in my car. Jackson is four hours from Shreveport, give or take. I can be there by sundown.

I get there just as rush hour is glutting I-20, but things move faster than in some cities I've been to, so I just plow through, following my GPS to the address I've gotten. The guy's name is Alvin Rossi, and he lives on the north side of Jackson. It takes me about half an hour to get through the traffic and follow the stack to I-55, to the north side of the city. My GPS directs me to get off at County Line Road, which is a pain to navigate this time of day. But my GPS finally spouts out, "You've arrived at your destination."

I look at the building the voice has indicated. It's a shopping center. The address is a UPS store. He must have a PO box there.

So it's a decoy address. I'm going to have to dig further.

There are a lot of shops up County Line Road, and I drive until I hit Old Canton and find a barbecue place that advertises free Wi-Fi. The parking lot's remarkably empty for this time of day. I take my laptop in and order a meal, then take my time checking all my databases to find Alvin Rossi.

Everything I find on him has that decoy address on it, but finally I locate his place of employment. He works at a Nissan plant a few miles up 55, in a bedroom town called Canton. Maybe he lives around there.

I drive over there and pull into the parking lot. The place is massive, and it's not likely that they all know each other. This is probably one of the biggest employers in the area. How am I going to locate this guy?

It's seven p.m. by now, but there's clearly a night shift, so I go to the front entrance and step inside. There's a guard at the front, so I give it a shot. "Hi, I need to see one of your employees. Alvin Rossi."

The guard shows no recognition. "What department is he in?"

"Not sure."

"I'll look him up." He punches something on the computer, and I fiddle with my phone as though uninterested. But I'm really opening my camera, ready to click when his info comes up.

My shutter is silent, so he doesn't realize I've done it. I lean toward the screen after I've gotten the picture, and study the guy's face. My eyes skim down, and I try to get the phone number, but he shuts it down before I can find it.

"He's not on the night shift," he says. "Doesn't work till morning."

"Oh, my bad," I say. "I thought he said nights. What time does that shift start?"

"Seven a.m."

I thank him and leave, checking my phone to make sure I got a good shot of the screen. Yes, his information is there. He's still using the same address, but I got his phone number.

Hoping it's a cell phone, I quickly add it to my Contacts, then send him a text.

> Alvin, you don't know me, but I need to talk to you
> about your time at the Shreveport PD. Can we meet
> somewhere? Very important.

I drive back toward Jackson and look for a motel that isn't too expensive and isn't in crackhead territory. I pull into a Motel 6.

I'm just about to go in when he texts me back.

Who is this?

I don't want to give him my real name, just in case he's in touch with Keegan. The phone I'm using isn't the one Keegan knows about, so he won't know it by my number.

I use my middle name.

Name's Ward. Like I said, you don't know me.

Before I press Send, I add a line:

I can be at your place within a few minutes. I won't keep you long. I think we might have some things in common.

I hope I've made him think I have his address and will show up at his house if he doesn't agree to meet me.

There's a longer silence than I expected, then finally, he says, I'm tied up right now. No can do.

Now what? I blow out a sigh, then go in and get a room. I'm just walking into it when my phone vibrates again.

Meet me in the parking lot of Buffalo Wild Wings, eight o'clock.

I type back, I'll be there.

I get there fifteen minutes early and park with my back to the restaurant. It's a popular place, and there are few empty spaces. It's not dark yet, so I watch every car that comes in. Finally, a white Nissan truck pulls in at about ten till eight. A guy gets out, wearing sunglasses even though it's dusk, and I'm pretty sure it's him. He taps a cigarette out of its pack as he walks up to the front, then stands there with his hand in his jeans pocket, smoking as he looks out toward the street.

I get out of my car and walk toward him. "Alvin?"

He turns and looks me over. "Yeah."

"Thanks for meeting me." I start to shake his hand, but he thrusts out his cigarette pack. "Take a cigarette and light it."

I take one and he flicks his lighter, and I inhale although I don't smoke. He's paranoid, looking from one end of the parking lot to the other, clearly worried someone might be watching us, wanting it to look like I'm a stranger bumming a smoke.

"See that bar across the street?" he says. "Meet me in there. I'll be in the back booth."

The clandestine stuff sets off my alarm. The guy seems ultra-careful, too careful for his story to be that he just got tired of police work. I leave my car where it is and watch him get in his truck and drive it across the street. I wait a few minutes, smoking, then put my cigarette out and cross the four lanes of traffic. When I go in, I use the restroom first, giving him time to get settled, then I stride back there.

He's at the back booth, his back to the wall, and when I slip in, he keeps watching the door. He finally settles his gaze on me. "Who are you and what do you want?"

I don't know quite where to begin. I didn't expect it to go

this way. Again, I leave my name out of it. "I'm a private investigator, and I'm working on a case that involves Andy Cox."

His ears redden. "He's dead."

"Yes, but I got curious about the circumstances of his death. I noticed you quit working for the department that same year. I wondered if you could tell me why you left."

"I don't know anything about his case," he says, but his Adam's apple is a little too active. He lowers his voice. "Look, if you're checking on me for him, you can tell him I haven't opened my mouth in all these years. I'm not going to start now. All I want is to be left alone. How did you even find me?"

I don't answer that question. "I'm not working for Keegan," I say. His reaction when I use the name is interesting. His hands are trembling now, and he waves for a barmaid, orders a beer. I ask her for a Coke.

While we're waiting, I watch him. He's sweating, and he doesn't take his eyes off the door. It's like he's sure Keegan is out there, about to enter and blow his head off. He's scared to death.

This isn't a guy who's buddies with Keegan. He's hiding from him.

I lean toward him and keep my voice low. "Gordon Keegan is still getting away with everything he's done. So is Sy Rollins. But I want to take them down. I need information from you to do that."

His eyes harden. "Take them down? You don't know who you're dealing with."

"I think I do." I pull out one of Brent's crime scene photos that was released to the press and lay it down on the table. "I have good reason to believe they recently did this."

Rossi stiffens. "Another cop?"

"No. A journalist who was looking into that case."

The barmaid brings our drinks, and he takes a gulp, then holds his mug like it's his lifeline. "This was Brent Pace, wasn't it? I saw that girl on the news. It's Cox's daughter, right?"

"Yes," I say.

"She didn't do it, did she?"

"No."

"They'll find her," he says.

I don't tell him that I'm going to find her first. "Help me take them down," I say. "Tell me who else in the department is involved."

"I don't know. I haven't been there in twelve years."

"Who was involved then? You must know."

"There were a few guys. One almost turned, wound up dead. One-car accident. Nobody even questioned it. The rest made so much money being their allies that none of them ever would have flipped."

"But you. Why did you leave?"

"Because I knew Andy Cox. I knew he didn't kill himself. Andy told me about the stuff he'd found out about them—extortion like you wouldn't believe—and he was getting ready to report them."

"Then he wound up dead?"

"Yeah. I told Maroney—he was the captain of my precinct back then—I told him what Andy had been working on, that I knew it wasn't suicide. That night, I pulled into my driveway, and two men wearing ski caps grabbed me and beat me. Bashed my head into the concrete. I went limp, acted like I was dead. Almost was."

He turns and points to the scarring on the side of his head. "A neighbor saw me and called an ambulance, and they got me to the hospital. Soon as I woke up, I realized the captain must have been involved and let them know I snitched on them. I didn't know who I could trust, so I got up and walked out of the hospital. Disappeared."

"Did they ever come after you?"

"No, they didn't know where I was. I wasn't married then, so I went from one place to another, just hiding. I finally met my wife here and got married. Enough time has passed that I didn't think they were after me anymore. I took precautions, but you found my address. I thought it was impossible."

"I didn't, man. I lied to get you to come out."

He takes in a deep breath, lets it out in a huff. "You're sure they haven't followed you?"

"Yeah, I'm sure. Look, I need names. And if this ever goes to court, I need for you to testify."

"No way. I have a family now."

"What if we get all of them? What if we clean out that department? Do you have any evidence it was them who beat you?"

"Just a voice. Keegan's voice."

"No other evidence?"

"I have what Andy Cox had."

I catch my breath. "Extortion victims?"

"Yeah, that and bank accounts, and how they were laundering the money. Others they'd terrorized."

"Can you get all that to me?"

He takes another gulp. "I don't want to stir things up. I like it here. My kids like their school."

"The sooner we get these leeches off the street, the sooner you can let your guard down."

He's sweating now. "I'll think about it."

"Don't take long," I say. "A girl's life depends on it. She's been through a lot. Think of all the other families they've threatened. There are probably even more murders than we know. You've managed to hide out all this time, but you constantly look over your shoulder because you know they could catch up to you eventually."

He looks at the booth behind me, as if thinking through his options, trying to figure out how this could go. Finally, he says, "Where you staying?"

"Near here," I say.

He leans forward, whispering again. "If I decide to help you, I'll leave you an envelope under the trash can at the 7/11 a few doors down from here. The can at the number three pump. It'll be there by seven in the morning if I'm going to leave it."

"They won't know I talked to you."

"You don't know that."

"I do. I've been hired as a consultant to find Casey Cox. They think I'm only focused on that."

"You really think you can do it? Take those maniacs down? You really think you're a match for them?"

I meet his eyes. "Try me."

He looks down at his drink again. "I'd wanted to be a cop since I was a kid. Loved it, most of it. But after that, I didn't dare join a force again. I had to keep my head down. I didn't want to get it bashed in again."

"You didn't have any allies," I say, trying to make him feel better. "You were injured. You did what you had to do."

"But look at all they've gotten away with since then."

"You can change all that now. Help me."

He draws in a deep breath, calls the barmaid for our check. I can tell that he hasn't made up his mind yet.

"Leave me the envelope," I say, "and you won't hear from me again until the prosecutor needs you to testify. And trust me, I won't out them until I know we've got them good. All of them."

He's somber as I pay our bill, then he tells me to wait and let him leave first. I give him fifteen minutes just for good measure.

I go back to the motel, but I don't want to sleep. I spend most of the night finding out about Captain Maroney, who was captain of the precinct at the time of Cox's murder. He's retired now and has moved up to Tennessee where he lives in a nice house on a lake in the Smokies.

When morning comes, I've only dozed a few times, but I've snatched myself out each time. My body aches, and my brain seems fuzzy. I finally go have breakfast and make my way to the 7/11 at five after seven. I fill up my car at the number three pump and look under the trash can.

The manila envelope is right where he said it would be.

17

─────

DYLAN

The file Rossi left me under the trash can is full of things I've been wanting to see. Crime scene photos of Andy Cox's death, pictures of Rossi's injuries after his beating, lists of extortion victims, the money laundering flowchart, and a picture taken through glass at a café downtown. The photographer has zoomed in, making the subjects blurry. But I see Keegan and Rollins and three other cops. The photo itself isn't evidence of anything. They could have been just shooting the breeze over lunch. But the fact that Rossi gave it to me tells me these are men who were part of Keegan's money-making scheme thirteen years ago.

I don't know any of them—except for the two I already knew about—and since these were taken over a decade ago, I can only guess there are more involved now. Keegan's son is suspect, for instance. I played football with him in high school—he was a decent guy and now is a cop—but it's hard to believe that his dad wouldn't cut him in on the action. One of these guys might be Maroney, the captain of Rossi's precinct then. I'll have to look them all up and make sure I have their names.

I flip the page. The next bit of evidence is a statement given by Casey Cox, then twelve years old, telling Rossi about an anonymous phone threat against her family. The person on the line told her that she needed to shut up about her father's death, that if she kept insisting it was a murder, she and her mother and sister might wind up "committing suicide" too. Casey interpreted it exactly as she should have.

No wonder she ran after she found Brent. Who would she have gone to with this allegation? She'd clearly trusted Rossi with that information, but if she knew he'd been beaten for his push-back, and that he'd now disappeared, she might have feared he was dead now too. She might have kept her mouth shut for the next decade to protect her mother and sister, and now her baby niece and her brother-in-law. She'd have no choice but to disappear to stay alive, and she'd also think it would keep them from going after her family. No wonder her family was so quick to tell me they believed in Andy's suicide. It was self-preservation.

The file isn't conclusive. It's not enough to put them away, but it's a start.

I can't help wondering about Casey, if she's scared, or tired, or lonely. She seems like a social person, so being on the run might take its toll on her. But I still have no clues as to where she is.

I tell Jim Pace I'm following some leads in the Great Lakes area and have him set up a charter flight to Michigan. I want to find the other man on my list, Gus Marlowe.

Marlowe seems to have gone off the grid, too, but the guy is ex-military, so I manage to get an address through my military database, something I hope Keegan hasn't had access to. The man gets a military disability check every month. Surely that address will get me close to him.

When Keegan asks where I'm going, I tell him I've worked out where she might have gotten off a train, and they buy it.

I get into Grand Rapids near ten o'clock at night, eager to seek out the address I have for Gus Marlowe. I get a rental car and program the GPS on my phone. I follow the directions, but halfway through, the road disappears and my GPS says that it can't continue.

So the guy lives off a dirt road south of town. Not easy to find at night. I decide to get some sleep and try again in the morning.

I check into a Drury Inn off 28th Street and turn the TV to Fox News. I turn it down low while I'm trying to fall asleep. Sometimes it helps; the background noise stops my brain from processing, and I'm able to relax.

Then I hear Casey's name. I sit up and grab the remote, turn it up.

"So if Casey Cox is apprehended, do you think what she did to help that girl will be admissible in court? I mean, that was heroic. She risked her life . . ."

"She didn't risk her life," some attorney says. "She saw the girl after breaking into a house to rob it."

"We don't know that. The grandmother of the girl says that Casey had reason to believe the girl was there. She knowingly walked into danger to get her out, even after being arrested for breaking into that same house once. She knew she could be outed by all this, but she chose to save the girl. I'm just saying that the jury might—"

"It'll never be admissible," someone else interrupts. "She'll be tried on the murder she allegedly committed. Period. No sane judge would allow the waters to be muddied by what happened in Shady Grove."

They move on to political talk.

I'm sick that the publicity will make it much harder for her to hide. If I were her, what would I do? She has probably already dyed her hair some color that would distract people from her face. She has likely cut it shorter. I try to imagine her hair in different colors. Which one would she try?

As tough as she is, she's also fragile. I hope she doesn't feel hopeless. If only I could talk to her again.

I open my laptop and check the email account we've communicated on before. Nothing. I don't blame her.

I turn off the TV, letting darkness envelop me. I'm so tired that this time I don't fight sleep. I fall into a surface slumber, the kind where my nightmares have a field day. Suddenly I'm back there, in the Humvee that day, and I get that feeling where the hair on the back of my neck rises, and Tillis curses as he sees something up ahead, and before I can even look, I'm flying back, my ears bursting with the sound, the smell of flesh and fuel burning and the metallic taste of blood . . . then that silence as things seem to go into slow motion.

I wake up drenched with sweat, and I've wet myself, as I did that day. As we all did. I'm shaking, so I clean up, then wrap myself in the bedspread, tight enough that I can't move. It doesn't help.

18

DYLAN

When morning comes, I find Gus Marlowe's house. What was impossible after dark is a little easier in the daytime. He isn't home, so I get back on my computer and locate the cell phone numbers associated with this address. When I call the first one, a woman answers. I ask her if I can speak to Gus, and she says he has a different number. I have another number, but just in case, I ask her for it. She hesitates a moment, then says she'd rather not give it out. Assuming she's his wife, I ask her if he was a detective on the Shreveport police department. She hangs up. Before she can warn him, I dial the other number.

"Hello?"

"Gus!" I say like a long-lost friend. "How's it going, man?"

"Fine," he says. "Who's this?"

I decide not to carry on with that ruse, and choose another one. "I'm Greg Houser, a private investigator working on a case having to do with Andy Cox, a cop who used to be on the Shreveport Police Department before he died. I was wondering if I could meet with you and ask you a few questions."

He pauses for a long moment. "I'm busy. Can you ask them on the phone?"

I don't want to lose the opportunity for a face-to-face. "Look, I know this is out of the blue, and you've been gone a long time from that place. But I'm looking into some of the activities of the people involved in the Andy Cox case. I noticed you retired a few months after that. It may not have had anything to do with the case at all."

"It didn't," he cuts in. "I retired because I was of age."

"But still, you must remember it."

"What do you want?" he asks.

"I'm just trying to get some information. There's another case I'm working on that might intersect. If you could just give me ten minutes, we could meet at a neutral location or restaurant or someplace. I'm not going to bother you after this. I just want to ask you a few things."

There's another long pause, then finally I hear a woman

speaking in the background. I can't hear what she's saying. He finally comes back on. "All right, I'll meet you at ten o'clock at the IHOP on 28th Street."

I'm there at nine forty-five, waiting in my car, when I see a man drive up alone. He scans the parking lot, clearly looking for someone, so I assume it's him. I get out and say, "You Gus?"

He grabs me then, twists my arm behind my back and kicks my feet apart, and throws me over the hood of my car. I almost fight back, but he's frisking me, making sure I'm not armed. I wait, my forehead pressed against my hot hood. "I'm not carrying," I say through my teeth. "I just want to talk to you."

When he's satisfied, he jerks me back up. "Who do you work for?"

"Not who you think. I just want information," I say.

He lets me go and starts into the IHOP, and I follow him. Like Alvin, he takes a booth at the back and sits on the side where he can see the door. As I take the seat across from him, I say, "Looks like you still have some skills. What are you? Seventy? And you had me over the hood before I could even react."

"What's your name again?" he asks, unamused.

I almost don't remember the name I gave him last night, but I come up with it suddenly. "Greg." The waitress comes over and takes our orders. I tell him it's my treat. He orders pancakes and sausage, a large coffee.

"I wasn't involved in the Andy Cox case," he says finally.

"I didn't think you were. I just thought that maybe the timing of your retirement and your moving out of state could've had something to do with it. I have reason to believe there are some corrupt officers who worked on that case, and things don't add up."

He shakes his head. "Got that right. Things never did add up on the Andy Cox case. He never would've done what they said. No way."

"So you knew him?"

"Yeah," he says. "Worked with him for years. We were partners for a while back in our younger days. Andy was a positive person. Loved people, loved police work. He wasn't one to be depressed. Never, even when he had reason to be. When his mother died, she had a long bout with cancer, really bad. She suffered a lot. He worried about her all the time, but even so, he wasn't dragging around. He just took care of her, did what he had to do, stayed positive. He had a way with people. And he loved his girls."

"I've heard that."

His mouth twists as emotion works on him. "You know, it's horrible the way he was found. That's the biggest clue I had that things weren't right. No way Andy Cox would've hung himself in his living room and expected his daughter to find him. That would never happen."

"Did you say anything about it at the time?"

He looks down at his hands, takes a sip of his coffee. "By then I knew not to."

"Were you afraid there'd be payback?"

"I feared hanging myself in my living room for my children to find."

The waitress brings our food, but he doesn't dig in.

"Did someone threaten you?"

"Andy Cox's death was a threat to everybody who had anything to say about certain people in the department. An object lesson. And we got it loud and clear."

"Was Gordon Keegan one of those people sending that message?" I ask.

He stares at me, his eyes locked with mine, and I know the answer is yes.

"I'm trying to make a case against them," I say. "I need your help. Can you tell me who else was involved at the time, who else covered up, who else might have been responsible for Cox's death?"

I wait quietly as he doctors his pancakes. He cuts into them and takes a bite, chews for a long moment.

"I guess what I'm trying to figure out," I say, "is whether Keegan's current captain or the chief of police has anything to do with it."

"I don't know who they are," he says. "I haven't kept up."

"Chief Gates is in charge now," I say. "Captain's named Swayze."

"Swayze," he says, almost spitting it out. "Probably."

"And what about Gates?"

"I don't know him," he says. "He was probably hired from

outside. There's no telling, but Keegan has a way of cutting people in. I wouldn't trust anybody."

"So do you know anything about Keegan or Rollins or Maroney or Swayze or any of the ones who were involved that I could use in a case against them? Anything at all. How they're spending the money they're extorting from people, things they may have bought that I could use as evidence . . ."

"You know about the mistress," he says, then takes another bite.

"What mistress?" I ask.

"Keegan has a hot little mistress. I was in Dallas last year visiting my boy for a Cowboys game, and I saw him there with her, right out in public. I got out of there as fast as I could. He didn't see me. When I got home, I did a little digging to see if he was still married, and he is."

"Yeah, he is. Did you find out the woman's name?"

"No, I didn't really care. Haven't thought much about it since then."

We end on much calmer terms than when he came in, and I feel like a dog with a bone. I can't wait to sink my teeth into the things he's given me. Especially the mistress.

19

CASEY

I check my look twice before I leave my motel, making certain that while I'm watching Candace Price, she won't recognize me. My black hair is pinned up close to my head, and I cake on the eyeliner and smoky eye shadow.

I have no trouble finding her house. A lot of the houses in Dallas are big, but this one qualifies as a mansion. From what I can tell about her recent real estate sales, she doesn't make that kind of money.

It's just before seven a.m. when I park, sip my Starbucks and eat my muffin, and watch for her to come out. At around eight, an older man drives up and parks at the curb in front of her house. He gets out and hobbles up to her door. She lets him in and he stays for an hour or more.

While I'm waiting, I take a stroll on the sidewalk like a neighbor getting exercise, and as I pass his Pontiac Bonneville, I see a stack of mail on the dashboard. I slow enough to get the name on the address. Morris Price. He must be her father. I make a mental note of his address, then go back to my car and look him up. He's a retired teacher who lives in a neighborhood a few miles from here. A Google Earth search shows that his house is much more modest than hers, so she must not have inherited her money, at least from that side of her family.

At around nine, she comes out with him, dressed in yoga pants and a tank top. Her platinum-blonde hair is cut like Marilyn Monroe's. She walks her father to the Bonneville, then gets into her own car and leaves.

I follow her to a Planet Fitness and watch her go in. She has the body of a model, so I'm guessing she works out a lot. I wait in the car, reading her Facebook page on my phone and taking down notes. When she comes out an hour later, she heads back home. Another hour passes, then she comes out, showered, her hair looking like she's been to the hairdresser. She's wearing a maxi dress and high heels. I expect her to go to her real estate office, but instead she drives downtown to Neiman Marcus and parks in the garage.

I pull into a vacant space about twenty cars down from her. I almost lose her, but I catch up to her as she's going into the store. I step into the air-conditioning and pretend to look at a dress. She goes to the handbags, peruses each one, takes a few pictures of them with her phone.

I pretend that I'm browsing as she goes to the women's section and holds up a few outfits as she gazes into the mirror. She takes their pictures too.

Did she send the pictures to friends and ask their opinions? Finally she makes some decisions. She chooses an expensive handbag, pays for it, then goes back to buy all of the outfits she photographed. I guess she's spent at least a couple thousand dollars, if not more.

She goes back to her Mercedes and I head to my car, adjusting my sunglasses, looking at my phone as I pass her so she doesn't notice my face. I follow her to her office, then sit outside and watch for her for the next couple of hours.

She comes out finally and drives off. I follow her until she parks in front of a house that's for sale. Another car drives up. I can't stop, so I pass by the house as they go in.

The day creeps by slowly as I tail her, and several times I almost give up and go home. She hasn't done anything that seems Keegan-related. As it's getting dark, she heads to a club.

I'm not in the mood for a place like that, but I decide to follow her in and get something to eat. The place is hopping since it's happy hour. I ask for a seat at the bar and order a Diet Coke and an appetizer. There's a mirror behind the bar, so I watch her meeting some girlfriends at a tall table.

Their laughter is loud enough to be heard throughout the club. They order a round of drinks and some food.

I'm trying to hear what they're saying when a man sits down next to me. "You waiting for someone?" he asks.

"Yes," I say.

"You've been here a while. You haven't been stood up, have you?"

I want to ignore him, but when I glance back in the mirror, I see Candace coming to the bar, right toward me. I turn to the man, smiling. "He's not late. I got here early."

"I'm Hamlin," he says.

"Miranda."

"You're dry. What are you drinking?"

She's standing right behind me now, leaning so close I can smell her perfume. The bartender asks her what she needs. "Can we get a round of shots for my table over there?" she asks in a southern lilt. "There are five of us."

He goes to pour them. I shake my thoughts back to the man next to me and keep my hand over the left side of my face so she won't see it in the mirror. "What did you ask?"

"Your drink. Want another one? What is it?"

Distracted, I look at my drink as if I can't remember what it is.

"You don't know what you're drinking?"

I look at him and laugh, as if I've had a brain slip. "I'm sorry. It's Diet Coke. I don't want another one."

When the bartender brings Candace the tray of shots, she

takes the plate and clomps in those heels back to her table. My mind checks out and I don't hear another thing the man is saying.

Finally, I give up. I'm sick of this. Keegan is nowhere in sight, and this is a waste of time. I'll try again tomorrow.

⌒

I watch Candace for most of the weekend, and there doesn't seem to be a husband or boyfriend around. She comes and goes in her shiny new Mercedes, zipping around town like she's in the Million Dollar Club.

There's no sign of Keegan. I don't even know for sure if he's still in her life.

After a while, I realize that this could take some time. I need to stay in Dallas for a while, so I'm going to have to find a cheaper place to live and get some kind of job.

I remember the Help Wanted sign in Cole Whittington's family's business, and the truth is, I'm curious about his situation. Maybe it wouldn't hurt to apply for that job.

Monday morning I drive over there and go inside. His mother is at the front desk again. "Hey, sweetie," she says in a comfortable drawl. "You're back. Don't tell me you found another Bible."

I laugh. "No, I was just . . . I'm looking for a job, and the other day I noticed you were hiring. I wondered what you're looking for."

Cole walks in, and he recognizes me and comes to the desk. "Hey . . . Miranda, right?"

"Yes, Miranda Henley," I say.

"Miranda was just asking about the job," his mother says.

Cole takes over. "Well, we need help packaging and shipping our orders."

"What are the qualifications?"

He hesitates. "Warm bodies who show up on time every day."

"I can do that. I'm a good worker and people say I'm reliable."

"I think we can trust her," he tells his mother. "She found my Bible after I lost it, and she made the effort to bring it back."

"It's a family business, darlin'," his mother says, "and we have about twenty other employees. We're always looking for more. You available to start tomorrow?"

"Sure," I say. "I'll be here."

I fill out some paperwork with my new name and social security number. I tell them I'll have to give them my address later, because I'm just moving into a new apartment and don't have the address yet. That'll give me time to get one.

Maybe I can get to know Cole and somehow convince him that suicide is not the way to go. Or at the very least, if he still seems bent on going through with his plan, maybe I'll let his family know so they can intervene.

Having this job will at least mean that I don't have to keep leeching from my cash while I'm watching Candace Price.

It will be a nice distraction.

20

CASEY

Since I've got a job now, I set to work to find a cheaper place to live. I've got to conserve what's left of my cash. I start out looking for a garage apartment, but everything I call about on Craigslist has already been taken. Then I find a room for rent about two miles from work. I make the phone call and get an appointment to go see it. When I get there, it's a two-story house. A chubby, retirement-aged woman comes to the door, old-timey curlers in her hair.

"Hi," I say. "My name is Miranda. I called about the bedroom for rent?"

The woman invites me in and I'm struck by the scent of lemon drops. It feels good in here, clean and fresh, and I'm thinking maybe this could work out.

"It's not much," she says, "just a room upstairs. You'd have to come in through the house, but you could have kitchen privileges. You'll have your own bedroom and your own bathroom. We share chores, and your food will have to be marked in the fridge."

"How much is it?" I ask.

"Four hundred a month," she says. "You won't beat that anywhere in this part of town."

"I'll take it. When can I move in?"

"Don't you want to see it?" she asks, chuckling.

I realize that I'm being impulsive. "Sure," I say.

She leads me up the stairs, but she clearly has knee problems, because she pauses every step and pulls up with only her left leg, favoring her right knee. "I try to keep it clean in here," she says. "That's my biggest fault, my daughter tells me."

"That's okay," I say. "I'm kind of a clean freak myself."

We get to the top of the stairs and she shows me a sitting area with a TV, then off to the side the bedroom that's furnished. It's small—just enough for a dresser and a bed, and the bathroom has a shower, a commode, and a sink. No frills, but perfect for me.

"I'd like a six-month lease," she says.

I don't plan to be here for six weeks, much less six months, but I go ahead and sign it.

"You can move in as soon as you want."

"I'll move in tonight."

As I leave the house, I'm excited about having a place that feels like a home, even if it isn't mine. I hope I'm not going to get her into trouble for harboring a criminal, but since it's a business transaction and not a favor, she'll be able to say she had no idea. She just rented me a room. She didn't aid me in any way. I'll have to bend over backward to make that true.

I go back to the hotel room to get the few things I've left there, pack up my car, then go to the grocery store and stock up. When I get back, there's another car in the driveway. I park on the street. I grab my bag and some of the groceries and carry them to the front door. I knock but no one comes, so I open the screen door and step inside. "Hello," I call. "It's me, Miranda."

I see the lady through the back screen door. She's sweeping the porch, and I realize I never even looked at the backyard. I walk into the kitchen, set my duffel bag down, and quickly unload my groceries, marking my name on each item with a Sharpie. When I put them into the fridge, I see that there are two other names on the items there. Miss Naomi who owns the place, and another name—Lydia. Is there another tenant?

When I'm done, I step to the screen door. "Miss Naomi, I'm back. Just wanted to let you know."

"Sure, honey, go on up," she says. "Let me know if you need anything."

I carry my duffel bag upstairs and, as I reach the top

landing, I run smack into a girl with waist-length hair as black as night and a toddler on her hip.

"Hi," I say.

"Who are you?" she asks in an irritated voice.

"I'm Miranda. I just rented the room."

"What room?"

This isn't going well. I point to the room I've just rented, and she rolls her eyes. "You'd think she could have told me she was giving my room away."

I want to ask if she's freaking kidding me, but I try to sort through it as I hear Miss Naomi stepping slowly up the stairs. "Oh good, so you've met my daughter Lydia."

"Who *is* she?" the girl asks in a biting voice.

"She's Miranda," Miss Naomi says. "Your new roommate. I told you I was going to have to rent out one of the rooms if you couldn't pay your rent on time."

"What did you do with Caden's stuff?" Lydia snipes back.

"I moved it all to your room." There's a note of satisfaction in Miss Naomi's voice, and I feel like I'm stepping into a family fight.

"I can't sleep with him! He sleeps sideways and kicks me in the ribs."

"I'll make him a pallet on the floor," Miss Naomi says.

"Mom, I did pay the rent!"

"You didn't pay what I told you it costs."

"So sue me," Lydia says. "It's not *worth* that."

"You paid me half, so you get to live in half. You don't get the whole floor anymore."

I freeze on the landing. "Look, if my being here is a problem, we can tear up the lease."

"No," Miss Naomi says. "Stay. Lydia, be nice to your housemate. You have to live with her."

I'm thinking that I don't want to live with this girl and a toddler who's looking at me like he's about to cry.

"Miranda, do you like children?" Miss Naomi asks.

"Yes, sure. I have a niece."

"Well, this is my grandson Caden. He's two and a half. He's the best thing in this house. He'll entertain you for hours."

I frown, hoping that's an exaggeration.

"So, let me get this straight," I say. "Lydia and Caden and I are going to be sharing?"

"The floor," Miss Naomi says. "That bedroom and bath are yours. You'll share this TV room. Lydia and Caden are in that bedroom over there."

I look and see the other room across the TV room. It looks like a toddler's room, with toys everywhere. "Oh, okay. I didn't realize . . ."

"I was going to tell you more, but you snapped it right up, no questions asked. You signed the lease."

"I know," I say. "No, it's fine, really."

I try to console myself as I move my stuff into the drawers, but Lydia comes to the door, leans in. I glance past her and see Caden sitting on the floor, watching an episode of a show with little mermaid cartoon characters floating around in the water. It's *Bubble Guppies*, something Emma used to love to watch. I think maybe it won't be all bad being around a child.

"So you don't have much stuff," Lydia says grudgingly.

"No," I tell her. "I like to travel light. I'll have the rest of my stuff sent later."

"So you're new in town?"

I shrug. "Yeah, I just got a job."

"Where are you working?" Her question sounds like an accusation.

"At the UpDown Seat Company. The Whittingtons own it. Do you know them?"

"No," she says. "There are over a million people in Dallas. I don't know everybody."

This girl has quite a mouth on her.

"It's only a couple of miles away, so I thought maybe you were familiar with them." I stop unpacking, because I don't want her to get suspicious by just how light I travel. At least my wigs are in my emergency bag in the car, so she won't see those. I take out the bag of toiletries I've bought and go into the bathroom to put them away.

Lydia follows me and leans against the door. "Believe me, if I could live anywhere else, I would. She's got this idea that she's been enabling me. To do what, I don't know, but she's using you to manipulate me."

I look at her reflection in the mirror. "So you two don't get along?"

Lydia just rolls her eyes. "My mother is grudgmental."

"Did you say *grudgmental*? Like *judgmental*?"

"Kind of," Lydia says, "but it's based on a past grudge. She's kind of a mental case."

That's not very kind to say about your own mother, and it makes me miss my own mom back home, with her rituals of pairs of everything piled so high that she can't walk to her bed. Lydia doesn't know how lucky she is.

"Don't worry," Lydia says. "I'm not gonna be like this all the time."

I try to smile. "Like what?"

"Snarcastic. Like Godzilla's angry stepsister."

"I wasn't thinking you were like that."

"It's just that my mother likes to do things. Grand gestures that are supposed to shake me to my senses. Taking in a tenant was one of those things."

"I feel bad." I put my shampoo in the shower, then turn back to her. "But there was an ad on Craigslist. Doesn't seem that spontaneous."

She sighs. "At least it'll get her off my back about the rent. Oh, and by the way, you need to know that Caden does not like closed doors, so unless you lock it, he's probably gonna come bolting in. He's fascinated by doorknobs."

Caden toddles in, smiles up at me, and asks, "Why she in my room?"

"Because your grandmother is a crazy woman," Lydia says.

He takes flat, duck-like steps toward me.

"What your name?" he asks.

I almost say Casey, but I catch myself. "I'm Miranda," I say, and I reach out to shake his little hand. He slaps it like a high five. I wonder if all kids come out of the womb knowing how to do that.

He reaches up to me before I know it, offering himself. "Hold me."

I pick him up, glancing at Lydia to make sure she's okay with it, but she's looking down at her phone, probably texting her friends about the girl who just invaded her home. I have to make sure she doesn't take my picture.

Caden grins up at me, and I can't help liking him. "Are you watching *Bubble Guppies*?" I ask.

Remembering the show, he squirms to get down again. He hurries out and plants himself back in front of the TV. I leave the door open as I put the rest of my things away and try to make myself at home.

I can't help singing "Bubble Guppies" under my breath as I work.

21

DYLAN

Today Hannah didn't go for her walk earlier in the day, so I'm guessing she will right after dinner. I go to her walking park around five thirty and meander up the path to the wooded area that she'll pass. I wait there, reading old newspaper articles about the Shreveport PD on my phone.

An hour later, I finally see her walk by. I get up and walk behind her, waiting until she's deeper into the wooded area, too deep to be bugged. I check to see if she has a cell phone in a pocket through which they could be listening, but she's wearing pocketless yoga pants. She seems to have left her phone in the car. She carries her keys, dangling from her hand.

"Hannah," I say, coming up behind her, and she jumps and swings around.

I hold out a hand and say, "I'm sorry. It's me, Dylan."

She touches her chest and expels a breath. "You scared me!"

"I know. I'm sorry."

"Are you following me?"

"I was waiting for you. I know you come here most days. I wanted to talk to you. It's really important."

She turns around to walk away. "I have nothing to say to you. I've already told you everything I know."

"I believe Casey," I blurt. "I know she didn't kill Brent."

She stops and slowly turns back around, studying me. A woman jogs past, and Hannah's quiet until she's out of sight. "How do I know you're not just saying that to manipulate me?"

"She didn't do it," I say in a low voice. "I've already told you I read all the stuff she sent me, all the files Brent had, the interviews. I have no doubt in my mind. I need your help."

She looks behind her, in front of her, all around us.

"You're right to be cautious," I say. "They could be listening. They have your cell phone wiretapped."

"I figured."

"They also put a GPS tracker on your car, but I moved it to your mailbox so they'll think you're just staying home."

"You've tampered with my car?"

"It's a magnetic tracker. I just went into your driveway last night after the media went home. I was trying to help you." I step toward her. "Look, if you hear from her, if you know how to reach her, I need for you to tell her to email me."

"I told you, I don't know where she is!"

"She'll touch base with you when she can. Hannah, this is a matter of life and death. You could be in danger, too, and you're the one who told me *she* was in danger if she's caught. The police are still looking for her. If they find her before I do, she's going to die. You know that as well as I do."

Tears shine in her eyes, and she turns away.

"She's asked me to protect you. Now I need for you to protect her."

"I have a baby," she whispers, turning back around. "I have to think of my family. Casey wants me to."

"I know you do," I say. "But if I can just work with Casey, we can take them down." I step closer to her, almost whispering. "I've found out some things that will help her case. We need to work together. You have to trust me."

"I don't trust anybody," Hannah says, "especially when they've been hired to find my sister."

I back away now, several steps. "Look, I understand where you're coming from. I know exactly."

"I have to go." Hannah turns and walks away.

"Did she tell you that I let her get away?"

She stops and turns back. "No."

"I had the chance to arrest her in Georgia and I didn't. She's free right now because of me. They didn't report that on the news, because they didn't know it. But Casey is a hero. She saved the lives of a girl and her baby. She's not the person they want people to believe she is. The tide is turning. People are wondering how she can be a psychopath and still do something like that. The time is right. If we just get enough evidence, we can clear her, Hannah. We can take them down. I know we can."

I know she'll ask Casey if what I'm saying is true.

This time when she walks away, I let her go. I sit down and lean back against a tree, exhaustion from lack of sleep aching in every joint. I wait for her to be long gone before I emerge from the trees, hoping that if anyone is staking out the area, they'll think I'm here to follow her myself. When I get to my car, I want nothing more than to go home and drop into bed.

That night, I fall asleep lying on the couch, fully clothed, and my dreams instantly go to Brent's body at the foot of his stairs. I see him get up, and his face morphs back into his childhood face, but with blood streaks and stab wounds. He's running ahead of me, telling me to hurry and catch up, and we're in the woods, tripping over branches and zigging between trees. I run to reach him, and he leaps into a hollow tree. I get in with him, and suddenly it's a Humvee, and he morphs into my buddy Blue Dog, joking with Dex. Unger drives and Tillis watches the road.

Tillis says, "What's that?" when the blast deafens me, hurling me back. Thick smoke makes everything go black, and suddenly I'm on my knees, reaching, groping, yelling . . .

Something crashes and startles me awake, and I realize I'm on the floor under my end table. The lamp that was there is in a dozen pieces on the floor.

I'm soaked and shaking, and I hate my life like I hated it then. I sit back on the floor, an elbow on my knee, and I try to get a grip.

When I can move again, I take a shower, trying to wash the images out of my mind, trying not to loathe the fact that I'm still breathing. I pray that God will fix this.

I get out of the shower and look at my bed, and though my body is still tired, I don't dare go there. I won't sleep again tonight. I can't take that chance.

I don't fear Keegan, but I do fear sleep. I want to avoid it until I can't take it anymore.

I can't go on like this.

I finally call my shrink and make an appointment.

I'm late for my appointment with Dr. Coggins, and I hope she hasn't given my slot away. When I check in, she comes out pretty quickly and ushers me in.

"I can't sleep," I say before she even takes her seat. "It's bad."

"You can't *fall* asleep?"

"No, I can fall asleep, but I can't stay asleep. And I dread it, like it's life or death, like it's . . ." My voice trails off, and I try to find the words.

"Night terrors?"

"Yeah." I feel like an idiot. Aren't night terrors something little kids have when they're afraid of monsters?

"That's common, Dylan. Tell me what you see. Is it the original trauma?"

"Yeah, that, and a few other things. My murdered friend seems to work his way in. I just can't quiet my brain. It goes there no matter what I do." I get up, pace across her office. "So I avoid it for days until I can't anymore."

"You can't do that, Dylan. You have to sleep."

"I know that, but it's not worth it."

"I can prescribe you something."

"No, I don't want drugs. But . . . you said something about that patch thing. Is it voodoo?"

"No," she says. "It's science. Researchers at the University of California, Los Angeles, are studying this. It's called trigeminal nerve stimulation." She gets up and goes to her cabinet on the wall, pulls out a small case. She lays it on the table and opens it, then takes out the device.

I sit back down and try to figure it out.

"The device has a nine-volt battery. It's wired to the patch. You put the patch on your forehead, and it sends these small electrical currents to the largest nerve in your brain—the trigeminal nerve. The device sends a little current to some of the forehead's cranial nerves that are connected to the amygdala and prefrontal cortex, where mood is regulated. It calms your brain so it's not dragging up all those traumas."

"When do you wear it?"

"Just while you sleep. They're studying it with military veterans, and some of my patients participating in the study say it helps with depression and insomnia. Some even say it helps with cognition. A quarter of them stopped having any symptoms. Some have reported improvement; some haven't. I can probably get you enrolled in the study, if you want to try it. You're a good candidate."

I don't have time for a lot of paperwork and waiting to get started, but I guess I don't have a choice. "Yeah, I'll try it," I say.

She knows me too well, so she makes me fill out the paperwork right there in her office. They'll call me and ask some questions, she says, then if I make the study, they'll send me my own patch.

I don't know how I'll survive until then.

22

CASEY

My new job seems easy enough. I'm tasked with loading the UpDown Seat into a box, sealing it up, and getting it ready to mail. There are three others who work on that task with me. Because of some press they've gotten in the last few weeks in some kind of geriatric magazine, they have more orders than usual, which is why I was hired. We work in a big warehouse that's pretty noisy, because in one corner they're working on parts of the hydraulic lift that makes the seat what it is. In another corner they're using molds to make the plastic parts. By the time it gets to us it's all put together, and we have to put it in a clear plastic bag, then in the box, then in a shipping box. It gets pretty tedious and my back hurts, but I do my best even though it's the least amount I've ever been paid. But I can't expect more than minimum wage. I just hope it's enough to help me fill back in what I've already spent of my cash.

There's kind of a family environment here, and every couple of hours the people doing the hydraulics take a break, so it gets quiet and we can talk. Blake, the inventor, is hands-on, making sure nothing is overlooked. He jumps in wherever he's needed. But Cole is different. He works in the office most of the time, and from time to time he walks through, looking distracted. I can't help looking for the sadness in his eyes, wondering if he's still contemplating suicide.

At lunch in the break room, I get to know my coworkers better. I find out that one of them, Alice, is a gluten-free vegan about my age, who has a weakness for bologna. It seems that her doctor has her on the G-free diet, but she eats the meat like candy that she's sneaked into her car. The two other people in my area in charge of packaging are Trey, who dropped out of high school in the tenth grade, and Sully, who's around thirty-five and used to work offshore on an oil rig, until the economy turned and he couldn't find work. Though they're pretty quiet and focused when they're working, they relax a little at lunch.

"So does anybody know how Cole's wife is doing?" Alice asks the guys at our table in a whisper.

I look up.

"She came by here to talk to him the other day," Trey says. "I saw her when she left and she was crying."

"Do you think he did it?" Alice asks.

Trey shrugs. "I don't know him that well, but he seems like a decent guy."

I want to ask what they think he did, but it seems like none of my business, so I look down at my food.

"How do you get over this, if it's not true?" Alice says. "You can't just move on. People are going to think he did it for the rest of his life." She glances at me. "It's Cole. He's only been working here a couple of weeks, since he lost his job as a vice-principal." She glances to the side, making sure none of the family are lurking nearby. "They're saying he molested a seven-year-old girl at his school."

I catch myself before I gasp, and then I remember that line in the suicide note, where he mentioned a false accusation. "What has he said?"

"That he didn't do it and his lawyer is working on clearing his name."

"He goes to my church," Sully finally says. "I've been on mission trips with him. He's for real, man. He couldn't have done it."

"But isn't that how it goes?" Alice asks. "I mean, people who do that are never the ones you think."

"But I've seen him with his kids. He *has* a seven-year-old. No way he did that."

I finally have to ask. "Did he get fired, or did he just resign?"

"Got fired, I heard," Sully says. "And it's been all over the papers and local news."

"You know, the weird thing is that they usually keep the identity of a child abuse victim private, but this family has been giving interviews. They outed her themselves."

"He must be really depressed," I say, glancing toward the door. "Is his wife sticking by him?"

"Seems to be," Alice says. "But it's got to be hard."

About that time, Cole comes into the room. He stands in the doorway for a moment, looking around as if he's forgotten why he came in here. He has dark circles under his eyes, and his skin has a gray pallor. He looks like he hasn't had much sleep in days.

He meets my eyes, then quickly looks away, then back again. I look down at my sandwich and take a bite. I wonder if he realizes I saw the note. He finally leaves the room and doesn't come back.

When I get off work, I go into my room, crawl up on the bed, and turn on my computer. I look up reports of the accusations against Cole. As my coworkers mentioned, there are several articles that have interviews with Nate and Tiffany Trendall, the parents accusing him and suing the school.

I watch the interviews they've done on the local news, astonished that they went into such detail about their child's abuse. Doctors have confirmed that she was molested.

I hear knocking on the door and I get up and open it. Little

Caden is holding on to the doorknob, wanting to close the door. I smile and let him close it, then he knocks and opens it again. He's delighted by the game as he stands on his toes, opening and closing my door. "Caden, what are you doing?"

"I told you he loves doors." Lydia is sitting in a chair, legs crossed in a yoga pose, and she's on her phone texting furiously. I bend down and speak to him, throw his ball, and let him run after it and bring it back. He seems starved for attention, and she's not interested in giving it. It's a small thing, playing with a child, but it means a lot, and it makes me miss my little Emma even more.

He brings me a book and I ask Lydia if she minds if I pull him up onto my bed and read it to him. She says it's okay— without looking up from her phone—so I pull him up. He gets into position, snuggled next to me, eagerly waiting for the story to begin. Because I don't see him following every word of the book, I abbreviate the words and concentrate on the pictures. He sucks his thumb as he listens.

Before I've finished the story, he demands "milt," which I'm pretty sure means *milk*. I go to the door and try to get his mother's attention. "Lydia, he's saying he wants some milt."

"Yeah, I guess it's bedtime," she says without looking at him. "I'm going out. My mother is keeping him. I'll make her get him some milk and put him to bed." She finally puts her phone in her pocket, then grabs Caden and takes him downstairs. I'm relieved because he's wearing me out after I've worked all day, but I don't want him to know it. I hope his "milt" lulls him to sleep.

23

CASEY

By Sunday morning, I wonder if my time following Candace Price has been wasted. I'm bored following her as she zips around town for home showings and goes out every night to clubs. I haven't yet found anything that will help my case against Keegan. Maybe they've broken up. I wonder if I should even keep trying.

It's quiet in the house. Lydia and Caden, and even Miss Naomi, are still sleeping. Loneliness hits me like the flu, and I think I'll shrivel up and die before tomorrow comes when I can get back to work. My spirit feels dry, like drought-dead fruit, and I'm hit with the sense that I need to attend to it. Churches all across town are meeting this morning. I've only been to church a few times in my life, mostly for funerals and weddings. But I feel like I owe God something, since he's answered some of my most urgent prayers lately.

I get in the car and drive around to some of the churches I've seen on the way to work. I'm drawn to a small one, but then I realize that I might attract too much attention if I go there and they're not used to visitors. I decide on a bigger church with hundreds of cars in the parking lot. A sign out front says "Visitors Welcome." Maybe I can get lost in the crowd and not be noticed. The sign says the service starts at 10:30, so I wait until 10:35 and go in, hoping no one will pay attention to me or speak to me if I'm late.

I don't know Episcopal from Baptist, and when I sit down, I can't remember which one this is. From the back row, the huge room looks like a theater. The people in front of me are dressed nicer than I am. For a moment I think of slipping back out, but then the singing starts, and I decide I'll wait a while longer.

The congregation is sitting when the choir opens with a song I've never heard, and the sound is soothing and calming. The music director turns to the audience, indicating we can sing along. I pick up on it after the first chorus and find myself singing. I don't remember when I've sung as an adult, except to the radio. It's nice. Halfway through the song, someone near the middle of the room stands up, as though he can't contain himself. Slowly, others pop up, then more, then finally the rest of the crowd is on their feet, including me.

I like the feeling that comes over me, and I wonder if that's God.

The guy at the front leads them into another song, and I watch the lyrics on the screen.

What can wash away my sin?
Nothing but the blood of Jesus.

I don't sing to this one. I just study those lyrics. How can blood wash away anything? The thought is a little disturbing.

Oh, precious is the flow
That makes me white as snow.
No other fount I know,
Nothing but the blood of Jesus.

As we sit again after the song, I pull out a pen and a notepad and jot down those words. As performers sing solos, I think through each line of this verse. The flow of blood, making someone white as snow. I don't get it, but I really want to.

They sing a few more songs that don't tax my understanding, then after the offering, all gets quiet as the preacher takes the podium. He tells a joke, then a story, and my mind drifts to those in front of me in the pews. I see a family—a husband and wife and two children—and a little girl leaning against her father, and suddenly I miss mine. We never did church when I was young, but I would have liked sitting on a pew next to my dad, his arm around me. I wonder if he and Mom ever talked about taking us.

I wonder if he lives on now . . . somewhere.

I tune back in as the preacher gets to the meat of his sermon. It's mostly clear to me, as he talks about Sunday Christians who change on Monday morning. I think of Miss Lucy, who was the same all the time. If I ever decide to convert, I want to be like her. I think of Dylan, who talked of God in our email. I doubt he's a Sunday-only Christian.

My gaze travels again and snags on a familiar face in the third row from the back, down to the right of me. It's Cole Whittington with his wife and his daughters, who look about five and seven. His wife sits shoulder-snug to him.

I wonder if it was her idea to come, or his. It would be so easy to stay home as people judge you for the worst accusation ever made about you. The fact that they're here says something about them. I'm not sure what.

But as the sermon ends and we sing another song, I see him wiping tears. I feel bad for him and hope that he isn't considering suicide again. I can't see his wife's face from this angle because he's blocking her, but I see him reach into his pocket for a handkerchief and hand it to her.

Something about that moves me.

The family gets up and leaves quietly after that, clearly avoiding the others. There are a few announcements, then the congregation is told to hold hands for the closing song. I take that moment to slip out too. I get to the parking lot and see Cole and his family pulling out.

Instead of going back to Miss Naomi's, I go to Candace Price's house and watch her again. Her father's car is back, and there's no activity for a while. Sitting in my car and using my phone as a hotspot, I go online to look for more information about Cole's accusers. I guess I'm still obsessed with his plight. I really need a hobby.

24

DYLAN

'm pulling into my apartment parking lot after church when I see my buddy Dex is waiting for me in his van. I pull up beside him and open my door. He rolls down his window.

"'S'up, dude?"

I get out and go around the car to fist-bump with his hook. "Dex, how long you been waiting?"

"Half hour or so. You got a girl or something?"

"No, man. Church. You should come with me someday."

"Yeah, someday."

I wait as he gets out of his van, wearing shorts, and limps

to the steps, one leg perfect, the other a tangle of steel rods. He has papers rolled up and sticking out of his back pocket.

"Still don't have elevators, huh?" he asks as he pulls himself up with his left hand.

"They'll never get elevators here. But I could move."

He laughs. "You'd do that for me, wouldn't you, Pretty Boy?"

We get to the second floor, and I unlock my door. I wish he wouldn't call me Pretty Boy. I wasn't Pretty Boy when we hung out on post, eating in the same mess hall. *He* was the pretty boy then, the one all the girls went after, the one who was once Mr. July in a calendar that women hung on their refrigerators.

But I'm Pretty Boy now because I have two legs and two arms. How I escaped injury is a question I'll never have answered. Every time he refers to me that way, I wonder if it's because he resents my surviving unscathed as much as I resent it.

We get into my apartment and he goes to my fridge and takes out a bottled water. "So how's the job?"

"Okay."

"I've been following Keegan," he says. "This guy is interesting. He gets around."

"What does that mean?"

"He's in and out of businesses all day. Not just going to crime scenes." He tosses a report of his observations down on the counter. "I went into one establishment when he was in there and saw him taking cash. Seemed to be a little fear there. Owner didn't want to cross him."

"Which one was that?" I ask, studying his report.

"Catalina Convenience Store," he says, pointing to it. "I didn't want to go in any others, because I'm sorta recognizable."

"Ya think?"

"And of course he coulda been working on cases, talking to witnesses, whatever. I only know for sure that he took cash from this guy. But I made a list in case you want to check them out."

I pick up the report and scan it. "Was Rollins with him when he made these visits?"

"His partner? Yeah, on a few of them."

I smile, glad I hired him. "That's just what I needed. Good work, buddy."

"Need me to keep on?"

"Yeah, if you have time."

"Nothing but."

I write him a check for the hours he's put in. I hope it makes his life easier.

"So what do these guys have to do with Casey Cox?"

"They're the detectives on her case."

"And you think they're dirty."

I don't know whether to answer, so I just look at him.

"How dirty?" he asks.

I turn away and flick on the TV. The news channel comes on.

"I mean, like, skimming a little under the table dirty, or worse?"

"I can't really talk about it," I say, looking back at him.

"No problem, man." He leaves it at that and lowers to the couch. "Did I tell you I had an interview the other day? Tried to point out that they didn't have enough handicapped people working for them. Hate that word, you know, but if it checks off a box they need checked off and gets me a job, then I'll use it."

"You're the least handicapped guy I know." It's true. He tackled his amputations with gusto. He went through the depression and grief that all amputees endure, but it focused him on rehab. He waited so long for his prosthetic limbs, then suffered pain and frustration as he tried to make them part of himself. And those were just his physical challenges. If it were me, I might not have wanted to push through that pain. I might have just opted for the wheelchair and drugs.

Truth is, I may be more handicapped than he is.

"So how you doing, really?" he asks me, as if I'm the one to be worried about.

"Good. This case is keeping me busy. Hey, I took your advice and signed up for that clinical study with that patch thing."

"Did, huh? They send it to you yet?"

"No, but they called. I've been approved. Just waiting to use it."

"Got mine last week. It's helped me, man. I sleep. I'm not as gloomy. And hey, my wife tells me I'm better looking."

"I noticed that right away."

"So are you still hunting that girl, even though you doubt she did it?"

"Yeah."

"Any leads?"

"No, not this time. She's smart. Really, really smart. She doesn't go where anyone would expect her to. She picks places randomly, with no rhyme or reason. That makes things harder. Last time it was a small town. This time it could be a big city. Impossible to know."

"Any idea where she's getting these identities? Is she counterfeiting driver's licenses herself?"

"Doubt it. There are lots of places where you can get fake driver's licenses."

"But how would she know them?"

"I wish I knew. It's not like she has a history of hanging out with criminals."

He grabs the remote and finds a ball game as I look at his list again.

"Want to get lunch?" he asks after a few minutes.

I decide to go, even though he should probably be with his family today. I don't ask questions about that, because it would sound like I'm judging. Sometimes you just need to be around other PTSD victims.

25

CASEY

When Candace goes to the airport, I hope she's picking up Keegan. I circle the garage for a couple of hours, waiting to see if she's coming back out. She doesn't, so I park and walk over, look into her car for clues. She's neat, so there isn't anything on the seat that would give me any info about where she's gone.

Since I doubt she'll be back today if she really flew out of town, I use the rest of that day to follow the Trendalls—the family accusing Cole Whittington of molesting their daughter. I don't know why that family is plaguing me, but Cole's suicidal thoughts worry me. I want to know if he deserves what he's getting. My snooping has turned up their address, which isn't far from here.

I've also learned that Tiffany Trendall accused her boss of sexual harassment two years ago and won a cash settlement, and just before that, Nate, her husband, accused his employer of religious persecution. Again, there was a settlement. Tiffany was also married before and has older children with that husband, and during that divorce, she accused her ex of child abuse and won custody.

And it looks like she has a problem with people rear-ending her. She's been hit from behind three times. I read a .pdf file of the brief of one of the cases, and it cites the police report. The person who hit her claimed Tiffany slammed on her brakes and forced the collision. But in all these cases, she was awarded settlement money.

Now this family is suing the school system for their child's abuse. Their past doesn't necessarily negate the possibility that little Ava was abused by the vice-principal, but it makes me doubtful.

I find their house, which is in a middle-class neighborhood. The house is nice, but the yard is grown up—the only yard in the neighborhood that looks neglected. Two doors on the passenger side of their gray van are open. They're either coming or going. As I drive by, I see a little girl in a pale blue T-shirt with her name—Ava—in black text. She's playing by the mailbox, way too close to the street. She's a cute little thing with curly black hair and huge brown eyes, and she looks younger than seven. I would have figured her for a five-year-old.

I round the block, then before getting to their house again, I pull over a few houses down. I watch as the couple comes out and the three of them pile into the van. Then I follow them to a children's indoor playground called Bouncy House Heaven.

They go in, so I wait a few minutes and follow them. I'm surprised that there's security at the front. As they check in the family in front of me, I realize I've got to have a reason for being there without a kid.

I step up to the turnstile. "My sister's family is already here," I say. "I'm late."

They accept that and take my money. I go in and look around. There are inflatables all over this place, with a bunch of tables in the middle. On the side is a concession area, next to a bunch of arcade games. I go to the counter and order a drink, then glance around to see where the Trendalls are. Tiffany and Nate are sitting at a table, both of them reading their phones. I scan the building for little Ava. I don't see her. She must be inside one of the bounce houses.

I walk over to one of the rubber houses and see Ava through the netting, trying to jump among bigger kids who knock her down. I glance back at the parents, hoping they'll intervene and direct her to a place where she's safer, but they still aren't watching her.

That disturbs me too. If their child has already been abused, you would expect them to be overprotective, not checked out.

I watch as a pizza is delivered to the table. Tiffany and Nate start to eat without trying to find their daughter.

I take a seat and watch for another hour or so. In the time that they're there, Ava comes over and eats a few bites of pizza, but most of the time she's off playing, out of sight, and her parents never check on her. But maybe that's normal for a child that age. It's not like she's a toddler, though she isn't much bigger than one.

When they finish the pizza, Nate and Tiffany get up as if to leave, but they don't go get Ava. I watch through the front window as they go outside to smoke, not bothering to tell her where they're going. I expect them to come back in within minutes. But then they get in their van and drive away.

They've left their daughter behind.

Alarmed, I watch Ava more closely now, afraid she'll come out of the bounce house and look for her parents and be terrified that she's been left. But she just goes from one inflatable to another, bouncing around with other kids.

I go to the castle she's in and peer through the black netting. Some kids who look like they're too big to be in there tumble down from the second level, bobbing and squealing. Ava doesn't move fast enough, and one of them lands on top of her.

She screams as the girl rolls off of her. Alarmed, I find the flap and crawl in. "You hurt her!" I tell the girl. "You have to watch out for the little kids!"

The older girl ignores me and bounces away, but Ava keeps

screaming. Her face is crimson and her mouth is stretched with heartbreaking wails, and tears stream down her face. She crawls past me to the doorway and gets out, then looks around for her parents. I get out behind her, glad to be on solid ground.

"Mama!" Her cry shrieks over the building.

I stoop down in front of her. "Are you all right, honey?"

She shakes her head, hiccupping sobs.

"I think your mom walked outside." I look her over to make sure nothing's broken. She's standing on both legs and moving her arms and fingers, so everything seems to be in working order. "How about I buy you something to drink?"

She sucks in a sob and wipes her eyes. "Okay," she says in a high-pitched voice.

I lead her to the concession area and buy a piece of pizza and a strawberry-flavored drink, and I give her the drink. She slurps it and follows me to the table where her parents had been sitting. I don't want them to come in and notice me, so I don't sit. I put her pizza plate down and check to make sure it's not too hot. "Is that better?" I ask her.

She nods, perches on the edge of a chair, and takes a big bite of pizza. Her front two teeth are missing, so she bites with her side teeth.

I stroke her corkscrew curls and look toward the big glass window. Her parents are pulling back into their space and another black, beat-up van pulls in next to them. Tiffany gets out, so I point Ava's attention to her. "There's your mom."

Ava looks through the glass as she slurps her drink, but as

the driver of the black van gets out to talk to Tiffany and Nate, Ava drops her drink. It splashes on the tile, and I stoop to grab the cup. "Oh, honey . . ."

But Ava hasn't noticed the spill. She's staring toward her parents, a look of terror on her face. I look from her to the window.

Ava whizzes past me and shoots to the bathroom. I look back at Nate and Tiffany. They're coming in now, and the greasy man from the van stays outside, leaning back against his fender.

I hurry into the bathroom. Only one stall door is closed, and I glance under and don't see feet. But I hear Ava sniffing.

I want to ask her if she's all right, but the bathroom door flies open. I slip into the stall closest to me and lock it.

"Ava? Baby, are you in here?"

Ava doesn't answer. I watch under the door and see Tiffany duck her head down to look under the stall. "Ava, get out here!" she yells when she sees the little girl. "Unlock this door right now!"

I hear the door clicking, but Ava doesn't come out. Tiffany shoves the door open and jerks her out.

"No!"

"It's time to go. You straighten up or we're never coming back!"

"I don't want to go with him, Mama!"

"Hush!" Tiffany says, dragging Ava to the door. "Dry up right now. Do you hear me?"

I close my eyes as Tiffany walks her out.

I wait a minute, giving them time to leave the building before I come out of the bathroom. I look through the big front window again and stand in utter amazement as the greasy man takes Ava's hand and puts her in his van.

Tiffany and Nate get into their own van.

I hurry out the door to my car, and as the man with Ava pulls out of the parking lot, I follow him. I use my phone to take pictures of his tag.

Is he a relative? A babysitter? Could he be her father rather than Nate?

I follow a block behind him, watching as he pulls into the parking lot of a junkyard. He gets out, carrying Ava, and takes her into the office that seems to be closed.

She doesn't seem to be crying anymore. Her little face just looks blank.

I drive around the block several times, trying to see if Ava's in the junkyard or standing at the window, but there's no sign of her. I park at the tattoo parlor half a block away and watch for them to come out.

An hour passes, when finally I see the man walking out with Ava trailing several feet behind him. He opens the sliding side door and she gets in. He doesn't buckle her in, just slams the door and gets behind the wheel.

I get a sick feeling as I follow him back to the parking lot of Bouncy House Heaven. Nate and Tiffany have moved their van to deeper in the parking lot, and they're standing outside it as if waiting. I pull into the first space I see, several rows away, in front of a grocery store.

Nate drops his cigarette and stomps it out as the black van pulls up behind them. I see Tiffany slide the back door open. I expect her to get her daughter out, but instead she retrieves a brown paper sack, opens it, and looks inside. Apparently satisfied with the contents, she grabs out Ava.

The man in the van takes off, and Nate and Tiffany put Ava in their van. They don't leave right away. They sit inside the van for a few minutes. I'm soaked with sweat as I sort through what I just saw. Was this a drug deal? If so, what was the payment?

I feel the contents of my stomach rising up, and I open the door and throw up on the pavement. The van pulls away.

Could this man in the black van have been the one who actually abused Ava, rather than Cole Whittington? If so, this can't be allowed to happen anymore. I have to do something.

⌣

My head is splitting when I get back to Miss Naomi's. I'm not in the mood for Lydia or Caden. Lydia's car isn't there. I go in through the front door. Miss Naomi is sound asleep in a recliner, and Caden is playing on the floor in front of her.

"Manda!" he says, springing to his feet.

"Caden," I say. "Where's your mama?"

He shrugs, then points to his grandmother, who's snoring. "She seeping."

I go over to Miss Naomi and touch her shoulder, try to wake her. She doesn't rouse. I look down at him. I can't leave him here.

"Come on upstairs with me, buddy," I say. "I'll read you a book."

Delighted, he holds my hand as we head upstairs, but it takes a while because he wants to hop up each step. When we finally make it to the top, he runs to climb on my bed. I'm not in the mood for entertaining a child, but Caden shouldn't be left alone with a sleeping grandmother.

When Lydia finally comes home, I hear her bounding up the steps. She comes to my door.

"Mama!" Caden bounces down and runs to her, and she lifts him.

"Your mother was asleep," I say. "He was playing by himself when I got home."

"And she calls me irresponsible," Lydia says. "Thanks for hanging out with him. He likes you."

"I like him too," I say, hoping this won't make him come back to my bed and start things up again. I really want to get on my computer. I grab it and open it. Maybe she'll get the message.

Thankfully, she does, and she closes my door. I hear the TV going on outside it. *Bubble Guppies* again.

I lean back against my headboard and type in the black van's tag number. Nothing comes up. I don't have access to the DMV's database, and the man may not own the junkyard.

Somehow I've got to find out who that man was and why Ava's parents handed her over.

I tell myself that it can't be what I fear, even though I know better. I don't know what to do. What if I go to the police and risk exposing myself, only to find he's an uncle or something? I could emphasize how afraid she was of him, but I can't prove that anything happened.

I can almost hear my sister's voice, begging me, *pleading* with me, to let this go and mind my own business. She would tell me that I have catastrophic problems of my own, and that I need to focus on them if I ever want to return to my family.

The *Bubble Guppies* theme song plays from the other room. I think of my little niece's soft hair on my lips and her head swaying to the beat of the music, laughter in her eyes.

She's probably walking by now. I imagine her holding a chair and pushing it across the room as she learns how to pick up one foot, then another. I picture her falling, then getting back up, reaching for her mom and lifting that right foot again, then the left, then toppling over. I ache as I think about catching her up before she hits the floor, and cheering like she's just run a 5K.

I'll never be able to see her milestones. She's out of my reach now.

And the idea that I will ever be a mom myself seems even more out of reach. Even if I did manage to find a good, stable hiding place and start a new life, how could I ever bring a child into my fugitive world? It would only put her at risk of emotional trauma, or worse. No, that's not a possibility anymore.

I know that Hannah has probably posted videos of Emma's milestones, but I fight the urge to use one of my fake Facebook accounts to go see those latest pictures, because I know they'll be watching for me to do that. I don't know how much information they can get from something like that, but I suspect that they can trace my location via my server. I'm just going to have to miss all of her milestones. I may miss her whole childhood.

But within the context of all the other losses in my life, I should be glad that she's sheltered from the pain. She probably won't feel as though anyone has been ripped from her life. I'll be the aunt who's mentioned in hushed tones, the one in pictures at her grandmother's house, the one people don't want to talk about openly. As long as she's protected from Keegan and his schemes, it will all be worth it.

26

CASEY

I'm at work, just clocking out for lunch, when Cole stops me. "Miranda, can I talk to you for a second?"

I turn around. "Sure."

He leads me into the break room. No one else is there. Leaning against the table, he rakes his fingers through his brown hair. "I just wanted to thank you again for bringing back my Bible."

I can't meet his eyes. Instead, I look past him out the door to where my coworkers are clocking out. "Sure, it was no problem. I got a job out of it, right?"

"I just wanted to ask you, though . . . if you might've read the note that was in there."

I think of lying to keep him from feeling awkward around me. But this could be life or death, so I embrace the opportunity. I take a step toward him and lower my voice. "I did. I wasn't trying to pry. It was none of my business, but I was really glad when I found out that you hadn't gone through with it."

His eyes glisten as he pushes off from the table. "Yeah, it's a little embarrassing. I was at a really low place. It was a couple of weeks ago, right after I lost my job. I didn't think I could bear to go home and tell my wife what had happened, so I got a hotel room, then I just sat there all night, thinking about it."

"Look, I know a little bit about what's happening with you," I say. "Someone told me and then I Googled a few articles. I'm nosy that way. I wondered if you knew that the Trendalls have done this kind of thing before."

"What kind of thing?" Cole asks.

"I mean, they haven't accused anyone else of abusing their child. Well, Tiffany Trendall did accuse her ex-husband of abusing her older children, during a custody battle. But they've sued a lot of people, and they've made a lot of accusations. They seem to live on the settlements."

Cole doesn't seem surprised. "Yeah, my attorney found a few things like that too. It's just that I'm between a rock and a hard place. If I go back at them with public accusations of my own, I'll look like an even worse monster than I already do."

I stand there looking up at him, trying to see any guile

in his eyes, but I don't see any. He seems like a genuinely troubled man.

He sighs. "I just wanted to tell you that it's okay that you read the note. But I appreciate that you haven't brought it up to my family."

I almost let him off the hook, but then I think better of it. "I won't bring it up if you'll promise me you're not still thinking about it."

"I'm doing what's best for my family," he says. "I'm going to be there for them. I don't want them to worry I'm going to jump off a bridge."

That last phrase is a little weak, but I want to believe it. I draw a deep breath. "It's not worth it, you know. There's always a way through it somehow. Even the worst accusations. I know, because there've been times when I've been accused of things I didn't do." I cut myself off, knowing I'm going too far.

"I appreciate your concern," he says. "I just wanted to break the ice, get the awkwardness out of the way. If we're going to be working together, there's no use walking on eggshells around each other." He reaches out a hand for me to shake. I take his hand as I hear children's voices, and I turn to the doorway. His daughters are running through the workroom, and the five-year-old is skipping.

"Daddy, look what I learned!"

He laughs as he heads toward her, and I see what he must look like when he doesn't have the weight of the world bearing down on him. "No way! You learned to skip!"

She's skipping toward the break room when the toe of her sneaker catches on a crack in the concrete floor, and she tumbles forward, hitting the door casing. In one step, he's over her, gathering her up in his arms as she starts to wail.

I stand back, watching as her mother dives toward her, checking her for injuries. There's a red spot on her forehead, and in seconds it's already forming a goose egg. I slip out the door, knowing I'm just in the way. I get my purse from under my workstation and glance back. The crying has stopped, and Cole is flying his daughter around the room like an airplane, distracting her completely from her fall.

It reminds me of what my dad used to do. I remember falling off my bike as he was teaching me to ride, and my mother hovered over me with hydrogen peroxide and Band-Aids, while he told me the scrape was nothing, that I could do it again and better this time. He had tried for months to get me to try, and he wouldn't let me give up. He carried me on his shoulders back to the bike and told me that I had to show that mean old ground that it couldn't get the best of a Cox girl. He told me there was always a crash-up before the success came.

He had me back on that bike before I even stopped bleeding. I rode my bike without his or Mom's hands steadying me, rode it all the way down the street, and finally managed to stop and look back. He was running after me, just feet behind me all the way, dripping with sweat and cheering as though I'd just won Olympic gold.

Cole seems to be that kind of dad, and as I watch, I see his little girl forget all about that big knot on her head, and she's asking if he has any gum in his desk.

I glance at his wife, who's talking quietly to Cole's mother. "They say if it swells out like that, that it's probably not serious. It's when it swells *in* that there are problems. But look at it. It looks awful."

"Where'd she learn that skipping, anyway?"

"They taught her that at preschool."

"Who would have thought? Skipping."

They seem like such an ordinary family, not at all like the people you would expect to be sheltering an evil child molester.

As I go out to my car, I say a prayer for justice for Cole Whittington. But I wonder if that's as much a pipe dream as praying for my own.

27

CASEY

We're nearing the end of a big deadline for getting an order for five hundred UpDown Seats shipped to a major department store chain, and the machines have gone quiet, when I hear loud voices in the office. "You can't think that I did this!"

"We just need to look over your children, Mr. Whittington. If you would show us someplace that we could go that's private . . ."

I look at Trey and Alice. They've turned toward the office and are listening.

"But why do we have to do this here?"

"Because you're not at home. We went by your house and no one was there. Please get your wife on the phone and have her bring your children here."

Trey is the nosiest of the four of us in my department— even nosier than I am—so he walks to the doorway and peers into the front office area. He comes back a few minutes later. "I heard him on the phone with his wife. He said they're from Child Protective Services. You were right, Alice."

"They want to see the kids?" I ask. "Why?"

He shrugs, but just then, Cole comes bounding through the workroom with two female caseworkers on his heels. They go toward the break room. "I want to know who called you," I hear him say.

"We're not at liberty to give you that information."

He stops at the break room door. "She fell right here, yesterday. She was skipping, and she slipped and hit her head right here on the door casing. There were multiple witnesses!"

"We just need to see her, Mr. Whittington. Where is your wife?"

"She's on her way. I told you."

"And she has the children with her?"

"Yes."

We all try to go back to work, but none of us can ignore what's going on in there. This could be dangerous. Someone at her preschool must have reported to them that she had the knot, and since her father is being charged with abuse, of course they had to take it seriously. But I saw this. I know he didn't do anything wrong.

I abandon my work area and go to the break room, knock on the door. Cole looks up at me. "Yes, Miranda?"

"Um . . . I'm sorry, but I couldn't help overhearing." I look at the CPS workers. "I just wanted to say that I was in here when his daughter hurt herself yesterday. That's exactly what happened. She was skipping and tumbled into the doorway. It was no big deal. She didn't even cry for long."

The women don't look like they want to hear that. "Thank you. We'll talk to you again if we need you."

"Okay," I say. "I'll be right out here."

In a few minutes, Cole's wife comes in, clutching the hands of both of her daughters so tightly that her knuckles are white. Her face is ashen, and I can see the fear in her eyes. She goes into the break room, and the social worker closes the door behind her.

We all go back to work, whispering. "They're blaming him? They won't even listen?"

"Do you think they'll take the kids?"

"Surely not. It's just a bump. All kids get bumps."

But after a few minutes, I hear Cole's wife's voice, rising up from the other side of the wall. "No, you can't! Please!"

The children start to cry, and I hear Cole begging the caseworkers. "Please, listen to the witnesses."

There's an exchange of voices again, all talking on top of each other, then the door opens and each of the caseworkers comes out holding one of the screaming children.

I stop what I'm doing and step toward them, horrified.

"What do we have to do?" his wife cries, reaching for her children. "Please . . . who can we talk to?"

"We'll have to go before the judge for a shelter hearing," one of the women says over the child's screaming. "I'll let you know when it is."

"You'll let us know?" Cole asks, trying to block them. "This is ridiculous. These are our children. The government can't just come in here and take them!"

The younger daughter, the one with the knot, screams, "Mooommmmmyyy!"

Cole's mother emerges from the front office as the caseworkers get out the door, and all three follow them out. I look through the window and see a struggle, but the women get the children into their car. I touch my chest as the sounds of their cries seem to linger in the air, even after they've driven away. I look out the window and see Cole's wife collapsing in the parking lot. He picks her up and holds her. Mrs. Whittington rushes back in as if there's someone she can call.

"We have to go after them!" Cole's wife screams. "We have to go get them!"

He lets her lead him to the car, but as he gazes into the distance, I know what he's thinking. He's thinking that he's lost all control, that his life has entered some kind of new dimension, where nothing makes sense and everything is upside down.

I know that look because I've worn it myself.

They get into the car, and Cole backs out of the parking lot and drives in the direction they went. I hope he finds someone there with common sense.

I'm crying by the time I turn to my coworkers. Alice is weeping, too, and everyone on the floor is staring at the front door.

28

CASEY

I don't want to go back to my room when I get off work, because I don't want to chat with Miss Naomi or Lydia, and I don't want to entertain Caden. Instead I drive out of town so my phone will ping off a different tower, and I call my sister. She doesn't answer, but calls back within minutes.

I cry as I tell her what happened to Cole, without using names. She's quiet as she listens, then she says, "Casey, you're doing it again."

"Doing what?"

"Getting involved. It's going to get you killed. Please, just walk away from there. Don't even look back."

"I can't do that. I'm a witness. I may need to go before the judge so he can get his kids back."

"Go before a judge?" she says, her voice falling to a stage whisper. "Are you crazy? You can't do that! The judge might recognize you."

I know she's right, but I sit in my car clutching the phone to my ear, and grow quiet.

"Casey, tell me you're not getting in their business. You're not watching them or snooping or . . . Oh my gosh. I know what you're doing. You're watching the family accusing him, aren't you?"

"No," I lie.

"You're not everybody's hero," she says. "I need you to focus! I need you to clear yourself so you can get back here. I'm getting scared. Not just for you, for us."

I sit stiffer now. "What do you mean? Why?"

"Because they keep coming by here, questioning me. Detective Keegan and that other man . . . Rollins . . . came yesterday. They want to know where you are, and they said they know I've been in touch with you. I denied it, but what if they have proof?"

"That's it. I'm not calling you again."

"No, you have to! Don't you dare disappear on me! I can't handle that. Already I can't walk out of my house without reporters yelling at me. Jeff is getting sick of it and threatening to leave."

"Oh no. Hannah!"

"I'm not trying to guilt you, Casey. I just want you to understand that you have to clear your name. You have to be able to come back so this can end. Mom is going to wind up in an institution if you don't! And I might too."

"What about Emma? Is she feeling any of this?"

"She does wonder why people scream at us everywhere we go. The other day we were at the grocery store and this woman started yelling, 'Your sister is a murderer!' at me."

I put my hand over my mouth.

She's crying now. "I didn't mean to tell you any of this. It's just . . . it's not just you being accused. We have to deal with it too. You can't distract yourself with someone else's tragedy when you have one of your own. Oh, and Dylan Roberts caught me when I was walking the other day. He wants you to email him. He says he believes you."

"Did anyone see him?"

"No, I was on the walking trail, in the trees. But Casey, let him help you. You could have told your story to someone by now. You could have gotten someone on your side. But no, you're out there rescuing other people when you're the one who needs rescuing!"

"Hannah, I'm not rescuing anyone. I'm gathering evidence. I am. I'm keeping my head down and getting the proof I need."

"You swear?"

"I promise. I'm doing the best I can."

"What happened to those children is wrong, Casey. I know that. But let their family figure it out. You have much worse things going on. I need you. You have to beat this."

I know that Hannah's life must be getting unbearable if she's revealing any of this to me. It's not like her.

When I get off the phone, I'm shaken. I force myself to go get something to eat, then I drive back to Dallas, to Candace Price's street where I eat in the car. As I sit there, I wonder what I'm doing. What if she never does anything that helps my case? She has a life, and other than the old pictures on Facebook, I haven't seen it intersect with Keegan's. But Brent had a reason for having her name in the file.

I can't stop crying, so I drive away before some neighbor sees me sobbing out in my car and comes to comfort me. Or worse.

I drive around, wasting gas, until I feel I can control myself enough to walk through the house and go to my room. I wait late enough for Caden to be sleeping. Then I walk quietly into the house and make it to my room without having to see anyone.

It's a good thing. When I get into my room and turn on the light, I see that I've cried all my makeup off. For the first time in days, I look like myself.

But that's the last person I want to be right now.

29

CASEY

I'm having trouble sleeping tonight, so I get up at one a.m. and work on my computer, organizing the evidence I have in a format that would be easy to hand over to someone. When I put it all together in one file, I see that I don't have that much. Not enough to convict cops of murder.

By the time I get to work, I'm exhausted but glad for some mindless work that will get my mind off Hannah and our conversation last night, plus I hope to get an update on the kids. Surely they were returned to their parents by now. But Cole and his mother aren't there, and Blake, his brother, is keeping a low profile.

Friday morning, I see that Mrs. Whittington's car is back. All the faces of the employees are long, and when I go in, I can tell she's been crying all night.

Finally, when I'm close to Cole's mother, I gather up the nerve to ask her. "What happened with the kids? Are they back with their parents?"

She sniffs and wipes her eyes. "No, hon. They put the kids in a shelter. They can't get before the judge. He's at a convention or some such. We've called everybody we know who has any pull, but nobody can do anything. They won't even give them to me." She stops and blows her nose. "Cole left Daphne last night, hoping CPS would return the kids if he isn't in the home, but it hasn't worked. Now I can't find him. He didn't come in this morning, and I don't know where he is."

That shakes me. She doesn't know about the suicide threat. Now he has even more of a reason. I try to work, but I can't focus on it. When the machines are quiet, I hear her on the other side of the wall, leaving voice mail messages for him to call her. He never does.

I feel nauseous, and I have to run to the bathroom. I wash my face and try to calm down, and I restore my eyeliner. When I come out, I start toward my workstation, but then I just keep walking into the front office, where Mrs. Whittington is still crying at her desk.

"Mrs. Whittington," I say, hating to invade her privacy, "would you mind if I go drive around and look for him?"

She wipes her chin. "Blake and their daddy are looking, sweetie."

I consider telling her he mentioned jumping off a bridge when we talked about suicide, but I think better of it. "But . . . it wouldn't hurt to have more of us. I don't know where he hangs out, but I could look for his car around the area."

She finally waves me off, letting me go. I get my purse and go out to my car, then look on my phone for the closest bridge. I get to it, but he's not there.

I find three more and drive to each of them. No luck.

I try driving through the motel parking lot where I was staying when I found the Bible, since I know he's stayed there before. His car isn't there. I drive to other motels, looking through every parking lot, searching.

Finally, I go to Miss Naomi's, feeling like a failure. Exhausted, I fall into a light sleep until Lydia and Caden come home, and the toddler's voice rises above the household. I check my makeup again, cake on more eyeliner. Then, while they're in the kitchen, I grab my purse and leave.

I get something to eat, then as it grows dark, I drive to the biggest bridge again, just to check one more time. Then I see.

His car is parked at the end of the bridge, but he's not in it. My stomach turns. I pull in behind his car and get out. There's a walkway the length of the bridge, so I start up it, hoping it's not too late, praying he's still there. I walk slowly at first, then faster and faster, jogging toward the center.

And there he is, sitting on the edge, leaning on the lower bar of the guardrail, his feet hanging off.

"Cole," I say, and he jerks his head up at me.

"Cole, don't do it."

"Miranda! Go away!"

"No." I walk toward him and reach out my hand. "Get up. Come on. Everybody's looking for you."

He doesn't take my hand. I finally drop it and look over the bridge railing. The water is a long way down. I wonder what would happen if he hit it from this distance. Would he break his neck? Plunge so far down that he knocks himself out? Would his lungs fill with water even before he's unconscious?

I feel powerless, but I'm not going to leave. Light-headed, I sit down beside him. "Cole, it's not hopeless. Your wife needs you. Your children need you."

"They won't give them back," he bites out. "That little girl lied, or she didn't even lie, but her parents made up a lie, and now I've lost my job and my children are terrified, in the hands of strangers. The parents accused me to get even. I told them that things Ava had said made me think she'd been abused. They got defensive instead of concerned. Next thing I knew, they'd accused me. I didn't even see it coming."

"What did Ava tell you?"

"She said a man did bad things to her and hurt her. She

called him Fred. Her parents said they didn't know anybody named Fred."

Cars whiz behind us, and the wind whips our hair. "I know it's bad. It is. There's no denying that. But what if you do this and the next day the family admits they lied and the judge comes home and they return the kids . . . and it would all be over . . . except they have a funeral?"

He sniffs hard and looks to the side, and I know he hears me. "Miranda, I know you mean well. But this is none of your business."

I know I'm making him mad, and it's risky, but I'm not getting anywhere with him. He already intends to jump. I have to try. "I'm not leaving you here," I say. "So you're gonna have to listen to me ramble."

He closes his hands around the rails. I know he could simply slip his body under the horizontal bar and he'd be gone.

"Most people don't know this," I say, "but I found my dad's dead body when I was twelve."

He lifts his head and looks at me. "Is this a story you're making up to distract me?"

"No, it's true. He was hanging from the fan at the center of our . . ." My voice cracks and I swallow hard. "Our living room. The police ruled it suicide. So that's what it was, officially. We had to take phone calls where people tried to comfort us. We had to go to the funeral and stand there in a line, shaking hands, and people tried to tell us happy stories about him, but there was no joy in those stories. There was only such heavy, heavy . . . sadness."

I don't tell him how I tried to talk to police and convince them it was foul play, because that would only confuse the issue. Or make it too clear.

"From then on, we were *that* family. My mother got a terrible case of OCD, so bad that she hoards everything in sight, and my sister developed this inferiority complex, sure that people were whispering about her and asking what kind of horrible children we must be, what kind of dysfunctional family, to have driven our father to do such a thing. But no one knew the truth. They only knew what they'd heard. That he committed suicide, and that it came out of nowhere, with no clue, with no time to get ready."

He lets go of the bar and is looking fully at me. "I'm sorry," he whispers. "That's awful."

"Your children can overcome this if you're alive," I say. "If you're alive to tell them, then they'll know the truth, no matter what anyone else ever thinks. But if you're gone, it'll be years before they find their way through the darkness, and there will always be that black fog that descends when they don't expect it. Is that the legacy you want to leave?"

He's quiet as he stares out at the water. "I'm marked as a child molester, an abuser. I've never even spanked my kids. They'll never let me be around them again. Supervised visitation, maybe, in some government worker's office." Tears come to his eyes, and he wipes them on his sleeve.

I have to think fast, because he's getting to that point where he could just slip under and fall. "Your wife," I say. "What's her name?"

"Daphne," he says.

"How do you think the funeral will be for her? Is she the kind who tries to comfort everyone even when she's suffering? Or will every word from mourners be like a knife in her?"

"Miranda, please."

"Do you think she'll need to be sedated? Will she be angry at you? Or will she understand?"

He's seething, and I hope he'll get up and storm back to his car, but he just sits there. On the off chance that he's listening to me, I go on. "The night of my father's funeral, I could hear my mother in her room, screaming into her pillow. She thought we couldn't hear. My sister and I sat on my bed hugging each other."

"This isn't helping me." Moonlight illuminates the tears on his face.

"Do you think the kids will go to the funeral? Will they stand with your wife as people come by? Will they have an open casket? Will they have to look at you?"

He's silent now, biting his lip. I realize I'm crying too.

"Children have to learn about death sometime. Usually it's a hamster or a goldfish, but your kids will learn when they never see their dad again."

"Stop it!" he cries.

"No!" I wipe the tears off my face. "I won't, because I've

been where they're going to be. I saw you in church. If you're a man of faith, don't you think God knows the truth about you?"

"Then why hasn't he vindicated me?" he demands. "Why am I here?"

"I don't know," I say, because I don't have a clue. "All I know is, what kind of faith will they think you have if you give up this easily?"

"Faith that's not big enough to save my kids."

I hear a helicopter overhead, and I wonder if it's looking down at us, but there's no beacon light, and it's too far away.

"Your faith is big enough. I don't know a lot about God, but I know that he's working on this. Maybe you'll all be stronger for it. Maybe—"

"That's garbage and you know it. I don't want to be stronger. I want to have peace. I want my kids to have happy childhoods and not have to deal with this."

"Then don't make them deal with a suicide," I say. "Imagine that you suffer through this and stand strong and fight. When your kids grow up, they can look back and know that you had the world against you, but you fought for them. Whatever the outcome, they'll know you were a man of incredible strength. Not that you checked out and left them to deal with it all by themselves."

He seems to wilt, his face in his hands. He sobs for a moment, and I want to touch his shoulder, but somehow it seems inappropriate. I'm not the one who can comfort him. I'm just the one to talk him down.

He finally scoots back and pulls his feet up. "You're right."

I wait . . . hoping he means it. He gets to his feet, holds out a hand and helps me to mine.

"You're sure? You won't come back after I leave?"

"No," he says. "I have to man up, push through this. I have to be stronger than I expect *them* to be."

I wipe the tears on my face, hoping all my makeup isn't washed off. "I'm so glad."

We walk quietly back toward our cars, and as he gets into his, he looks at me over the roof. "Thank you, Miranda."

I nod. "Where will you go now?"

"To my mother's," he says. "I don't want to go home to Daphne because they may never return the children if I'm there."

I look at my feet.

"I'll just go to my mom's."

"Good. She's really, really worried about you."

He gets into his car, and I pull out after him. I can't help following him all the way to his mom's house, just to make sure he doesn't make a U-turn and jump off the bridge. I'm not satisfied until he goes in. He turns back and waves at me as he walks into the house.

30

DYLAN

'**ve just gone by the house to eat something when the UPS man comes to my door. He's got a box that I assume is the infamous patch for the clinical study. I sign for it and quickly tear into the box. I take out the patch. Will I really be able to fall asleep with this thing stuck to my forehead?

I toss it aside for now and get on my computer to finish what I've been working on. Time flies by as I dig through my databases, getting information about all those on my lists. But my body aches from lack of sleep, and my eyes begin to blur. I really do need sleep.

I dig around in the box the patch came in and find the instructions. It's not that complicated. You just put it on your head, turn the switch on, and let yourself fall asleep. If you can.

The patch is sticky, and I know it's going to make me sweat. But I dutifully put it on, route the wires off to the side, and put the device on the pillow next to me. When I turn it on, I don't really feel anything. I won't be able to sleep with this. It's going to bother me all night.

But my body is so tired that I can't fight sleep, and I don't try this time. I'll give this thing a shot.

I leave the TV on, turned down low, so the sounds of the voices will distract me from my thoughts. Sleep finally comes.

When I wake up, it's six a.m. and I haven't had a nightmare. I sit up and stare down at the device. I turn it off and peel the patch off my forehead.

Did it work? I don't really know yet. Maybe I wouldn't have had nightmares anyway. Maybe I was so tired that I slept too deeply. The thing could also be a placebo. As long as it works, I don't really care.

My brain feels clearer; my body feels rested. I feel like I can face Casey's situation with more zeal today. The device is worth it so far. I'll try it again tonight.

31

___

CASEY

Now that Cole is off the bridge, I spend the night worrying about his children.

It's a sickness, almost, this need I have to focus on other people's problems. I wonder if this is how my mother feels when she's doing the things she does. It makes me feel better, more in control, so I spend the night typing up a list of lawsuits and accusations the Trendalls have been behind, along with my observations about them giving Ava to a man she clearly fears. I write that I don't have his name, but I give them his car tag number and mention he may work at the Cumberland Auto

Parts Junkyard. I also write that Ava has mentioned to a friend that a man named Fred has been hurting her.

I get up Saturday morning and take special care with my looks, rounding my eyes with my eyeliner, shadowing them more carefully than usual, even contouring my nose a little so that it looks longer and narrower, and marking shadowed slashes under my cheekbones to make me look more hollow-faced. I tease my hair and leave it messy.

Then I find a Kinkos where I print out two copies of the list. When I get to the local TV station, I sit in my car and study myself in the rearview mirror again. I don't see myself through all the makeup and the darker hair and sunglasses, so I hope they won't either.

My stomach feels full of butterflies with flapping wings, and my hands are shaking. A voice in my head tells me this is crazy, to turn around and drive away. But I think of Cole sitting on that bridge, his children crying for their mother in a DHS shelter, his wife in agony and wondering how their family got here. And I think of little Ava's fear as she hunkered in a bathroom stall with her feet pulled up.

I grab the envelope where I've put the list and go inside. There's a little waiting area with a TV playing what the station is broadcasting right now. There's a woman at a desk behind a counter, and she glances up and pushes a notebook across the counter toward me. "Sign in, please."

I wonder who she thinks I am. "Um . . . I don't have an appointment or anything. I just—"

"Everyone here for *Midday Dallas* has to wait over there and the producer will come get you," she says.

I look at the others in the waiting room. A girl in an evening gown with a tiara and a sash that says "Junior Miss Dallas" is fidgeting next to a woman who looks like an older version of her, and there's a portly man with an index card in his hand. His foot is tapping with a staccato rhythm that tells me he hasn't gone on TV many times before. A couple of seats down is a woman who seems calm and is watching the TV screen.

I turn back to the receptionist. "Is it possible for me to see someone in the newsroom? Like a reporter or someone?"

"They're on the air," she says impatiently, pointing to the screen. "You can see them when they come for you."

I look at the TV and see that the anchor is on, and then they cut to the weather girl. "No . . . I mean someone who actually writes the news. Is there someone . . . ?"

A girl who looks like she's in high school, carrying a clipboard, comes to the doorway. "Miss Dallas?"

The beauty pageant girl looks up. "Junior Miss."

"Okay. Mr. Salahay?"

The man nods and stands.

"And Beth. Everybody come on back."

As they file out behind her, I leave the receptionist desk and fall into step, like I'm with one of the guests. When we get to the studio, she says, "Mr. Salahay, you're up first, then Junior Miss, and Beth, you'll go last. We might have to cut you or add depending on how the first ones go, like usual. Cute dress. Where'd you get it?"

"T.J. Maxx," the woman named Beth says. "Got it for forty bucks. Check out these shoes."

I look around for a newsroom, but I don't see one. There's a room next to us with computers and TV monitors on the wall, but only one guy in there.

The producer opens a door to a small green room and asks them to wait in there until they're called, then she takes Mr. Salahay with her. I go into the waiting room, but I don't sit with the rest of them. I stand at the glass door and watch the man following the producer into the lit-up area across the hall.

Then I slip out and walk up the hall, looking for a reporter. I finally find a room with people in it, sitting at computers. I recognize one of them as one of the field reporters who comes on at night.

I make a beeline to her. "Excuse me."

She doesn't stop typing as she looks up at me. "*Midday Dallas* is up the hall."

"No, I need to talk to a reporter. It's about a news story."

She stops typing and looks around, then calls, "Harris!"

A man leans out a door from another room. "Yeah?"

"Talk to him," she says, and goes back to her keyboard.

I step over to him. "Hi," I say. "I'm Miranda. I have some information on a story you guys are reporting on . . . the Cole Whittington story?"

He looks past me to another guy. "Run in there and tell them to adjust the lighting on Kay. She looks like death warmed over."

The guy goes, and the man turns back to me. "I'm sorry, which story?"

"Cole Whittington. The vice-principal accused of child abuse?"

He looks at me fully now. "Yeah. What about it?"

"I have some information you need to know about the family who's accusing him." I open my envelope and pull out the sheets I've typed up. "They're professional litigators," I say.

"Lawyers?"

"No, I mean they live off money from settlements from lawsuits they initiate. They've got a long history of accusing people and suing them."

I have his attention now, and he takes my sheets and looks at them. "That doesn't mean their child wasn't abused."

"No, it doesn't. But there's someone else who may have done it."

"What are you, a neighbor?"

I draw in a breath before I lie. "Yes."

He looks at the information again. "You could have emailed this in, you know."

"I know," I say, "but I didn't want you to overlook it. I wanted to make sure you understood. A good man . . . an entire family . . . is being horribly impacted by this. He's lost his job.

His children are suffering for it. If there's a chance that this accusation could be false, that these people are just using it as a reason to sue the school system for damages, and if you could keep a child from being abused, wouldn't you want to know? Wouldn't that be a story?"

He glances at the monitor, where the weather girl is wrapping up. "That's better," he says to the guy who went to see about the lighting. "But why did that guy wear that tie? You should've given him another one."

I look at the monitor. Mr. Salahay is fidgeting at a table, off-camera, as the anchor fixes her collar. On the monitor next to them is the screen with the news they're playing. It's national news from the network. They're covering a train accident in Portland. Suddenly the clip ends and I see my own face fill the screen.

"Police officials in Shreveport are still searching for Casey Cox, the woman who allegedly stabbed her friend to death . . ."

I freeze. I can't even breathe, or I'll give myself away. I wait for him to look at me and point and call the police or handcuff me himself, but instead he says, "Joanie, are you the one working on the child abuse story over at that school?"

"Yeah," someone says from the other side of the computer bank.

"Got something for you," he says.

"Thank you," I tell him. "It's all there. I appreciate . . . your time."

I stumble from the room, wanting to get out of there

before someone looks up and realizes that I'm the girl on the screen.

Will they pay any attention to the leads on the papers I just gave them?

I'll just have to wait and see.

32

CASEY

Because I have housemates, there is never a time when I can take off my makeup and see Casey Cox. I have to leave my eyes smudged and black, like some heroin addict who woke up in a gutter. At first it was messy at night, and I didn't like the feel of it. My eyes continually itched and I longed to wipe them clean. But now I've gotten used to it.

Sunday morning I wake up early, craving something to fill the emptiness in my soul, so I decide I'll go to church again. I don't have nice clothes, but I put on a pair of black pants and a shirt that doesn't look too bad, and I apply my heavy makeup and tousle my hair. I go downstairs and start toward the door, when Miss Naomi stops me.

"Where are you going, honey? Not to work on Sunday, I hope."

I turn around. "I thought I would go to church."

Her face changes. "Church? Hold on a minute. I want Lydia to go with you."

I don't know what to say, but I stand there for a moment, trying to think of a way out. She runs up the stairs, leaving her grandson at the bottom looking up at me.

I smile at him. "What are you playing with?"

He shows me the dump truck he's pushing on the floor and chatters in his minion-speak, using words and sounds I can't quite understand. As I wait for whatever it is that Miss Naomi is doing, I check my watch. I'm going to be late if I wait much longer to leave.

I imagine she's upstairs, trying to get her daughter out of bed, but the likelihood of Lydia agreeing to go to church with me is pretty slim. I just hope her mother will hurry and figure that out.

After a few minutes, she comes back down with Lydia dragging behind her, looking like a zombie. She's wearing jeans and a pullover shirt that her mother probably dug out of a drawer and forced her to throw on. Her eyes are bloodshot and puffy. When she gets down the stairs she looks at me. "Church? Really?"

"Thank you for waiting, sweetheart," her mother says to me. "She's been wanting to go to church, haven't you?"

"More than anything," Lydia quips. "I've told her that in multiple nonversations we've had."

"Um . . . what about Caden?"

"I'll keep him here with me," Miss Naomi says. "Just you two go on and have a good time."

"Right," her daughter says in a bitter tone. "But I need coffee."

Miss Naomi runs to the kitchen and comes back with two Styrofoam cups, hands them to us as we start out the door. I take mine gladly and drink it down as I get into my car. Lydia plops into the passenger seat.

"Why under God's blue heaven would you suggest that we go to church when I was sleeping?"

"I didn't suggest that," I say. "I told your mother I was going and she insisted that I wait for you."

"She told me she wouldn't give me gas money unless I went. Tyrant. It ought to be against the law."

As I drive, I try to push back my disappointment that she's going with me. I hope it doesn't call more attention to me. I had hoped to sneak in the back again after it had already started so that I wouldn't have to speak to anyone. I want to blend in. I want to see if I can capture that feeling again. But I doubt I'll be feeling anything with Lydia along, except maybe irritation.

We're ten minutes late when we get to the church. I find a parking place, then hurry toward the door. She lags behind. I tell her she can sit outside on the steps if she doesn't want to participate. I won't tell her mother. But she comes inside, a bitter look of annoyance on her face, her arms crossed as if to deny anything suggesting vulnerability.

We slip into the back row as they're singing a song I've never heard. I watch the screens at the front of the room for the words, hungrily taking them in, not singing but playing those lyrics through my mind, trying to understand. I glance at her standing beside me, looking around, disengaged. At least she's being quiet, which is something.

We sit down after the singing and they pass the offering plate. Our section leaders start at the front of our section, working their way back. By the time it gets to our row, there are paper bills stacked on each other, a twenty at the top. When it's passed to Lydia, she plucks the twenty out of the stack and wads it in her hand.

I gasp as I grab the plate. "You can't do that!" I whisper.

"Why not?" she says. "I thought it was for the needy."

"It's *stealing*!" I whisper. "Put it back!"

I can see that she has no intention of doing that. She only grunts as if to say, "Make me." I'm thinking her maturity must've stalled somewhere around the age of eight.

I'm still holding the plate, and the guy looks our way and reaches out for it. But I can't give it to him until Lydia puts the twenty back. When I realize she's not going to, I grab my wallet out of my purse, pull a twenty out, and put it in the plate. The usher smiles as he takes the plate.

I'm mortified. My face burns red as I sit through the next

few minutes of the service. I offer a silent prayer asking forgiveness for letting that happen. Surely God has some law that stealing from him has to be punished right here in the sanctuary. Will lightning come through the window? I can almost smell an electric charge as we sit here.

"Enough with the hypocriticism," she whispers.

This must be another one of her combo words, but I can't be a hypocrite when I never claimed to be anything. "I didn't criticize you," I whisper back.

Eventually, Lydia nods off to sleep, so I lock onto the preacher's words and try to absorb their meaning.

"We're not talking about some mythical messiah who used to live two thousand years ago," he says. "We're talking about a living Savior. What is he doing right now? He's sitting at the right hand of God, making intercession for us."

I'm not entirely sure what intercession is, but it's as if the preacher reads my thoughts.

"What is intercession?" he asks, then his voice dips almost to a whisper. "It's prayer. Jesus is praying for you. John 1:3 says, 'All things came into being through Him, and apart from Him nothing came into being that has come into being.' All things. The whole world! Yet what is he doing right this minute? He's praying for you. Translating your prayers to his Father. Listening to what's on your heart."

I try to imagine the Christ who died on the cross and was raised from the dead, now sitting on a throne next to his Father, talking to him about me. If that's true, then maybe my prayers aren't random thoughts that fly into the ether, then vanish if someone doesn't happen along to catch them.

"When you pray," the preacher goes on, "it's like you're whispering into the ear of God himself. None of those prayers go unheard. They might not be answered like you hope or think they should be. You might ask for a car, and God gives you a bicycle. Turn with me to Romans 8 and look at something with me."

I pull the Bible out of its pocket on the back of the seat in front of me and open it, looking for Romans. I have no idea where it is, but I quickly find the index, then make my way to it.

The preacher waits for us all to get there, then says, "Let's start with verse 26. 'In the same way the Spirit also helps our weakness; for we do not know how to pray as we should, but the Spirit Himself intercedes for us with groanings too deep for words; and He who searches the hearts knows what the mind of the Spirit is, because He intercedes for the saints according to the will of God.'"

The words are like balm to me, exciting me in deep places of my soul, making me want more. I look up, waiting for the preacher to go on.

"What is he saying? Paul is telling us that we sometimes pray for a new car, when Jesus knows that what we really need is self-worth. So Jesus takes those prayers that we pray for whatever we think will make us happiest, and he translates them into what really will make us happiest. Look at the next part of that passage. Verse 28 says, 'And we know that God causes all things to work together for good to those who love God.' How many things?"

The congregation answers, "All things."

"Some things?"

I smile and answer with them. "All things."

"Listen, people, that's how your prayers work. They come out of your mouth the way you want them to happen. Jesus translates them to the Father, telling him what it is we really need. And whatever happens, he makes sure that all things that happen are for our good, if we love him and—look at that last part—'are called according to His purpose.' That means that our very existence is for his purposes. That our lives have meaning to him. *Called* means *invited*. *Chosen*. We've been chosen for a purpose, and it's for our good. Does that just blow your mind, or what?"

Yes, it blows my mind. I don't know why I'm wiping tears, but I've never felt quite like this before. Sitting here in this place gives me the most peace I've felt in years—maybe a decade, maybe more. I haven't really had peace since my dad died. There's been a bitterness eating a hole deep in me, burning the edges of my insides. But here I feel as if that heaviness is lifted, as if I can think more clearly. I can feel a power greater than me working right in front of me . . . and even through me.

Maybe God does care about me after all.

The service is almost over, and the congregation is on their feet, singing the last song, when I grab Lydia's arm and tug her out. She slept through the sermon, then came awake when the singing started again. Now she blinks at me sleepily. "You gotta be somewhere?"

"I just don't like the traffic," I say as we get to the foyer and push through the doors.

"You know, you didn't have to put that money in. Twenty bucks won't break an outfit like that."

I don't answer her, just walk down the stone stairs a few steps ahead of her, trying not to lose the feeling.

33

CASEY

Sunday afternoon I don't have to work, and I can't decide where to spend my time. I haven't watched Candace Price in a few days, so I go to her street. I don't see her car where she usually parks it. She probably left earlier. I'm discouraged. I can't find anything to link Candace and Keegan, so I'm probably in Dallas—dangerously close to Shreveport—for no reason at all. The TV station hasn't yet reported what I took them Friday. I have a sinking feeling that they've tossed it onto a desk somewhere and covered it over with pageant queens and local events.

Curious, I use my phone and go to the news station's

website. My mood changes instantly when I see that the first story is the one I've given them. I click on the video that played at noon today when I wasn't home. They report the Trendalls' reputation, their history of lawsuits and accusations, and the fact that Child Protective Services has taken Cole's kids into custody. The TV station has even done an interview with him, and they have a clip of him saying that these baseless accusations have deeply impacted his family and traumatized his own children, since they've been taken from him and not even placed with a family member.

I bang on the steering wheel and whisper, *"Yes!"* That's something, even though they left out the part about the Trendalls giving Ava over to that man. Maybe they're sitting on that until they have his full name and more evidence. I drive over to the Trendalls' street, eager to see if they're showing any reaction to the news.

Little Ava is playing outside by herself again, digging in the yard with a small shovel. I watch her from my place several houses down. A half hour or so later, I see Nate storm out to the white four-door pickup in the driveway. He throws the back door open and yells for her to get in. Her hands are covered with soil, but she runs to obey anyway. Then I see her mother staggering out. She walks like a drunk across the yard, trips in a hole her daughter has dug, and falls in the dirt. Even as far away as I am, I hear her cursing as she gets to her feet. She doesn't go back in to clean up. She simply dusts herself off and gets into the truck's passenger seat.

They back out of the driveway and head away from where I'm parked down the street. I start my car and follow. They turn right at the stop sign. When I reach the sign, I see that they're three blocks away from me. I turn and try to catch up, keeping a couple of cars between us.

The truck veers off the road a couple of times, then quickly rights itself. I wonder if Nate, who's driving, is drunk too. Has anyone made Ava buckle her seat belt?

After several miles of driving through town, they turn into a neighborhood. I follow, closer than I'd like, and when they pull into a driveway of a corner house with a chain-link fence that goes around the front and back yards, I drive past as if I have business down the road. As I pass, the man I saw the other day—the one Ava was terrified of—emerges from the house, and Tiffany gets out and slides open the back door. Ava doesn't come right out, so Tiffany reaches in and jerks her out. Tiffany slams the back door, then turns back to the man and talks animatedly, arms flailing. She's clearly angry, though I can't hear what she's saying.

The man takes hold of Ava and pulls her into the house. Tiffany and Nate back out of the driveway, leaving her there.

I feel sick again. I think of calling the police, but what could I say? That the Trendalls just left Ava with a man? What if he's her uncle or her real father? What if I'm way overreacting?

I look for something to write on, but there's only a copy of the pages I gave the TV reporter, still lying on my passenger seat. I turn it over and write down the name of the street. I can't see the number of the man's house, but I scribble the numbers of the houses on either side—233 Cattonelle Avenue and 237 Cattonelle. I want to stay at the house to keep an eye out for Ava, but she's not where I can see her. I don't know how to help her.

When the Trendalls are almost too far away, I decide to follow them instead. I get to the closest main street and see them several cars ahead of me.

I follow them across town to the TV station. They both go to the door like they're on a mission. It's locked, so they bang on the glass, but no one opens it. I can't pull in, so I drive past, then go around the block. When I get back, I see that they still haven't been let in, so they're heading back to the truck.

I have to stop at a red light way too close to them, and I look the other direction so they won't see me.

Suddenly my passenger door flies open. I scream as Nate comes across the seat, shifts my car into park, and yanks me out. "Who are you?" he demands.

"Get your hands off me!" I scream.

Tiffany jumps into my driver's seat. "I told you she was following us!"

"What do you want?" he shouts, shaking me.

I twist and slip out of his grasp, but he knocks me to the pavement, and my chin and elbows scrape on the ground. I scramble back up, screaming as he throws me against the car, but it's Sunday and no one comes.

"Who are you?" Nate demands. "What do you want?"

"Are you crazy?" I shout back. "I was just driving by!"

"She's working for him!" Tiffany screams, jumping out of my car, waving papers. "Look what I found!"

She's holding up the copy I had on my seat—the stuff I gave to the TV station, with the address of the house where they left Ava. He holds me by my hair as he skims it, then grabs my chin and bangs me back against my car again. "So it was you who gave them that."

"Most of it's public record," I bite out. "They would have found out eventually."

His breath smells of tooth decay and alcohol. "What business is this of yours?"

"I know Cole Whittington," I say. "He's a decent man. They took his kids and now he's suicidal, and you've done it all for money! Meanwhile, you let that man molest your daughter!"

I bring up my knee and hit him hard, making him drop his arms and double over. Tiffany comes at me, but I shove her back, toppling her. I rush to my car and jump in. I slam the door and lock it, then screech away, leaving them behind.

I'm trembling so hard I can't even hold the steering wheel, but I get far enough away that they won't find me. When I get back to my house, I sit in the driveway for a while, until I can make my hands stop shaking. *I must be crazy*, I tell myself. *I must be as insane as them.*

What is wrong with me? My sister would absolutely die.

I get to my room without anyone seeing me. Then I jump

into the shower and clean off the bloody scrapes on my chin, my knees, my elbows and hands.

I stand in the shower, trying to decide what to do next. I finally get out, shivering, and get dressed and climb into bed. I pull the covers over my head and try to think.

I'm so tired of evil winning. I try to form a plan, but my thoughts race from my problems to Cole's . . . and then to Ava's.

I pull myself back together, and I sit up and try to think. I could leave town, but I haven't finished with Candace Price. I got sidetracked with the Trendalls, but I need to focus on Candace and her link to Keegan. Despite how things look, she has to be the link.

If I don't, I'll wind up on the run for the rest of my life. My sister is right.

I have to stick with the plan. The Trendalls don't know where I live. They don't even know my name. I got away from them before they had time to get back to their van and follow me. It's okay. There's no harm done.

By the time I hear Lydia and Caden coming home from wherever they've been, I've found some semblance of calm. I can do this. I have to. I'm not giving up this easily.

I go to the mirror. I look too much like myself. I quickly apply more eyeliner again before I get back into bed, in case Caden demands to talk to me.

Tomorrow I'll start again.

34

CASEY

The next morning when I show up for work, everyone in the workroom is standing around the TV. The morning news is on, and they're showing the weather. When I walk in, Cole looks up. He still looks tired, dark circles under his eyes, but there is a light in them that I haven't seen for a few days. "Hey, Miranda, can I talk to you?"

I'm probably in trouble. He must have realized that I'm the one who went to the media. I follow him into the break room, hoping he doesn't notice the scrapes on my chin and hands.

"Somehow the media got wind of all the things we talked about regarding the Trendalls."

"Yeah, I noticed that," I say.

"So . . . did you go to them with that information?"

I try not to indicate with my expression whether I did or not. "What difference does it make? The important thing is that people are aware of what they've done. If it gets you your kids back, your job . . ."

He sighs. "If you did, I want to thank you. I told you not to do it before, but if you did it anyway, I'm glad. You've been a good friend to me, even though I don't know you that well."

I can't manage a smile. "I'm glad to hear that," I say. "I just don't like to see injustice. It kind of got under my skin."

"Well, it's not over yet." He goes to the coffeepot, pours two cups of coffee, hands one to me. "We go to youth court about custody of the kids tomorrow. I'm hoping that since I've moved out, they'll let my wife have them back. At least then we'll know they're safe."

"It's just all wrong," I say. "It shouldn't be possible for you to lose your kids that easily. And to have them put in a shelter instead of placed with family members. That doesn't even make sense."

"Tell me about it," he says.

Out in the workroom, there's a cheer, and we run out and see that his segment is on the news again. A hush falls over the room, and we watch as they show new things they've uncovered about the Trendalls, things I didn't even tell them.

It was just what I'd hoped, that once I gave them the initial facts, they would go at it like a dog with a bone. I'm so thankful they did. Some of my coworkers mention that the other news networks are picking it up, and that it was in the paper this morning.

When the segment is over, my coworkers cheer again, and they all pat Cole on the back.

We head to our stations as the TV continues to play. Cole is near the set when a segment comes on about me. I quickly turn toward the wall and continue boxing the seat that I'm working on. I hear the anchorman talking about me, and I know they've got that notorious picture of me up on the screen, the picture where I look like myself, the one before my life fell apart. I hope I've put on enough eyeliner this morning, and the smoky eyes and teased black hair will distract people's attention. But hopes can only go so far.

Sources close to the investigation cite the suicide of Casey Cox's father Andy Cox when she was twelve years old as a contributing factor to her state of mind. Psychologist Bill Pennington said that sometimes an event like that can trigger flashbacks later on and result in a patient reacting in an unpredictable, sometimes violent, way.

I turn and glance at Cole, and suddenly his eyes turn from the screen to me. Our eyes lock for a moment, and I can almost see the wheels turning in his head as he remembers my telling him my dad's death was ruled a suicide when I was twelve. The hairs on my neck rise.

He knows.

He slides his hands into his pockets and, with a stricken expression, turns back to the screen. He stares at it, frozen for a moment, then frowns down at the floor. His ears redden and his breathing grows heavier as he works through it in his head. What will he decide to do with the fugitive standing in his workroom . . . the one who talked him off a bridge?

It's over.

I don't say a word to anyone. I just get my purse from under my station, leave the workroom, and walk through the office and out the front door. I get into my car and drive away before anyone can stop me, fully expecting police cars to surround me any minute.

I take back roads. When no one follows me, I begin to breathe again. But I know I can't even go back to Miss Naomi's. I can't count on him not telling the police that I've been there right under his nose. I can't count on him being loyal to me in any way. Why should he be? In a panic, I decide that I'll have to get out of town as fast as I can.

But first I want to go by Candace Price's one last time. I head that way, praying for a crumb of evidence I can use before I'm found.

35

CASEY

I sit in my car on Candace's street while I figure out what I should do next. Her car's in the driveway, and there's a red Jaguar convertible next to it that I haven't seen before.

I park in front of a different house where it looks like no one is home. If someone jogs by and asks me what I'm doing, I can tell them that I'm waiting for their neighbor to get home. I watch the house for a while and see no one. The sports car sits in her circular driveway, and I consider walking up to it and looking in the window, but that would be suicide, because she probably has a security system with cameras.

So I sit in my car and try to think what I need to buy before I get out of town. At Miss Naomi's, I've left my bag with my few clothes, most of my makeup, and the toiletries that I've bought since being here. There's food in the fridge that will go to waste.

I turn to my backseat and pull out the emergency bag I've kept in my car every day since the beginning. It holds my wigs and alternate driver's license and social security card, as well as a change of clothes and a few other things. I've also kept most of my cash there. I'll be okay.

It's so quiet at the Price house that I've almost decided to give up and drive away, when I see the front door opening. Candace bops out first, a man behind her. I catch my breath. The man is Gordon Keegan.

He's laughing. He catches up to her and puts his arm around her, then takes her to the Jaguar passenger seat and ushers her in like she's a princess. He bends over and kisses her, closes the door, then almost dances around the car. He gets in and backs into the street. I cannot believe this. It's too good to be true.

As I follow them, I take special care to keep several cars between us. It's not hard to see them up ahead in that red Jag. I try to take pictures with my phone, but I'm not close enough to get any good ones. When they stop at a red light, I'm about four cars down in the next lane over. I can only see the left side of their car tag, but I write down the three letters I can see. The Jag eases ahead slowly, and I get the rest of the tag number.

I'm no Jay Leno, but I figure the Jag is worth over sixty-five grand. Keegan is driving a little faster than the speed limit, and I fear that if I do the same I'll be pulled over, so I get farther and farther behind them, trying hard to keep up without calling attention to myself. He gets on an interstate and I follow, straining to see that red spot up ahead, zigging in and out of traffic. Then I see them turn off. The exit sign says Lake Ron Hubbard.

As soon as I can, I take the same exit. Then I manage to follow them down several roads until they come to a marina. I pull in on the outskirts of the parking lot as they go in deeper. Luckily, I can see the Jag as Keegan parks it. They close the convertible top, then jump out and grab stuff out of their trunk. They walk down a dock to a yacht that's moored there. A couple of other cars have just pulled up and families are getting out, so I quickly get out and follow the groups of people as they walk toward the lake.

I've never been here before, but it's beautiful and huge. I didn't know fresh bodies of water had yachts that sailed in them, but clearly they do. I stand among several people fishing over a pier railing and try to see which yacht Keegan and Candace got on. There they are. They're not pulling out; they're just sitting on the deck seats looking out over the water, drinking. Keegan is talking on the phone now, and I wonder whether he's finding out something about me. Has Cole called and reported me already? Has the call been routed to Keegan? Is he freaked out knowing I'm here, in Dallas? Does he realize that I'm here to get evidence on him?

———

I go back to my car. I sit there behind the wheel with my AC running to combat the heat. I watch the parking lot, waiting for him to come back up the dock, but he doesn't. After a while, I venture back to the water. They're still out there, this time with a couple of friends. If I could just get close enough to that boat to get the name or a number or some kind of evidence that would allow us to track the ownership of it . . . something I could connect to him and give to Dylan or whoever might care. I pretend to be checking my texts, but I take pictures of the yacht and the people on it, zooming in as close as I can with my digital limitations.

When they've been out there three hours and nothing seems to be happening, I get a surge of bravery, and I walk down the dock past the other boats until I get to the one Keegan and his girlfriend are on. I hear laughter, and his voice rising, just out of my sight on the other sundeck of the boat. There is a name on the boat—*Kandy Kane*—with K's. I take a picture and zoom in on the model name over the back deck, then I get the number painted on the side. I hurry back to my car.

I'm pretty sure Keegan didn't spot me, and I need more before I get out of town. I'm so close. I don't know anything about yachts—I don't know a stern from a prow—and I'm clueless whether their names are registered somewhere or just for private use. I write down the number on the side. Maybe there's a database somewhere that will tell who owns it. The boat is a Myacht 4515. That should help me narrow it down.

The fact that Keegan's still on the boat gives me reason

to wonder if Cole has called the police about me yet. Maybe he's hesitating because of what I've done for his family, or he's gotten bogged down in bureaucratic sludge and hasn't been able to get the message to the right person yet. Or maybe he hasn't called, since he knows what it's like to be falsely accused. Maybe he's giving me the benefit of the doubt.

But that's wishful thinking. It's more likely Keegan is supervising, via cell phone from his boat, a battalion of police who are searching the entire Dallas–Fort Worth metropolitan area for me.

I'm getting hungry, so I leave my car again, this time carrying my emergency duffel bag in case I can't get back to my car. I walk to a food cart where I buy a hot dog and fries, and sit at a picnic table that gives me a good view of them, my back to the sun. If they stay where they are, the blinding glare of the descending sun will keep them from seeing me.

After a while, I turn away from them for a moment and watch the sun going down. It hits the water with a splendor unequaled by anything man can produce, then descends beneath the waterline. I send up a prayer that God will give me the insight and evidence to do what I need to do to put Keegan and his co-criminals away once and for all. I wonder how Jesus will translate that prayer.

As twilight seeps into the sky, I keep my perch at my picnic table until I see the lights going out on the *Kandy Kane*. Maybe they're leaving now. I get up and walk slowly back until I can see them in the streetlights over the parking lot. Keegan is at the trunk of the sports car, loading up the things they brought, and Candace is putting her things into the passenger side of the car. Their friends, parked nearby, are talking to them, loading their own car. By the time I've walked the length of the parking lot, along the far side from them, I don't see the red Jag anymore, so I assume they've already driven away. I'll have to catch up to them at Candace's house.

I'm hurrying toward my car when headlights come bolting toward me. I can't see the car behind them, but it's about to hit me. I dive out of the way, hitting the ground and rolling under a car as the vehicle just misses me.

It's the red Jaguar.

I doubt that he can see me after I'm out of the headlights' glare, so I scramble up and get to my car, crouching and keeping my head down. I crawl into the driver's seat, and the interior light comes on for an instant until I ease the door closed. I see lights in my rearview mirror. Is Keegan rounding the lot again, looking for me? I glance out the back and see the sports car, so I duck.

He comes back around twice more, slowing as he gets to where he almost ran me over.

I hear children's voices and raise my head enough to see two families headed to cars near me. I start my engine, keeping my lights off. As both groups load their stuff into their cars, I see that the sports car is parked now on the other side of the lot. Keegan is probably looking for me on foot now.

I reach for my bag, grab the first wig I touch, and pull it on.

As the car two down from me pulls out, I turn on my lights and pull out behind it.

Keegan is standing between parked cars as I pull past him. With the short red wig on, I don't look like the girl he saw, and I smile and wave to the car in front of me, to give the illusion that I'm with them. He turns away from me and scans the parking lot as I drive away.

I fly through the streets, making random turns until I'm sure I'm not followed. It's half an hour before I'm confident that I've lost him.

36

CASEY

I'm in lots of trouble. If Keegan saw me, then he not only knows I'm in Dallas, he knows how I'm wearing my hair, how my eyes are disguised, and that I'm stalking him. I'm sunk.

I take a minute to swap my license plate with one from another car. I'm panicked, shaking. I need to leave town now, but I'm so close to getting what I need on him.

I want to go lock myself in my room with the covers over my head, but I don't think it's safe.

I have to get to Candace's house and see what Keegan does next. This is key to my case. I can't drop the ball now.

My mind races as I fly back to Candace's street. The sports car's back there now, so I sit in my car at my usual place, where the people still don't seem to be home. Nothing's happening, so I take the time to load my pictures onto my computer. Just in case I get arrested tonight, I send an email to Dylan, and I attach all the pictures and tell him that Candace Price is Keegan's mistress and that he was in Dallas with her tonight, that they have a yacht called the *Kandy Kane* docked at the Watershed Marina, and a Jaguar, a Mercedes, and a mansion. I've just hit Send when Keegan comes out of the house.

I slap my laptop screen shut, my heart pounding, sure he must be coming for me. I fully expect police cars to come from all directions and circle me, but they don't. Keegan loads his suitcase into his car. Candace turns on the porch light and comes out to give him a long kiss, then she walks him to the driver's side. She goes back inside as he pulls out of the driveway.

I'm afraid he's baiting me, but I follow him anyway, staying back and keeping my lights off until I turn onto the busier road. I have no idea where we're going, but it's not the same direction as before. He turns down several roads, then I finally see where we're headed. It's a small airport just a few miles from Candace's house. He pulls the Jaguar into the parking lot. Knowing he'll see my car when I drive in, I wait until another car pulls in, then I follow, parking off to the side. Keegan hops out and gets his suitcase. He pulls a protective slipcover out of his trunk and puts it on his car, as if he doesn't plan to be back for a while. I watch the other driver get out of his car and go into a building.

Keegan turns and heads out between the buildings to the tarmac where the planes are parked. I wait a few minutes, then get out of my car, close the door quietly, and follow between two other buildings. Pressing myself against the side brick wall, I watch him walk to a plane. He opens the cargo door and lifts his suitcase in, then unlocks the pilot door and does something inside.

So he has a plane too. This guy has made a lot of illegal money and he seems to enjoy spending it. Should I walk closer to get a picture? No, it's just too dangerous under the bright tarmac lights. I watch him do his pre-check and I take pictures, but I can't zoom close enough to get the tail number. After a few minutes, he starts the engine and begins to taxi out. I snap pictures as he takes off, but I know they're not clear enough to be useful.

When his plane is far enough away, I run back to the sports car and quickly roll back the cover. Using the flashlight on my phone, I find the VIN number and take a picture of it. Then I photograph the license plate.

I get back into my car. Before I even start the engine, I load the pictures onto my computer and send them to Dylan.

He still hasn't responded to the last emails I sent. Now that I've got the evidence I need, probably more evidence than I ever could've hoped to have, I have to figure out what to do next. Where will I go? I'm certain Keegan saw me, but maybe that's why he's hightailing it back to Shreveport. Maybe he's regrouping, getting backup, and returning to find me.

Still wearing my short red wig, I drive about an hour west of Dallas and get a hotel room there. I sink into bed, afraid to even check the news. I try to sleep, but the silence is too loud, and my thoughts race.

At two a.m. I turn the TV on. I flip the channels until I find a Dallas station, and try to sleep to the low sound of an infomercial.

Sleep still evades me, and I find myself listening to models and actresses touting the magic properties of the latest skin care product. It's so convincing that I almost call the number, but I don't have a credit card or an address, or even a name that's mine.

When the infomercial ends, one about a cooking implement comes on, then a Zumba DVD set.

Finally, I drift into sleep. A knocking on the door wakes me some time later. I sit up and ask, "Who is it?"

"Housekeeping."

"Can you come back later?" I call.

She goes away. I check the clock. It's noon. The midday news is coming on, the theme song playing.

Accused child molester Cole Whittington was found dead moments ago.

I come up in bed like I've been splashed with ice water. "No . . ." I grope for the remote and turn it up.

. . . one-car accident that took his life.

They show his mangled car at the bottom of an embankment. I drop the remote and hold my head to keep it from bursting apart.

. . . we've reported on all week. A family spokesman told us
that he had been to court this morning regarding the custody
of his children, who were returned to his wife, Daphne.
We will continue to report on this developing story.

Despair rushes up in me to mushroom-cloud level, bursting out of me in a scream I mute with my fist.

Minutes pass, but I can't move. I feel my heart pounding, noise screaming in my ears, reality crushing me.

Cole is dead. Nothing I've done has mattered.

37

DYLAN

My lungs lock when I see the emails that have come in from Casey. I take a second to breathe, then as I study each of the pictures she's sent, I realize that she's in Dallas, only three hours from here. When I see how close she got to Keegan, I get a little sick. The most recent email she sent was the one that contained the airplane pictures, sent last night, and I write her back to tell her that I have the tail number of the plane because I've seen Keegan in it before. I tell her to back off, that she's putting herself at too much risk. I tell her to let me take it from here.

As I pack a bag to go to Dallas, hoping to see a return email pop up, my phone rings and I see that it's Dex.

I click it on. "Hey, man."

"Pretty Boy, you're not gonna believe this." His voice is low, but behind him I hear Tim McGraw singing "Live Like You Were Dying" over the noise of a crowd. "I lost Keegan, so I wound up tailing Rollins, and he's in Marshall, drunk in a bar."

"Marshall, Texas?" I ask. "Who's he with?"

"By his lonely. Want me to make friends?"

"No, you'd be too recognizable if he sees you after this."

"Because I only have one leg and one arm? That's discrimination, dude. I might sue."

"It's reality. Just wait for me. I'll be there in thirty minutes. I was just about to head to Dallas. Can you hang and watch his car until I get there, in case he leaves? Maybe if I talk to him while he's drunk, I can get him to spill something."

"Will do. He might gush. Looks to be in a good mood."

I grab my bag and head out to my car. Marshall is forty-two miles from Shreveport. Rollins probably went there to drink so nobody he knows would be there to see him. If Keegan's in Dallas, maybe it's a case of the cat being away.

I drive faster than I should and get to the bar half an hour later. I find Dex in his car, and he tells me where Rollins is sitting at the bar. Dex leaves, and I go into the bar and sit on the opposite side, pretending I don't know he's there. I order a Coke with ice and see him at the bar, nursing his drink as he sings to the song playing. When I get my drink, I take my glass and go to the bar stool next to him.

"Detective? I thought that was you."

Rollins looks at me, and it takes a minute for him to focus. He groans when he sees me. "Man, I can't go anywhere."

"Hey, dude, enjoy yourself. I just stopped in for a drink. What you do in your off time is none of my business, right?"

"Right," he says, and bottoms his glass, then slides it across the counter for a refill. "Anyway, you're a chick magnet. Can't hurt to be seen with you."

I grin and glance around like I'm looking for some of those *chicks*. "So where's Keegan? I thought you two were joined at the hip. You guys both off this weekend?"

"He's out of town," he says. "I'm not really off. I've been working the"—he burps—"Cox case."

"Yeah? Learned anything new?"

"No, but I could ask you the same. You here on the case?"

"I was heading for Tyler, just stopped off on the way. I was going to talk to a relative of hers who lives there. A distant cousin, but it's worth a try."

He shrugs. "We tracked down all the relatives."

"Still . . . Got to earn my money, right?"

"Right." He leans toward me, almost falls off his stool. "Hey, how much are the Paces paying you? That guy's rolling in money."

I hide behind my glass and take a sip. "I'd rather not say. It's enough to pay my rent."

"But how much? Seriously, I bet he's paying you more than I make."

"He's not."

"But sometimes I think maybe I should go private, you know? Get out of all this. Get away from Keegan, with all his ideas and demands."

"Ideas? What kind of ideas?"

He gets quiet then as the barmaid brings back his glass. He swigs the whiskey and belches again.

I try again. "What kind of ideas are you talking about?"

He waves a hand at me. "Nothin', man. Just, do this, do that. Don't do this, don't do that."

I know I can't press harder, so I just wait, hoping he'll go on, but he sees a girl walk by, and he grabs her arm and pulls her toward him. She isn't flattered and jerks away.

He turns back to the bar, brooding, and curses her.

After a few minutes, he pulls out his wallet, drops a ten on the bar, then changes his mind and leaves a twenty. "I gotta go," he says.

"Sure?"

"Yeah. Work to do." He gets up and steadies himself, then pats me on the back. "Later, man."

"You sure you want to drive? You've had a little much."

"I'm fine," he says. "Don't be like him."

"Like who?"

"Gordon. Like he's my ol' man or somethin'."

I look back at the counter, but I can't tell how many he's

had. There's only the one glass. He may have been three sheets already when he got here.

He staggers out and, when the door closes, I follow him. He's already in his car, pulling out of the parking lot. As he drives away, I pray that he won't kill anybody.

～

It's an hour later, and I'm driving through Tyler on my way to Dallas when my phone rings. It's a number I don't recognize. I pick it up. "Hello?"

"Dylan, it's me. Sy."

I frown. This isn't the number I have programmed into my phone for Rollins. "Yeah, what's going on?"

"I was arrested."

"What?"

"DUI. It's not good. I need you to bail me out tonight."

I look at my watch, then I turn at the next exit, cross under the interstate, and head back the other direction. "All right," I say. "I'm in Tyler, but I'll be there in about an hour."

"Look, don't tell Keegan or the chief or anybody. Got it?"

"Yeah, sure."

"Hurry."

It occurs to me that I should leave him there to rot in jail, but I know he'll find some way to be out by tomorrow. Maybe I can take advantage of his vulnerability.

An hour later I show up at the Marshall Police Department

and find the bail bondsman who's waiting for me. I pay the 10 percent of Rollins's bond and wait until they release him. After a while, he comes out, clearly still drunk.

"Thanks," he grumbles.

"Where's your car?"

"Where they stopped me. It was at that grocery store . . . what's its name . . . I don't know, Kroger, maybe."

I walk him out to my car, and he heads to the driver's side, forgetting it's my car. "Do you think you should be driving?"

"I'll be all right," he says.

"But you weren't. And it's my car. Let me drive, okay?"

He acquiesces and goes around to the passenger side. We get to the grocery store that I figure would have been on his way home, and I pull in behind his car. "Look, there's a motel over there. Why don't you get a room and just sleep it off? Drive back tomorrow? Nobody'll know."

He considers that, rubbing his bloodshot eyes. "Yeah, maybe."

I don't wait for consent. I drive over there and stop at the office. He doesn't get out.

"You know," I say, "you have the same rank as Keegan. You don't have to let him call all the shots."

"You're right about that."

I'm thinking how to say that he should out Keegan for anything he's doing, but Rollins speaks first.

"You know, he doesn't trust you. He's sure you're a turncoat, that you're trying to help Casey. But I think you're okay."

My mouth goes dry. "Keegan thinks that?"

"Yeah, he's paranoid. Don't worry about it." He gets out of the car and staggers inside.

I watch as he goes to the motel desk. After a moment, I drive away.

So Keegan is on to me.

I've suspected this, but now that I know for sure, it changes everything.

38

CASEY

The news of Cole's death vibrates through me like an electric shock. I've been frozen all afternoon, not sure what to do. Little Ava's fear as she hunkered in the bathroom stall splits through my brain. Did he really go through with suicide? Ava's fate seems sealed. There's no one left to tell the truth about what's happening to her.

I check out of the motel and drive back to Dallas, knowing it's the last place I should be. But I can't just forget about Ava's problems, whatever mine might be. I drive from Cole's house to the UpDown Seat Company, trying to find the embankment he went over. I don't see anything like that.

I stop at a restaurant with Wi-Fi. On my laptop, I go to the news station's website and watch the clip again that I saw this morning, and also the updates they've filed since. Police are ruling it a suicide based on it being a one-car accident, and on his state of mind over the last few weeks. Family members have told authorities that he had talked of suicide and that he'd been talked down from jumping off a bridge just days earlier. I'm surprised he told them about that.

I'm thankful no one mentions me to reporters.

I try to imagine what would make Cole do such a thing after his children were back with his wife and the media were exposing the Trendalls. Just when things were turning around, when there was a chance to right things, he drove off a cliff? No, I don't believe it. The website identifies where his car went off the embankment, and I drive over there. There are flowers on the side of the road where it must have happened. They've been placed near a broken guardrail.

I walk up to the flowers and look down to the rocks below. There's paint where the car hit, but the car itself is nowhere in sight. I sit on what's left of the guardrail and look down the road. It's not on a curve, so it's not like he checked a text and forgot to turn. It's a straight stretch.

I get back in my car and turn it around. I drive slowly up the road. I see two sets of black tire tracks about a half mile from where he went off. They zig toward the dirt, then back onto the road. I frown. Surely the police saw that. Those could be Cole's tracks, and the other set indicates that someone might have run him off.

Suddenly I'm as sure as I was with my own father. Cole Whittington didn't kill himself. He was run off the road.

39

CASEY

drive aimlessly that afternoon, one moment thinking of going back to the TV station to tell them who probably made those tire tracks, the next thinking of calling the police to give them an anonymous tip. But knowing that Keegan is on to me, I decide that neither course is wise.

Instead, I create another alias email account and shoot a message to the reporter who followed up on my story. I tell her to check out the tire tracks and the Trendalls' vehicles, that I don't believe it was suicide.

My body is so tired that I don't feel I can go on, so I finally make myself eat. I pack carbs, trying to feel better, but every bite is dry and knots going down.

I go back to the town where I spent last night and check into a different motel with my alternate ID—Liana Winters. Then I collapse into bed.

But sleep still evades me. I can't stop thinking about Cole's death, and his children marked by that for the rest of their lives, and his wife seething with anger at him, unaware that it wasn't suicide, that he'd ruled that out.

And my head aches with thoughts of Ava.

When morning finally comes, I shower. As I'm packing and getting dressed, I turn on the TV, an old box unit with sticky fingerprints on the screen and a layer of dust on the top. I find a news station. They're covering something political as I dry my hair, and then it moves to national news.

I hear my name and dart out of the bathroom.

Casey Cox, the woman accused of murdering Brent Pace in Shreveport, Louisiana, is still at large, but her sister, Hannah Boone, was arrested today and taken into police custody.

I suck in a breath and rush to turn up the TV. I see footage of my sister being handcuffed and walked out of her home in front of everyone, cameras flashing all around her. Jeff stands in the background, yelling at the police as he holds Emma, screaming in his arms. I drop to the floor, my hands over my head. This is worse than my fear of being caught and dragged out through the press. Worse than me being murdered in my motel room. To have my sister paraded out of her house in handcuffs in front of her daughter . . .

I listen as the panel discusses whether Hannah was an accessory to my escaping, whether she's been communicating with me, whether she's going to bond out or spend a night in jail.

I know exactly what's happening. Keegan saw me at the marina in Dallas, and he's drawing me out. He's telling me that I'd better keep my mouth shut, that I'd better stop snooping, that I'd better be afraid of him. He's using Hannah to torment and control me. My mind races as I wipe the tears staining my face, my makeup dripping down my skin like mud. I have to put Hannah first, even if it means playing into Keegan's hands.

I don't stop to reapply my makeup. I don't even stop to check out of the motel and get my overpayment back.

I finish packing as fast as I can, pull on my short red wig, and turn off the TV. There's only one thing to do. I have to go back to Shreveport.

40

DYLAN

Because of bailing Rollins out of jail, I haven't yet made it to Dallas in response to Casey's email. For now, I get a room back in Tyler, and my investigation from there is productive. I get Candace Price's address from Casey's email and do a Google Earth zoom-in. The house is massive, with a pool in the back . . . not the kind of thing a cop would normally have as a second home. Maybe she has some high-powered job of her own.

I do a deeper search, find that she's a real estate agent. I get the address and look in one of my databases for public records on that address. The house doesn't have a mortgage. It was paid for with cash three years ago.

I search for the documents and see that everything is in her name. I dig a little deeper, looking for any kind of estate that she might've come into three years ago, but there isn't anything. I pull up her tax records, find that she only makes $60,000 a year. Not enough to pay cash for a house that's worth $2 million. I dig deeper through the mortgage records and find a copy of the certified check used to pay for the property. It's listed as L.W. Enfor Enterprises. I frown. L.W. Enfor? Then I realize it's a kind of shorthand for law enforcement. Some sense of humor.

So I dig for information on L.W. Enfor. It's owned by another business that appears to be a glass repair company. It's listed in Dallas, so I pull it up on Google Earth, zoom in on that address. It looks like it's out of business, like the building may even be condemned.

So this is a classic money laundering scheme. Somehow I have to follow it back to Gordon Keegan. I dig all the way back to Shreveport, then I finally get to a property deed that has his name on it. It's four businesses removed, and it's paid for with funds from an offshore bank account.

But his name is clear. He's not as smart as he thinks he is.

I stay up all night, making a record of everything I can find about Candace. As morning comes, I sip a cup of coffee and I don't even feel tired. I'm finally getting somewhere.

I turn on the TV, make some coffee, and as I drink it, I hear Casey's name.

I turn around and move closer to the TV.

Casey Cox, the woman accused of murdering Brent Pace in Shreveport, Louisiana, is still at large. But her sister, Hannah Boone, was arrested today and taken into police custody.

I grab my phone as I see the footage of Hannah, hand-cuffed and crying as her husband holds the baby behind her, media swarming like vultures as the police try to push them back. Keegan is right there, one of the cops doing a sorry job of holding back the media who are trespassing in her yard.

My heart is slamming so fast it makes me dizzy. I call Keegan's cell phone, but he doesn't pick up. I try Rollins and get voice mail. I call Keegan again, and again, hanging up each time the voice mail recording comes on, then immediately calling back. He will not ignore me! I grab my keys and head into the parking lot, still calling.

Scum of the earth! That guy has no business bothering Hannah. But part of me wonders if my conversation with her might have been overheard, or if they think she's an accessory because of what I asked her to tell Casey. Did she make a mistake? How did Keegan know?

I head back to Shreveport instead of Dallas, praying that nothing happens to Hannah in retribution for her sister's survival.

41

DYLAN

Reporters cluster on the front steps of the Shreveport Police Department when I arrive. I move through them, ignored, head up to the third floor, and ask someone where Keegan is. They point me to the interrogation room down the hall. My temples hurting from grinding my teeth, I stride down to that door and look in the window. I see Hannah in there with Keegan and Rollins. She's crying and frantic.

I knock on the door.

Rollins opens it and leans out.

"I want to sit in," I say quietly.

"Naw, you can't do that."

"Let me talk to Detective Keegan."

He rolls his eyes and shuts the door. I watch through the two-way glass as he whispers to Keegan. I see the smarmy smirk on Keegan's face as he gets up and opens the door. "This is not your case, Dylan," he says. "I don't know why you keep making me remind you that you're contracted help tasked with one job. Bringing back the killer."

"That's her sister," I say. "I want to know what you have on her. Did she contact her? Did you intercept communications between them?"

"Go find something else to do," Keegan says. "I'm busy." He goes back in and closes the door.

I swing my fist, almost hitting the wall but stopping short of it. I want to yell so loud that my voice shakes the building, but I stop myself. I'm covered with sweat and I can hear my heart pounding in my ears.

Did I somehow cause this? Did I get Hannah arrested? Did I set Casey up to do something that turned out to be stupid?

What is all this about?

I go to Chief Gates's office. His secretary stops me. "He's in a meeting. He can't see you now."

"Please. It's important that I sit in on the interrogation with Casey Cox's sister. I need to know if Casey has contacted Hannah. I need to know why they've arrested her."

"I can't interrupt him," she says. "I'm sorry."

I think of kicking down his door, demanding that he

help me, but I know that's not the way to convince him I'm a professional. Instead, I go out into the hallway and find Jim Pace's number. I call him and it rings three times. Finally, he picks up.

"Dylan? What's going on? I saw the news report."

"They've brought Casey's sister in. I can't get any information. Jim, I need you to call the chief and ask him to let me sit in on their interrogation."

"Have you asked?"

"Yes, and the detectives don't play well with others. I need to be there, Jim." I know I need an ace in the hole to convince him, so I pull one out. "Look, they've clearly uncovered something that could lead us to Casey. She's very close to her sister. I need to know what it is so I can find her."

Jim hesitates for a moment, then says, "Has the chief told you no?"

"Not yet. He's in a meeting. I can't get in there to see him. You have his cell phone number, don't you? Can't you call him?"

"Yes," he says. "Just hang on. I'll get back to you. Where will you be?"

"Right here, in the hallway in front of his office," I say.

"Okay. Let me see if I can get him."

I wait, pacing up and down the hall, doing the breathing exercises my shrink gave me, trying to make my heart rate slow. I feel that illogical sense of panic like I did after the explosion—as I groped around trying to save my friends. It's not the same, I know, but I'm sweating and feel like I'm on high alert, waiting for the next blast to go off, waiting for gunfire, mortar fire, waiting for something . . .

When my phone chimes, I jump. It's Jim, but as he calls, I hear footsteps in the chief's office, and he leans out into the hall. "Dylan, Jim said you were here. Go on up. I've called Keegan and told him to let you in."

I let out a breath. "Thank you. I really need to be there."

"I agree. Sorry for the confusion."

My phone is still ringing, so I swipe it on. "Jim, you did it. He's letting me sit in. I'm heading up there now."

"Let me know what you find out," Jim says. "Call me as soon as you can."

"Will do."

I head back up the stairs and hurry down the hallway. When I knock on the door, it flies open. Keegan stares at me, his jaw set. He steps out into the hall and closes the door behind him. "Just because you have an in with the chief doesn't mean you belong here. We do the questioning. You don't say a word."

"All right."

"I don't know why you couldn't just watch through the glass, but the chief says let you in, so *come on in*." He sounds like a circus master as he says those last three words.

I follow him into the room, and see Hannah's face change. Is that hope? I fear she's going to cry out for me to help her, but surely she's wise enough not to. I sit down, arms crossed, as they resume their questioning. It doesn't take long for me to realize that they don't have anything on her. They're really just filling time.

This was all to lure Casey out of hiding.

42

CASEY

As I cross into the Shreveport city limits, I check myself in the mirror, and I'm looking at a stranger. My strawberry-blonde wig is short and tapered around my ears like something out of the fifties, and dark sunglasses hide my eyes. I've drawn my lips bigger than my own, with a more puckered look. All the way here from Dallas I've had one thought in mind—saving my sister. But now that I'm here I'm not sure how I'll do that.

She can't afford a lawyer without mortgaging her house since she and her husband barely make ends meet. She used her money that Dad left to invest in her home. I suppose she could get a second mortgage, but that's out of my control. I think of driving by her house and talking to Jeff, but there are probably still media on the front lawn.

One thought keeps hammering me. I have to turn myself in to get the heat off Hannah.

I can drive straight to the police department—disguised—and walk through the media and up to the office where my dad used to work, where Keegan works now. The thought nauseates me, and I pull over into a Walmart parking lot. For a moment, I think I'm going to throw up, but then the feeling passes.

No, presenting myself to Keegan is suicide. I'd be dead before I ever have an arraignment. I don't know how he would do it given the public attention to the case, but he'd find a way. He'd probably hang me in my cell and tell them that he found me that way.

Maybe I need to leave what's left of my cash somewhere and get a message to Jeff that it's for Hannah's defense, then leave town again.

I get out of my car and pull my bag out of the backseat, lock it in my trunk. My cash is in there. If I can just hide my keys somewhere and get word to Jeff, he can retrieve the money.

I realize that a lot of things have to fall into place for *any* of this to work, and that if I turn myself in, I may be about to hand over control to the most evil man I've ever known. The thought scares me to death. I shut the trunk as a family of five trail toward me, their shopping cart piled high. They get into the van next to my car.

I sit there a moment, trying to decide how to get the keys and cash into Jeff's hands for Hannah. If I leave my car here for him, how will I get to the police station?

The truth is, I'm stalling. I don't want to do it.

My brave girl. Dad's voice plays through my mind like an old familiar tune. I'm not feeling all that brave, but I have to go through the motions. Isn't it worth my life to make sure Emma still has her mother?

I don't let another thought hang me up. I start my car and back out, then head to the police department. I'll just leave my car in their parking lot and do this. The money isn't the main issue. Getting Hannah released is, and if they have me, they'll probably let Hannah go.

I turn onto the road where Dad's old workplace is, and I slow as I pass the media glutting the sidewalk, with cameras and boom mikes, their vans double-parked along the curb.

No one looks in my direction. Wouldn't they be shocked to know that the girl they've all been looking for is right under their noses?

I turn into the parking lot, clinging to my dad's words. *My brave girl.*

I find a parking place near the back of the lot, on the side facing the hardware store next door. I pull in and sit there a moment. It's suddenly hard to breathe, and my heartbeat is hurting my chest. I look toward the front walk and try to plot my path. Should I walk right up to the media and tell them who I am, or just go into the building?

Suddenly the passenger door opens and a man slips into my car. I yelp in surprise.

It's Dylan Roberts.

"I thought it was you," he says.

I grab my door handle and start to open it, but he stops me. "Don't. Not yet."

"Don't what?" I ask him. "Don't turn myself in? Are you seriously telling me that? Have you forgotten what you were hired to do?"

"It's not time yet," he says, looking out the back window. "I got your emails. I've been compiling all the evidence. I have statements by some of your dad's coworkers, evidence about things Keegan and his cohorts did back then. Money laundering trails, bank accounts. Enough to convict him of extortion, but not murder. I need more time."

"You can have all the credit for finding me. Just take me in right now. Turn me over to Keegan. Then you'll get to be the big hero and you'll get your job."

"I'm not looking for a job," he says. "I'm looking for justice. If you go in there, you know you'll wind up dead. Keegan *can't* let you talk. It's too dangerous for him."

"I know that," I say, bursting into tears. I touch my tears and see the brown liquid, and I'm embarrassed that my makeup's running. "Don't you think I know that?"

"Then work with me," he says. "Help me help you."

"Why are you doing this?" I ask. "Why would you risk yourself this way?"

"Because it's the right thing to do."

"Is it? My sister is in there. They arrested her for talking to me. I got her into this. I have to get her out. She has a child."

"They'll have to let her go anyway," he says. "I've been in the interrogations with her. They don't have anything on her, and when I realized they were doing all this just to draw you out, I left the interview room and have been sitting out here waiting for you. I knew you'd come. She did call for a lawyer, and they're waiting for him to show up."

"Really?" I ask.

"Yes, and he's a good one. I don't know how Keegan got the arrest warrant when he doesn't seem to have anything solid. All he's doing is going over and over the information about the day you left. Hannah's doing great. She's been very consistent."

"So she's talking before her attorney gets there?"

"Yeah, but don't worry. She hasn't said anything that implicates her."

"That's because she's telling the truth. She didn't know anything about Brent's death, and she didn't help me leave. She learned about it when the police told her." I look at him, my hands on the steering wheel. "I have to get her out of there. They could hurt her, just to hurt me. She doesn't belong in jail."

"And you do? You didn't kill Brent Pace."

"But I *have* broken laws. You know I have. It's *me* who's supposed to be in there, not her."

"Casey, you know that Keegan can hurt Hannah even if she's out. The only way to stop him is to nail him on his corruption. I'm putting myself on the line here right now." He glances out the back window. "There are cameras on the eaves of the building. But you don't look like yourself, and they don't know I've flipped, so for all they know, if anyone's watching, you could be my girlfriend. I want you to come away with me right now. Don't turn yourself in yet. That can be done later if you still want to, when it's safe. This is the rest of your life we're talking about, so let's do this right."

I look out the window, and my eyes drift to the corners of the building. I do see security cameras, but they're all fixed, steady, not moving toward us. "What do you want me to do?"

"I want to get out of this car and watch you drive away. I want you to meet me tonight after dark."

"After dark? By then Hannah will be in lockdown . . . or worse."

"I don't think so," Dylan says. "Once her lawyer gets here and realizes they don't have anything to hold her on, he'll get her out of here today."

"Can you guarantee that?"

"No, I can't. But I have a strong suspicion that's what'll happen. Keegan didn't arrest her because he had probable cause. He arrested her because he saw you in Dallas. You can't let him win."

"So why isn't he watching for me? If he thinks he's drawing me out—"

"He has people watching I-20 just outside of Shreveport. Your disguise got you past them."

"Then they'll see me when I leave town."

"They're only watching traffic coming into Shreveport, not going out. I'm trying to get the names of the guys he put out on I-20 to watch for you, because I think they must be part of the corruption. He wouldn't have wanted just any officers to apprehend you, for fear you'd tell them everything."

I shiver at the thought that I was almost caught in their net. "I was going to the press first, on the steps outside the department."

"You wouldn't have gotten two sentences out of your mouth before they arrested you. We're not ready yet. I need more hard evidence before we can make this stick. I'm counting four murders now—your dad, Sara Meadows, another officer, and Brent. I'm sure there will be more if we don't nail him."

I think about it for a minute and realize he's right.

"Casey, you don't have much more time. Someone's gonna come out and see us talking."

"All right," I say. "Where do you want to meet?"

He hands me a phone, clicks to the Contacts, and types in a phone number. "This is a burner phone, and I've put in the number to my second phone. I'll hang out here until they let Hannah go, under the guise that I'm collecting information that will lead me to you. I think Hannah will feel a little more comfortable knowing I'm here. As soon as she's free, I'll text you to see where you are."

"Okay," I say. "I'll take a different route back west, but I'll be checking. If they keep her, I'm coming back."

"I know." He reaches for a tissue from a box on my floor-board and hands it to me. "Are you going to be okay?"

"I will be if she is."

"She will be." His words sound like a promise, but I don't believe promises. "Tell me one thing," he says. "What happened to your chin? And your hands? Did that happen when Keegan almost ran you over?"

I look down at my hands and remember the scrapes from my run-in with the Trendalls. "No, not that. It's a long story. Nothing to do with this, really."

"If you say so." He opens the door and slips out, looks both ways. I glance at the cameras. I watch him walk to his car, the same one that was on the street when he helped me escape from Willie Dotson's house in Shady Grove. I pull out of the parking lot before he starts his car, and I drive off. I watch in my rear-view mirror as he turns the other direction. I pray that I'm not making a terrible mistake.

43

DYLAN

When Casey is out of sight, I go back inside the department. I want to make sure that things are okay with Hannah before I make my next move. I find her with her attorney and a bail bondsman, and I'm told she's being released. The press will descend on her like vultures the moment she steps out the door.

I hope she's prepared for that feeding frenzy, and that she won't say anything. I go upstairs to the detective division, hoping to feel Keegan out about the direction of the investigation. When I get to the top of the stairs, I hear him talking on his way out the door.

"I won't be back for a few days. Anything comes up, call Rollins or me. Especially with the Cox case. And keep that tail on Hannah." He rounds the corner, sees me, and stops for a moment, his eyes burning into me as if he hates my guts and would like to break me in half.

"Where you going?" I ask.

"Like I'd tell you," he says.

I glance behind him at Rollins, who's following him out.

"We'll be available by phone," Keegan says. As they shoot past me, I have a bad feeling in my gut that they're about to go to the airport and hop back over to Dallas.

I text Casey from the new burner phone I've just activated.

Hannah released. Keegan and Rollins headed to Dallas, I think. Don't go there.

She types back, Should I go south or north?

South, I say. Try Palestine TX.

She texts me back: Ok.

I write back: Text me when u find a place & I'll stay there too. On my way to meet u.

I hope rerouting her throws them off.

I run by my apartment, grab a few things, and head out.

For the next three hours, driving to where Casey should be, I watch every westbound plane that passes overhead, wondering if it's Keegan and Rollins.

I think she'll be safe if she doesn't go to Dallas. Hopefully, tonight we'll be able to get to the end of this.

44

CASEY

I get back on I-20 when I'm far enough away from Shreveport, then I stop at an exit along the way to get a burger. I sit in the Wendy's parking lot to eat and use their Wi-Fi signal to get on the Internet. I want to check the news and see what I can find about Hannah being released.

There are clips of her walking through the media with her attorney holding them back. I'm relieved, but still livid that my sister has had to go through that at all.

It's all my fault. I never should have contacted her. I put her in a terrible position. What if they found the burner phone she's been hiding? It would give them evidence that we've talked, and it might lead them to me. I take the battery out of the phone I've been using and break it. When I'm done here, I'll toss the pieces into separate trash cans. I'll use the one Dylan gave me instead.

While I'm online, I check the Dallas TV station's site to see if they have anything else on Cole's death.

I go back to the list of sites with recent stories about him and see that they're all reporting his death. There's a video of one of his cousins I've never met. "We're asking police not to rule this a suicide. We just don't think he did this on purpose."

"He didn't!" I yell. "The Trendalls . . ." I think back over my confrontation with those people. I shouldn't have told them anything about Cole. But I told them he was suicidal, hoping they had consciences. Now I have a deep gut feeling that they used that information . . . set up his death and knew it would seem as if he'd gone through with suicide. And with Cole dead, there'll be no one to fight the charges in their lawsuit, and Cole's testimony about a molester named Fred will never be brought into court. Ava's fate is sealed.

No, someone has to hold them accountable. Those tire tracks . . . If they match the Trendalls'. . . If there's evidence on their van or truck . . . These people seem to be drug users. Surely they haven't been that careful. They must have made mistakes. Maybe I can find the evidence and report them anonymously. For Ava's sake, I have to at least try. How could good people be crushed this way?

I start the car, but before I drive out of the parking lot, I text Dylan. Change of plans. Have to get closer to Dallas. I'll let you know where I wind up.

45

DYLAN

When I'm almost to Dallas, I get Casey's text. It worries me, so I call her.

"Hello?" Her voice sounds cloudy, wet.

"Casey, it's Dylan."

"Yeah, you're the only one who has this number."

"Right. So what happened? Why would you risk going near Dallas?"

She's silent for a long moment. "Something happened. I just needed to . . . check on somebody. Nothing to do with my case. I'll tell you about it when you come."

"Bad idea," I say. "You need to get as far from Dallas as you can."

"It's a big city. I can stay hidden. This is really important."

She's stubborn, and I can see I'm not going to talk her out of it.

"If you can tell me where you're staying, I'll get a room there too. Then we can go over what we've got on these people and get something ready for the media."

She tells me she's staying at the Independence Suites, not part of a chain. I put it in my GPS. When I get there, I see it's among a cluster of other motels. Her car isn't in the parking lot. I check in. I would ask them if I can get a room close to hers, but I don't know what name she's using. I go toss my bag into my room on the second floor, then I text and ask her room number. She texts it back. She's only a few rooms away from mine. I go knock on her door. I don't like that the rooms open to the outside, that people can walk up from the parking lot to any door. I would rather she had picked one that was more secure, but this one's cheap and I suppose she's getting short on cash.

She opens the door a couple of inches, looks out into the parking lot for danger, then lets me in.

I feel like a guy who's crushed on a girl for five years and finally has the chance to talk to her. But of course it's a paradox—I'm supposed to be dragging her back for a crime. I step into her room and see that it's a suite. It has a sitting area with a couch and a chair and a little kitchenette. Maybe mine has that too. I didn't pay attention. Her front drapes are shut except for a ten-inch slit, but there's still sunlight coming through the back window.

"I'd bet that Keegan and Rollins are here in Dallas by now," I say. "I could go and try to find them, but I think it's better if I stay here."

"Maybe. I can't think."

"Where's your car?"

"I parked it at the Super 8, a block up." She's been crying, and her eye makeup is smudged. She looks like the person in the pictures everyone has seen. Her nose is red, her eyes puffy.

"Casey, what's wrong? Hannah got out, didn't she?"

"Yeah. It's not her." She turns off the TV and goes to her couch, drops down. "A friend of mine died yesterday. Nothing to do with this case . . . just a nice person who had some bad stuff happen to him, and he somehow . . ." She stops and swallows hard, then says, "Drove his car off a cliff."

I lower to the couch, angle toward her. "Casey, I'm so sorry. Was it someone in Shreveport?"

She shakes her head. "No. Dallas. That's why I came back. I don't believe it was suicide. I have to find proof."

I can't believe what I'm hearing. "Casey, you have to stay focused. I know this is hard, but you can't get sidetracked . . ."

"A little girl's future is at stake. This isn't just grief. But honestly, I don't want to talk about it."

She doesn't entirely trust me yet, and I can see that she's determined, so I switch gears.

"So . . . do you want to talk about the evidence we've each gotten?" I put my computer on the coffee table next to hers. "Maybe between the two of us, we have enough."

"Hannah's lost weight," she says. "I saw her on the news footage, leaving the station. She looks really depressed and pale. Poor little Emma . . . I know my mother probably stepped in, but she's not a big help. And Jeff has to keep his job. He can't just take off work every day to take care of Emma, and I don't know how they're going to pay for attorneys if this drags on." She's distraught and her eyes glisten, though she's holding back tears.

I touch Casey's shoulder and look into her face. "Casey, you can do this. You've come this far. You're smart. You can't panic now."

"I just want it to be over. I think I was a little relieved when it seemed like I was ending it."

"He would pay a prisoner to beat you to death," I say. "Or hang you with your sheet."

She shivers.

"You did the right thing. If we have enough evidence, we can end it soon."

She sighs. "I sent you everything I have."

"But you haven't seen what I have. And I need to talk to you about the crime scene photos."

"What about them?"

"Have you looked at the ones of Brent's body that were released to the press?"

Her face drains of color before my eyes. "I saw the ones

on TV that were blurred out. I couldn't stand to look at the unedited ones online."

"You need to," I say. "I want to know if the way they photographed him is the way you saw him. If anything at the crime scene was moved or changed. If we can point out inconsistencies, make them question the evidence as Keegan and Rollins left it, then we might be able to tie them to the murder."

I hate doing it to her, but she finally takes my phone and looks down at the photo. I can feel her trembling next to me.

"It was such a blur," she whispers, then goes silent for a long moment. "Those footprints are mine. I stumbled all over the place. I grabbed him, tried to revive him. I kept thinking he would wake up, but he was cold . . . But . . . he's a lot taller than me. This slash across his neck . . . How could I have done that?"

"If you had, there would have to be a downward angle—like you reached up, then slashed back down—but there wasn't, according to the autopsy report. This was very deliberate. It cut the carotid artery. The person who did this was his height."

"They left the front door unlocked for me," she adds. "When he didn't answer, I went in, and there he was. Maybe their prints are on the doorknob or the lock."

"The problem with the crime scene is that even if there were fibers or prints from Keegan and Rollins—or whoever actually carried their plan out—they can explain why their DNA was there. They can say it was from their investigation of the scene."

She nods. "And the knife they planted in my car is pretty

condemning. No reason anyone should believe they put it there when they found my car." She thrusts my phone back at me. "How could anyone think I could stab my friend? Or any human being, anywhere?"

She's staring straight ahead, and I know she's there . . . at the scene. As much as I want her to give me something I can use, I don't want her to stay there. I show her the list of things I've compiled against Keegan, get her talking about it, gently pulling her back. Slowly, the color returns to her face.

"The key here," I say, "is going to be the press. If we can give them the evidence they need, then Keegan can't ride in and do something to stop you from talking. It'll be too late. But it has to be enough."

She pulls her feet up onto the couch, hugs her knees, and looks out through the gap in the drapes, toward the parking lot below. The strip of light from the afternoon sun has illuminated one side of her face, but the other side is shaded. "Best case scenario, I probably will have to go to jail anyway, even if Keegan's group is exposed and I'm somehow protected from them. I've been thinking about it. If my sister can handle it, I can. It's probably not as bad as it sounds. Nothing ever is."

I turn to her on the couch, set my elbow on the back of it, leaning on my hand. "Why do you think you'll have to go to jail if we can get people to listen to the truth?"

"A lot of broken laws," she says. "I've used dead people's identities. I've stolen license plates. I've fled prosecution. Those things have consequences."

"You were trying to survive," I say. Her eyes fix on something outside and I know she's thinking about what's in store for her.

"Casey, look at me," I say. She does, and again I have that feeling that I could fall into her eyes and disappear and never be heard from again. Those blue eyes are so deep, so full of things I can't express. I swallow the knot in my throat. "You didn't kill Brent Pace. You don't deserve to be charged with murder."

"I know," she says. "But I'm scared." Her words are a whisper, almost inaudible. "My dad used to call me his brave girl, but I think it was to bolster me because I *wasn't* brave. I waited a year after I was allowed to get my driver's license before I took the test, because I didn't want to fail. My mother had a terrible time getting me to drive for the first time."

"Casey, your dad was right. You're the bravest person I've ever met."

She gets tears in her eyes, and her mouth twists as she tries to hold them back. She doesn't answer, and I can see as she looks away that she doesn't have any words.

"You know," I say, "God has been watching over you all this time. I know he has. I told you before, he's the one who's given me the gut certainty that you aren't guilty."

She nods and turns her gaze back to me. "I see that," she says. "But it confuses me." She wipes her face, then dries her hands on her jeans. "I went to church a couple of times here. There were things I didn't understand. Like they kept talking about being washed by the blood of Christ, and that didn't make any sense to me. I don't know if I'm up to speed enough to ever be a Christian."

"Washed in the blood means that Jesus shed his blood to take our punishment. It wiped our slates clean, as far as he's concerned. Without that blood, we wouldn't be clean."

She nods slowly. "Yeah, I thought it was something like that."

"You don't have to get up to speed to be a Christ follower," I say. "There isn't a test. There's only talking to God and telling him you believe."

"But believe what?" she asks. "Sometimes I don't know exactly what I'm supposed to believe."

"Forget *supposed to*," I say. "What *do* you believe?"

She gets up and walks across the room, crosses her arms, and turns back to me. "I believe there is a God. I believe he's been watching over me and that he hears my prayers sometimes. And when I was in church, I felt . . . something. I don't know what to call it."

"It's the Holy Spirit," I say. "He sometimes moves in you when you worship. I think you're feeling his prodding."

She comes back to the couch. "I just don't understand how God works. I was gonna read the Bible one day, and I reached for the hotel Bible in the drawer, and I found someone else's Bible. It had a suicide note. It derailed me."

"A suicide note?"

"Yeah," she says. "And I found out the guy was alive, then I looked him up and returned the Bible to him. I found out all this stuff about what would make him want to kill himself." She pauses and sniffs, and tears rim her eyes. "He'd been accused of child molestation, and it was all bogus. I found out the accusing family was a bunch of liars, that they accuse people all the time and live on the settlements. Their daughter had been abused, but not by him. Things were turning around for him, and then he just . . . ran his car off a cliff. I think it was like with my dad, when someone made it look like a suicide but it wasn't. And I think it was those people. The ones who accused him. I just . . . I don't understand how God keeps letting things like that happen. Evil winning." With the last few words, she crumples into tears, and I watch her bury her head in her knees. I move closer, not sure what she would want me to do.

"I don't either," I say, touching her back. "I don't understand why lots of things happen. But evil has a name. We live in a world where Satan has a lot of power, and he works overtime to wreak havoc, especially when people are moving closer to God. I'm sorry that guy died."

"I just feel like I might have had something to do with it."

"What do you mean?"

"That couple, the accusers, they cornered me and were trying to intimidate me—that's where I got all these scrapes from— and I told them they were ruining a decent man's life, that he was suicidal. I think they used that. They got the idea from me and then they made it look like that happened. Then they could sue the school for all the money they wanted and he couldn't defend himself. He died with that allegation hanging over his head."

It's a knee-jerk reaction, but I pull her into my arms and hold her as she cries against my shirt.

"This guy and his wife were Christians," she says. "I don't know why God lets things like that happen to people who are devoted to him. There's so much evil. It just never stops."

"And the only thing in this world that beats that darkness back is the light."

She pulls upright, wiping her face. "But that's another one of those clichés I don't get. The light. I feel it sometimes. It makes sense that you have to beat back the darkness, but I just don't understand why there's darkness in the first place. Sometimes I feel like the world has fractured into a million pieces and they're closing in on me, and I have to push each piece back with my hands and my feet and my head to keep it from squeezing me to death."

"I've felt that way myself," I say. "But . . . Satan doesn't get the final word. I really believe there's more to this life than just living and dying. We each have an eternity somewhere."

"Heaven's a hard thing to grasp too. My dad . . . He never said anything about Jesus or religion or God. He was a good man, but that wasn't one of our things. If you believe he had to be a Christian to go to heaven, then he's probably not there, and I'll never see him again."

"Casey, for all you know, your dad is in heaven because he cried out to Jesus in those last minutes. God doesn't make it complicated. It's very simple. And don't you think your dad would want you to know the truth about God?"

"Yes, of course."

"Then don't let that be one of your obstacles. Casey, this world can be a really terrible place. I've experienced it myself. But Jesus died on the cross to overcome it. We only make it into heaven because of him. He died so that we don't have to smother in the darkness. He made it so if we simply call out to him, we're his."

"But there is repentance."

"Yes, there's repentance. We all have to repent."

"If I repent, then it's over. I'd have to turn myself in immediately, no matter what."

"You can't turn yourself in until we get all our ducks in a row. Not until we've contacted every media person who's interested in this story. Not until we make sure that Keegan and Rollins are going to face justice for murdering your father and Brent, and Sara Meadows, and the cop who was on to him, and whoever else they've killed, and for all the money they've gotten from innocent people to finance their toys. You're not just doing this for yourself, Casey, you're doing it for a lot of other people. You're doing it for your father. You're doing it for Hannah and for Emma and for Jeff and your mom."

She's staring at me now, so intently that my heart breaks.

"You can get forgiveness from God and still make sure that you help bring about justice. It's going to be all right," I tell her. "This is only the beginning."

"What if all hell breaks loose?"

"Then I'll keep picking up the pieces," I say. "I'll keep

putting them back together. I'll keep beating back the darkness. But we can do this."

We're closer to each other now, no longer separated by awkwardness or nerves. We work together at the same pace on the same project, getting our paperwork done to give to the press. And for the first time since before I was deployed, I feel as though my life has clicked into place.

46

CASEY

When we get hungry, Dylan goes out to get us something to eat, and I'm left there alone in my motel room. I sit on the couch for a while, savoring the thought of him. I've never felt so attached to another human being. I was almost this way with Brent, and he was attracted to me, but I always held him at arm's length. It seemed that whenever I let someone in, something bad happened. When people are ripped out of your life often enough, you find ways to avoid that pain again.

But it's different with Dylan somehow. I lean back on the couch and look up at the ceiling as if I can see God's face there, and I ask him, "Is this from you, God? Did you send him for me?"

The thought that he may have makes me feel that, just maybe, God does see me and love me. That maybe there truly is a living Savior who sits at the right hand of God and intercedes for us, just as the preacher said in church.

I get up and scurry around the room, straightening up, trying to keep myself busy. In the bathroom, I check my makeup and brush my teeth. I feel like wiping off what's left of my eyeliner, showing Dylan who I really am, looking like myself for the first time in days. After all, I'm not going anywhere tonight, so maybe it's okay if he sees me as I am. But as I'm reaching for a tissue, I hear a car door in the parking lot. I go look out the window.

I jump when I see who's getting out of the car, bumping a table and toppling a glass that falls and breaks on the floor.

Gordon Keegan and Sy Rollins are getting out of Keegan's red Jaguar and heading for the motel office.

47

DYLAN

Casey said she likes the salads at Chick-fil-A, so I walk a block to get her one and throw in a piece of cheesecake for good measure. I walk back to the motel, looking forward to eating a meal with her. But as I round the building, I see Keegan and Rollins coming out of the motel office and heading to the staircase. I step back behind the building where I hope they won't see me, and I quickly call Casey. Her phone rings to voice mail, which she hasn't set up yet. I text her, Keeg&Roll on their way up!

But I don't know if she sees it. I watch them approach her

door. How did they find her? I have to do something. My mind races. I could run up and distract their attention, pretend I found her in another hotel down the street. Or I could say she was here but she saw me and escaped. I'm still trying to come up with something when they draw their weapons and use a key card to open the door.

Suddenly my phone shakes.

Got out back window.

I close my eyes and whisper, "Thank you, God." While they're in her room, I run to my car, back out, and take the closest exit from the parking lot. As I pass the Super 8, I check—her car is not in the parking lot. She must have gotten to it.

I text her and ask where she is, but she doesn't answer, so I drive around and try to work out in my mind what just happened. After an hour, I go back to the motel. The detectives' car is gone, so I jog up to my room and get my stuff.

My laptop was still in Casey's room when they went in. If they got it, would they be able to see that I've emailed her? I compulsively empty my cache, but I could have left the Yahoo account open.

I pray Casey got out with it, but it's doubtful.

My mind careens from one thought to another. They were there without a local police escort, a breach of protocol. If they'd intended to simply arrest her, they would have notified the local police and made the arrest together with them. The fact that they did it alone tells me how close Casey just came to death.

And if they found her here, will they find her again? Is it possible they saw her in Shreveport today and had her followed? It seems unlikely. If they'd seen her when she drove to the police station, things would have ended differently. I was watching out the windows the whole time I was in her car.

Then I wonder if it was simpler than that.

What if they're tracking *me*?

I pull over and look under my car for a tracking device. I don't see anything. I get back in and think. Then I look down at my phone—the one they know about.

If they had it tapped, they could have used it as a microphone to listen to my conversations. I don't think that's what happened, because they want me off the case, and they could have used the tapes of my conversations to get me fired by now . . . and even arrested. Or I would have had a tragic, mysterious "accident" myself. If they were listening in, they would have made sure I was with Casey when they arrived at the motel, so they could take us out together.

So maybe they're only tracking my phone's location. That can be done pretty easily with an app, and they wouldn't have had to get a judge or the department involved. Yes, that has to be it. And if that's all it is, it's possible that they don't yet realize I'm working with her. They could just be following me as I hunt her.

Whatever the case, this phone is dangerous. I have to get rid of it right away.

48

CASEY

I drive, not knowing where I'm going, wondering how Keegan and Rollins found me. I must have slipped up somewhere, done something wrong. Or maybe Dylan did. If they found me once, they will find me again. I'm trembling, and I know I'm going to have to get rid of this car soon, since they might figure out I parked at one of the nearby motels and get the video from the Super 8's security cameras. But if I get rid of it, then what will I do? I don't have time or money to buy another car, and I need transportation. I can't just expect Dylan to take care of me from here on out.

I try to calm myself. When I saw them getting out of their car and going into the office, that gave me time to grab the two laptops and our papers and throw them in my bag. I went out the back window, which was on the second floor, and I jumped to the ground. I hurt my ankle when I landed, but I kept going anyway. Now my ankle is swelling.

Dylan's text calms me. At least I know he wasn't caught, and we haven't lost contact. I just have to figure out where to tell him to meet me.

My mind races and anxiety is rising. I feel the world pressing in, and I try to think how to push it back. I hit I-30 going east. If my time is short, then what should I do next? I've already given Dylan all the evidence I've found, but it's on his computer—on the seat next to me. I have to get it to him. But time is running out for me to help bring justice for Cole and Ava, and that's important too. If I leave town, this evil will prevail. If God is with me, if he's watching me, if he cares enough to send Dylan, then he cares about Cole's family and Ava too. Maybe he will help me expose the Trendalls.

Dylan texts me finally. Where can we meet?

Lake Ron Hubbard at 9:00, I type back. At the Watershed Marina. I have laptops.

He texts back, Thank God.

That allows me enough time to go by the Trendalls' so I can get a look at their vehicles and see if there's any evidence on them that they ran Cole off the road. I get to their house. The porch light is on. The garage door is open. Their van is sitting in the driveway, and it doesn't have any dents from what I can see. The white truck I've seen there is gone. Suddenly, the van's headlights come on and it starts backing out.

My heart jolts. Have they seen me?

I fly around the corner and speed up as I race away. I drive back to the interstate, zigzagging in and out of cars in case their van is behind me. All I see in my rearview mirror are dozens of headlights. I think I'm safe. I slow to the speed limit so I don't draw the highway patrol's attention, and I head for Lake Ron Hubbard.

49

DYLAN

Before I get on I-30, I find an eighteen-wheeler parked at a nearby truck stop and duct tape my phone that Keegan is probably tracking to the undercarriage. Now he'll think I'm going wherever that truck is heading.

I follow the GPS on my burner phone to Lake Ron Hubbard, then Google the dock where Casey told me to meet her and follow the directions. As I cross a spillway bridge, I see Casey's car just a few vehicles ahead of me. Relief floods through me. They haven't gotten to her yet.

I pass the person in front of me. Now there's nothing but a

gray van between us. I turn off my GPS since I don't need route
guidance from here.

Suddenly the van in front of me swerves into the passing
lane and accelerates quickly, drawing even with Casey and
sideswiping her car. She jerks toward the bridge rail, then
rights herself. The van moves over again, scraping her good,
sparks flying as metal grates metal. They're trying to push her
over, and they just might succeed—she's up against the rail
with nowhere to go.

I lay on my horn and stomp my accelerator, ramming the
van's bumper. Casey slams on her brakes and the van turns
sideways. Cars screech to a stop behind me. I back up and go
around the van, getting between them and Casey's car.

Who are they? Keegan and Rollins were in Keegan's red
sports car, not a gray van. They must have others in Dallas
helping them.

I turn my car sideways on the bridge to prevent them from
reaching her, but the van turns around, then screeches back the
way we came across the bridge and out of sight.

Cars are coming, so I move my car in front of Casey's and
back up toward her, my emergency lights blinking. Someone
will call the police soon if they haven't already. I get out and
run back to her car, try to open the door. "Casey!"

Her door's bent and she can't get out. I run around to the
passenger side and get it open. "Are you okay?"

"Yeah," she says, but I'm not sure she is.

"Get out," I say. "Can you climb across?"

She hands me her bag and I take it. It's heavy, and something clunks inside. I slide the strap over my head, then help her climb out. Her shoulder must be hurting. She's holding her arm close to her body, and she's limping. I help her to my car and get her in, then I run around to my side. My car is still running, so I shift it into drive and go.

I get off the bridge and mix into the traffic as I hear sirens.

"They almost killed me, just like they did him," she says.

"Brent?"

"No!" she cries. "That was . . . the Trendalls. I went by their house to see if their car was dented . . . and they saw me and followed . . ."

I want to go after them, but more than that I want to get Casey to safety. "Do you need a hospital?"

"No. I'm fine. Just . . . don't go to the dock. Don't go anywhere I've been before. Just go . . . somewhere else."

She's breathing hard. There's blood on her temple, and a knot forming there. She's still holding her arm carefully.

"I got the computers and papers," she says. "They didn't get anything back at the motel. But how did they know I was there?"

"I think they were tracking my phone, so I got rid of it."

I drive, not sure where to go. I probably should pull over and check my car. I can tell one of my headlights is broken, and the front end is dented. But the car seems like the safest place for Casey right now, so I drive into the darkest part of the night until I'm sure no one is behind us.

50

CASEY

Tell me about those people in the van," Dylan says. "Don't leave anything out."

I tell him again about my finding the Bible and getting a job where Cole worked, about my talking him off the bridge and going to the media. "Cole is dead now, and I know he didn't kill himself. I feel responsible."

"Just because you told the Trendalls he was suicidal?"

"Yes! I was trying to help and I made everything worse. The least I can do is make sure they don't get away with it. Those poor kids. Thinking their dad killed himself just when things were getting better. And little Ava, being so scared . . . and that sleazy man . . ."

He's quiet for a long moment, and I watch the headlights illuminating and darkening his face. I wonder if he's thinking what a fool I am.

He reaches across the seat and takes my hand. It quiets me, and suddenly I can't think about anything except his thumb stroking my skin. His eyes shimmer as he looks straight ahead. "You're the best person I know."

My heart hitches. I look down at his hand and fight the tears. I feel my trembling subside as gratitude falls over me, and with it, a stunning calm.

"We're going to Wichita Falls," he says after a moment. "It's about a hundred miles from Dallas. I've been there before. It's big enough that we can easily find a place to stay, and small enough that it might not be the first place they'd think of to look for you."

"If he knows you're involved with me, don't you think they'll be looking for your car?"

"Yeah, but I may have thrown them off track. I taped my phone to an eighteen-wheeler. He's probably headed somewhere on I-20. That'll keep them busy for a while."

"Do you think they'll do an APB or something?"

"You mean a BOLO? Be on the lookout? No, I don't think so. I think they're going rogue. There were no police escorts with them at the motel. Just the two of them. I'm sure they used their badges to get the cooperation of the motel manager, who probably showed them a surveillance video of you checking in, but I don't think they're wanting this to be a police-wide effort. They don't want anyone else apprehending you and getting your story."

"That's something. But what if the manager recognized me and called them?"

"Again, he would've called local police, not two Shreveport detectives' personal cell phones. No, I think it was my phone."

"When you went back into the department after I left Shreveport, did Keegan say anything to you about me?"

"No, but he had this look." I can see the wheels turning in his head. "But the other night, same night you saw Keegan in Dallas, I found Rollins in a bar in Marshall. I didn't get a lot out of him, but I guess I got his trust. Little while later, he gets a DUI driving home, and he calls me to bail him out. He tells me that Keegan doesn't trust me, but he—Rollins—does."

I look at him. "Keegan doesn't trust you? He knows?"

"I don't know how much he knows. Just that he's suspicious. Probably enough to keep close tabs on me. Or maybe he just thought I had a better chance of finding you than he did, especially when I headed to Dallas. I think we're okay. Your car is ditched. My phone is gone. I know this car isn't bugged or tracked. But just in case, I'll get a rental car when we get to Wichita Falls."

"Won't they track your credit card? Rental car companies won't take cash. I could buy a car on Craigslist. I've done it before with cash and there are no questions. But I'm running low."

"I have some cash," he says. "Brent's dad gave me some for travel. I guess this qualifies."

"He gave it to you to hunt for me."

"I look at it differently. I think he gave it to me to find Brent's killers and bring them to justice. That's what we're doing."

I stare at him for a long moment, taking in the myriad emotions packed into the expression in his eyes. "Do you feel guilty? Deceiving them?"

"Sometimes. But Brent would want this."

I swallow. "Yeah, he would. I never should have told him about my dad. I never should have opened up. I'm not a drinker. I hardly ever drink, because I don't like to lose control. But one night we had dinner and I had some wine, and it loosened me up, and he got me talking about my dad's death and all that happened."

"And he latched onto it like a dog with a bone? That was Brent. I remember when we were around twelve or so, he developed an interest in the JFK shooting, and he spent a year reading everything he could get his hands on, culling out every conspiracy theory. He even talked his parents into taking us to Dallas that summer so he could walk on the grassy knoll and figure out where everything happened. He was convinced he was going to get to the bottom of the shooting."

I smile. "That sounds just like him. Did he?"

"He finally agreed with what the government concluded. Once he was satisfied, he wrote this long report in history class for extra credit and moved on to something else. Guess he was a born journalist."

"That's how he was with this, and honestly, the more he found out, the more grateful I was. I really thought he might find the evidence I needed to take down the people who killed my dad. And that morning, he called me, so excited. He said he had something for me, that he'd put the flash drive in the mail to me, but he couldn't wait so he wanted me to come by. I went by on my lunch hour . . . and that was when . . ." My voice falls off.

"Yeah," I say. "They must have found out what he was doing. He had probably just done that interview with Sara Meadows."

"And somehow they knew I was going to find him."

"They knew somehow that he'd called you. They may have tapped his phone. Or maybe they would have set up *whoever* found him—didn't have to be you. His mom, his cleaning lady, a coworker . . . We may never know that."

"They're bloodthirsty animals," I whisper. "They have to be stopped."

He squeezes my hand, then strokes it with his thumb again. "They will be," he says. "I promise you that."

51

CASEY

We get to Wichita Falls, and I wait in the car as Dylan goes into the office and gets us a suite with two bedrooms. At first I worry about the intimacy of sharing a suite, and I tell him so, but he insists that he's not leaving me alone tonight. He wants to stand guard. After he gets the key, we drive through a fast-food place and get some salads, then go to our suite. It's a small suite with a tiny sitting area and a TV, but there are two bedrooms and two bathrooms. I suddenly feel so tired.

When we put our things down, he grabs my hand and leads

me to the couch. He sits on the coffee table, facing me. "You've hurt your arm or your shoulder, and your ankle is swollen like a bowling ball. Let me see."

I put my foot on the table next to him, and he examines it. "Was this from jumping out the window?"

"Yeah," I say. "It's okay. I'll put some ice on it."

"I'll get you some. What about your shoulder?"

"It's okay. Just bruised when they were ramming me in the car. I slammed against the door."

He moves my foot around, and I suck in a breath through clenched teeth. "It probably needs X-rays," he says.

"Well, that's out of the question."

"Yeah. Let's hope it's just sprained." He gets up and grabs his room key off the table. "I'll go get the ice. Want anything else?"

"No thanks," I say.

He finds the ice bucket. "You're low maintenance. You just may be my dream girl."

I laugh now.

He pauses at the door. "I like how at home your grin lines are around your eyes."

"I used to use them a lot."

He brings the ice back and fashions an ice pack out of the bucket's plastic bag so it doesn't hurt my skin. He takes the pillowcase off his pillow and puts the ice pack inside it. "You should go put your foot up. Get some sleep while you can."

"I don't know if I can sleep," I say. "I keep thinking about

Ava . . . and that man . . . and this just becoming a way of life for her while her parents get away with everything. She's only seven."

I tell him again about her hiding in the bathroom stall, then being handed over to the man.

"It's not right, Dylan. I know I need to lay low with all this stuff going on, but I keep thinking of her. Is there something you can do to investigate? Some way you could go to the accident scene or look at his car or something?"

"I'm sure the police are investigating."

"I'm *not* sure," I say. "Why would they? He had reason to kill himself, if they don't consider that things were turning around."

"They will consider that, Casey."

"But they've already told the press it was a suicide. And they know Ava was abused, but they think Cole did it. Now that he's dead, if they just close the case, that man will keep doing it. I can't stand it."

Dylan lets out a long breath, but I see him thinking it through. "You're sure he's abusing her?"

I tell him everything I saw again and what Cole said about Ava accusing a guy named Fred.

Finally, I see that he's coming around. "If I promise that in the morning I'll go back to Dallas and see what I can find out, will you go lie down?"

"But how will you do that?" I ask.

"I don't know exactly. Let me think about it."

"And if I fall asleep, you'll wake me up if . . . ?" My voice trails off.

"You're kidding, aren't you? You know I'll wake you up if anything happens."

Our eyes meet and hold for a moment longer than necessary. I'm losing it, I tell myself. Just because he's helping me doesn't mean he's in love with me. I'm lapping up his attention like a drug.

I make myself get up. He takes my hand, looks up at me. Again, I meet his eyes.

For a moment, I think he might kiss me, and I feel the magnetic pull of his wet lips. I could just bend down a few inches and kiss him myself . . .

Then he drops my hand and whispers, "Get some sleep."

I feel safer than I've felt since Brent was murdered, and I fall into a deep sleep.

52

KEEGAN

The photoshopped rendering I've gotten back from our forensic artist is better than I could have hoped. I enlarge it on my laptop screen and lean back and laugh. "This is perfect. Black hair, heavy eye makeup."

Rollins is driving our rental car tonight, since I don't want to attract attention in my Jag, and he glances over at me. His breath smells like cough drops, which he sucks on every waking moment, probably to hide the alcohol smell. "Is that how she looked?"

"I only saw her in my headlights for a second, but this is it, man. She just came out of nowhere. Freaked me out. I didn't know how long she'd been there, what she saw. I tried to find her but she got past me. There were families pulling out of the parking lot, and it was dark, and I looked into each car and didn't see anyone who looked like her. I still don't know if she left on foot or drove right past me."

"Here's the list of local media who are waiting for the email," Rollins says, pulling an index card out of his pocket. "Want to send it now?"

"No, the motel guy said she was in a red wig. I'm waiting for that rendering. Maybe I should get a picture of Dylan to send them too."

Rollins stares through the windshield at the traffic ahead of us on I-20. "Listen to me for a minute," he says, rubbing his chin.

I turn and look at him. "What?"

"I think you're making a mistake. You can't name him as an accessory when we don't know for sure he's helping her."

"Then explain to me how our tracking him led us right to her room tonight. He's about to lead us to her again, mark my word."

"But what if that's not what happened? What if he was tracking her too? We need to talk to him and find out if he saw her."

"Rollins, what is it with you? You got a man-crush on this guy?"

"Come on," he says. "I'm just saying that the chief is not

going to like it if we make a big stink about him outsourcing the hunt for Casey Cox, and insinuate that his guy flipped, when we don't know that he did. Why would he, anyway?"

"Okay, the alcohol is addling your brain, dude. You need to dry up."

He grunts and looks at me. "What are you talking about? I haven't had a drink all day."

I twist in my seat and reach into the backseat for the Igloo cooler. I open one of the bottled waters and take a swig. "Vodka."

He broods for a minute. "I didn't drink it," he says. "I'm making sense, Gordon, and you know it."

"Okay, you want to know why he would turn on us? Maybe he figured the whole thing out, idiot! Maybe he's talked to her. Maybe he *believes* her! And if that's true and he rats us out, then we're sunk, you and me. Do you get that?"

He gets quiet as he always does when I rag on him. I bite my lip until I taste blood, then I check the GPS locator app that I've linked to Dylan's phone. We're catching up to him. Should be another fifteen minutes or so.

I think over what Rollins has said. Maybe he's right about Chief Gates getting a burr in his saddle over our outing Dylan to the world. It would be an embarrassment and would upset Jim and Elise Pace. Maybe it is an overreaction.

A new email appears in my inbox. "Here's the other picture of her. I'll just send her pictures for now."

Rollins is still sulking. I get the index card and turn on the interior light so I can read it. I type the addresses of our contacts at the news outlets, draft the official statement I'm giving them about her recently being seen in their area, and attach her picture.

Then I press Send. "You sure they're waiting for it?"

"Yep," Rollins says. "With bated breath."

"So how close are we to him?" I click on the GPS banner and enlarge it so it fills my screen. I try to locate the blue ball that indicates Dylan's location, but I don't see it anymore. "Wait a minute."

"What?"

"The location. It's dropped off. Are you kidding me?"

"Maybe he stopped."

"It's tracking his phone! There's no reason it would go off just because he stopped. What the—"

"His battery died?"

I let that sink in, then I slam my hand on the dashboard and curse. I punch the light back out and put my hands over my face. "I don't believe this. How can this moron let his phone die in the middle of an investigation!"

"So what do we do?" he asks.

"Keep driving. Maybe he'll realize it's dead and plug it in."

But we drive for half an hour more and never find him. Finally, we give up and I seethe as we head back to Dallas.

53

_____

DYLAN

Casey sleeps hard all night. I doze off and on, sitting in the dark at the hotel window, watching every car that comes into the parking lot. I wonder if Keegan has caught up to the eighteen-wheeler with my phone yet, or if the trail ended when the battery died.

It's six a.m., and I turn on the TV. I flip around until I find a Dallas station. They cover a city council meeting and the governor's speech at an NAACP meeting. Then I hear Casey's name.

I spring to my feet and see the artist's sketch of Casey's face with her current black hairstyle. I go to her bedroom doorway. "Casey, wake up!"

She jumps too fast out of her sleep and sits bolt upright. "What?"

"In here!"

She gets out of bed and stumbles into the living room, and sucks in a breath as she sees the rendering. "It's me."

"You have to change your hair."

She looks around. "The wigs."

"Not the red one. They have that too. It's going to get harder and harder to disguise yourself. They have you with long blonde hair, shorter blonde hair, black hair, short red hair, heavy makeup, no makeup . . ."

"I'll wear the long brown one. Sunglasses. What if someone saw me here last night? What if security cameras got me?"

"You didn't go into the office. I scoped out the cameras. I don't think they got you."

"But what about you? What if they're looking for you?"

"They didn't put me on the news. The hotel managers won't be looking for me."

"Where is this broadcast from?"

"Dallas."

She sinks onto the couch, rubs her eyes. She's still wearing the clothes she was in last night. I wonder why she didn't put on her pajamas. Maybe she doesn't have any with her.

"They'll call. My landlady, her daughter. The people I

worked with. They'll see this and know it was me. What number is that?"

I look at the number they're showing on the screen. "Unbelievable. It's Keegan's cell phone."

"Can he do that?"

"He's not supposed to. He'd probably rather get forgiveness than permission. It shows how desperate he's gotten."

"He'll hear from them anytime now."

"It's okay. Put the wig on now. Just keep it on. Don't ever take your sunglasses off."

She goes in her room to grab her duffel bag. When I step into the doorway, she's putting on the brown wig. Casey looks good no matter how she wears her hair.

"Yeah, that one," I say. "It's a little different." I don't tell her, but she still looks too much like herself.

"I'll work on it," she says.

54

KEEGAN

'm a genius," I tell Rollins as we sit out by the pool at my Dallas house. Candy has gone to show a house, and I don't expect her back for a while. I left Rollins sleeping in a guest room, and as he comes out to find me, I can't help crowing. "The media idea was perfect. Calls have been coming in all morning."

He sits down at the patio table, looking a little hung over. "Any leads?"

"Tons of leads, man. I heard from two people who worked with Casey who say she left work in the middle of the day a few days ago and never came back, and a landlady who says she's been renting a room but hasn't been there in a couple of days. And there's this guy who died while she was working there. I'm trying to figure out—"

"Someone died? Who?"

I show him the webpage I've pulled up about Cole Whittington. "Drove his car off a cliff the other day. Police are calling it a suicide, but maybe we can use it."

My phone rings again, and I check the readout. I don't know the number, but I click it on. "Detective Keegan."

"Yeah, is this the number to report sightings of that Casey Cox woman?"

The voice is a woman's, husky and hoarse, and slightly slurred. "Yeah, what you got?"

"We had some . . . dealings with her."

"Yeah?"

"She was stalking us. That man Cole Whittington molested our daughter, and she was friends with him and started following us everywhere. She assaulted my husband."

"Wait." I stop her and jot the information down. "What's your name?"

"Tiffany Trendall," she says.

I put it on speakerphone so Rollins can hear. "What do you mean she assaulted your husband?"

"That's not the worst of it," she says. "She killed that guy . . . Cole Whittington. She ran him off the road."

I get to my feet, locking eyes with Rollins. "Didn't police rule that a suicide?"

"Yeah, but it wasn't. She was obsessed with him. I bet she killed him."

"You bet?" Rollins cuts in. "You don't know that for sure?"

"What do you think?" she says. "You think it's a coincidence that a known killer is here in Dallas, working at his family business, and he winds up dead?"

I ask to speak to her husband, and he seems a little less slurred, but equally adamant that Cox must be the one who killed Cole Whittington. When I'm finished with the conversation, I cut the phone off and let out a laugh that rises over the whole neighborhood. "Are you kidding me? This is too good to be true. A dead guy?"

Rollins laughs for the first time in months. Maybe years. He lifts his hand to high-five me. "I'll call the media. This story just gets better and better."

55

DYLAN

I find Casey a car for sale on Craigslist for only $1,500. I ask the guy to bring it to a Walmart parking lot a mile from our hotel. Casey gives me a thousand dollars and I put in five hundred of my own money. The car's got 200,000 miles, but it's a Nissan. I think it'll hold up for Casey.

I pay the cash and sign the title over to Liana Winter, the ID that Casey will be using now. I shake his hand and watch him leave, then I leave the car in the Walmart parking lot and go get Casey. I leave my car down the street from our hotel, just in case, and we wind up back at the motel in hers. We're

eating drive-through burgers and fries in the room and trying to make our next game plan, when the news story on TV
changes. The Dallas station cuts in with breaking news, and
Casey's rendering comes up next to Cole's face.

Casey sucks in a breath.

We listen as the anchor excitedly tells of the connection
between Casey and Cole Whittington, who police now suspect
may have been run off the road by the fugitive killer.

Casey springs up. "*What!*" Terror and shock drag on
her jaw.

I get up and pace, trying to think. This will change the
whole narrative. The stuff we've been compiling won't be considered seriously if they think she's killed more people.

"They think I killed Cole?" She's almost hysterical now.
"How could they think—"

I start pulling on my shoes. "Tell me where the Trendalls
live," I say.

She gives me their address. "Dylan, I know they did it.
I know they did. They probably called Keegan themselves,
maybe even the media, and told them this. They ran me off the
road, and they did the same thing with Cole. And now they're
taking advantage of the media coverage to get the heat off
themselves." She goes into the bedroom, and I hear her throwing her things into her bag.

I go to the door of her room. "Casey."

"I have to go back. I have to find their truck. I know it's
got evidence on it. It wasn't at their house after his wreck—I

looked for it. They hid it somewhere so the police wouldn't connect them."

"Now they'll have dents on their van too," I say.

"And those should show paint that connects it to my car. They've probably identified it by now."

"Casey, I'll go back. You have to stay here. I'll pretend I'm still on your case, looking for you. I'll find out what the police know. I'll look at Cole's car. Maybe I can find that truck."

"This is out of control!" she cries. "My family . . . what are they going to think?"

"They'll think you've been framed again!"

"It's got a life of its own. I can't keep hiding."

"You can today."

She looks at me, suddenly present again. "Take my car. Yours is dented. It might connect you to my wreck."

I nod. "Yeah, okay." I get her keys and leave her mine.

I go to the door, open it, and stick the Do Not Disturb sign in the key slot. I close it again. "You don't open this. If anyone knocks, you call through the door and say you're trying to sleep. And you don't even *think* about leaving here to work on Cole's case."

"What if they come in anyway? If it's the police?"

"Go out the window again and text me." I grab my computer and make sure she has all the information I have on hers. "I'll get you more food before I go. But I have to hurry."

I get her more vending machine food. I hear vacuum cleaners up the hall, but no one is watching me. I go back in and leave everything on the table. She's parked, frozen, in front of the TV.

"Casey, are you gonna be all right?"

She nods and wipes her face. "Yeah."

"I'll call you. Keep your phone charged."

"Yeah," she whispers again.

I'm not sure if she really is okay as I leave the hotel and go to her car.

56

DYLAN

I get to Dallas a couple of hours later, go to the police head-quarters, and show them my credentials. "I'm Dylan Roberts, contracted to work on the Casey Cox case with the Shreveport PD. Are you familiar with that case?"

The sergeant looks me over with disgust and picks up the phone. He walks a few steps away as he talks into it, and I can't hear him. Finally, he comes back. "The captain and the detective on that case are coming to talk to you." He leans over the counter. "They're not happy."

I brace myself as the captain emerges from a hallway. I extend my hand to introduce myself, but he rejects it.

"Why don't you just tell me who you think you are, coming into my jurisdiction without giving us the courtesy of a phone call letting us know that a known fugitive is here? Going into a motel with guns drawn without once looping us in!"

"That wasn't me," I say quickly. "I'm just a private investigator, contracted to find Casey Cox. I saw the report on the news."

"Just like us. You know how we look when the media calls to ask us about something this huge, and we don't know anything about it?"

"I recommend you call Chief Gates in Shreveport to complain. That's not how he wants things done. But I came to you as soon as I heard. Ask him about me. He'll vouch for me."

"I've already called him," he says. "First thing I did. But the damage is done."

"Well, maybe it can be undone when this case is wrapped up. I was hoping to talk to the detective who's working on the Cole Whittington case," I say. "I'm investigating the possible connection."

"She's coming," he says. "But if you do anything else in my jurisdiction without notifying us, you and me are gonna have a problem. You got that?"

"Yes, sir," I say.

A few minutes later a female detective comes down. She has a shock of bright orange hair—a color not known in real human follicles—and she looks about fifty. She has lines on her face that testify to the years of detective work she's done, and an air of confidence as she reaches out to shake my hand. "I'm Detective Powers. And you are?"

"Dylan Roberts," I say, and show her my credentials, then go over the situation again. She leads me back to her office and I follow her as we talk.

She's not as angry as the captain. "Yeah, we were treating the whole Whittington case as a suicide," she says. "Guy's been depressed, he's being accused of molesting a child, his kids are taken from them, he has to leave his wife so he can get them back. Stands to reason that he might decide to remove himself from the picture. After all, it was a one-car accident, and he drove off a cliff."

"Did the news reports change all that?"

"Well yeah, because we didn't know that a fugitive from a murder rap was working with Whittington and stalking him. She'd already been with him during one suicide attempt."

I look at her. "How do you know that?"

"Apparently he came back and told his mother that he'd been sitting on a bridge, thinking about jumping, and Cox had talked him down. You know, that girl sounds a little crazy in her head. Who knows why she'd be talking him down one minute, then running him off a cliff the next? Sounds like it's a game to her."

"Are there witnesses to Cole's crash?" I ask carefully.

"No, but we've given the case another look, reopened it, and we're calling it a *possible* homicide now. He'd been to court that morning and the kids had been returned to the wife, and with all the negative reports about his accusers, it seems like things should have turned around for him. I mean, of all the days to commit suicide, that was probably not the most likely one."

"Would it be possible for me to see the car?"

"Which one? Cole Whittington's car?" she asks.

"Right. Were there other cars?"

"I thought you might have been talking about Casey Cox's car. We found it parked on a bridge, smashed on both sides. It looks like she had a wreck there and abandoned it. Titled under the name Miranda Henley."

I try to look surprised.

"There were witnesses to that wreck, but no one could tell for sure what was happening."

"Did she hit another vehicle?"

"Looks like it, though it drove away. Witnesses say she got into another car and left the scene. We've gotten different accounts about the make and model of the car she got into."

I'm so glad I didn't drive my own car here. "So did you examine her car to see if it had any evidence of ramming into Whittington's car and running him off the road? Did you look at tire tracks at the cliff where he went off? Did they match hers?"

"Both are negative," she says. "No evidence of her car striking his, although whoever she rammed on that bridge, their gray paint is all over her car. Seems like it was a van or something, from where the sideswiping took place."

She offers to take me to the place where they have the Cole

Whittington car, but first she takes me by the spot where he went off the cliff.

Knowing what I know, that it was probably a truck that's missing from the Trendalls' house, I study the tire tracks.

"They're not from Whittington's car," she says before I can point that out. "Probably they're from a vehicle that sits higher up than a car, and they're big, like those of a full-size pickup truck. We don't know if these tracks are connected to his crash or if they were already there."

I look at how far the embankment is from the tire tracks. Then I study the rock that Cole's car would have bounced off, then rolled over, before dropping to a jolting stop. "Was he dead on impact?"

"Probably not, but he bled out. The side and the top of his car were smashed in. When we found him, he still had his seat belt on."

"Seat belt on? A guy who wanted to commit suicide wouldn't have put on his seat belt."

"That did give us pause, but we figured it was habit. Now we know better."

When we're done, she drives me to the garage where Cole's car has been towed.

She takes me in through an open bay. I see the mangled metal in which Cole Whittington was found, and I walk around the car, examining it. He would've been traveling north, so the cliff was to his right. A car that ran him off the road would have been ramming him on the left. I find some white scrapes around the height of the door handle, but much of the rest of the car is crunched up like a wad of paper.

"This right here," I say. "It looks like whoever ran him off the road sideswiped him right here. It's a white vehicle, probably a truck. It's too high to be a car."

"Casey was driving an Accord, right?"

"Yeah, black," I say. "This couldn't have been her car."

The detective nods. "Yeah, and as beaten up as her car was, it didn't have any paint on it the color of Whittington's car. But she could have been in a different vehicle. The girl's resourceful, I understand."

I don't comment on that. "So have you searched for the truck?"

"We're working on that right now. Maybe when we find it, it'll lead us to Casey Cox. Do you have any information that could help us with that?"

"No, but from the reports I've heard, Whittington's accusers should be looked at." I hesitate, then go on. "The media had just put out some negative information about them, and they were probably getting a little desperate."

"Yeah, we'll look at them. But in my experience the most obvious conclusion is the one we should draw first."

"In my experience, that works just fine until people start staging and framing. The most obvious conclusion is often the one that the killers want you to draw."

She bristles. "That's why we've just reopened the case. We're working on it. But we're really good at what we do."

———

"I don't doubt that at all," I say. "I'm just thinking that as I've worked on the Cox case, I've developed a pretty sound profile of her. This doesn't look like her. She seems more measured, less emotional."

"Are you getting that from the girl she rescued in Shady Grove? Or the best friend she stabbed to death in Shreveport?"

I don't dignify that with an answer. "I just don't want my investigation to get muddied up by this if Cox is not really involved." I thank her for her time and tell her I'll be in touch later to check on the investigation and see if she's learned anything about Casey. When she asks for my phone number, I give her my old one, the one that is taped to the bottom of a truck. I'll have to replace it soon anyway. I know better than to give her the new one, in case Keegan comes along. But I've gotten all I need to know from her for now.

57

CASEY

can't tear myself away from the television. When local news goes off, I switch to cable and see that they're treating Cole's case like an active murder investigation. You would think that the police had locked down the city of Dallas and were hunting for me in every home and business.

I can't believe my life has come to this. When Dylan calls to tell me what he's learned, I'm more sure than ever that the Trendalls are responsible for Cole's death. I know they're hiding that truck somewhere, and I try to give him the address of

Ava's abuser's house, but I'm not sure I've got it right. I'd written it on the papers the Trendalls took from my car.

"It was Cottonella, I think. It had a chain-link fence around the front and back yards. And there was a junkyard a couple of miles from the Bouncy House Heaven. Maybe it's there."

He takes it all down and says he'll get back to me.

On Fox News, they've assembled three attorneys who are discussing what detectives might be looking for in order to find me and stop my killing spree.

Then they bring in a psychologist who discusses my state of mind, what I was thinking when I helped the girl in Shady Grove, how I might be bipolar or schizophrenic, following the orders of voices in my head.

I force myself to turn off the TV, and I sit there a moment, my knee pulled up to my chest. I bury my face and cover my head as the chattering goes on. I *am* hearing voices. They *are* making me crazy.

A knock sounds on the door, making me jump.

"Housekeeping," someone says.

I jump up and go to the door. Without opening it, I call through, "I don't need service today."

The woman thanks me and goes about her business.

I pace back and forth across the living area of the suite, trying to decide what to do. I picture my mother watching television, shocked to see this new accusation coming against me, wondering how I got involved in this one. The media will be even more rabid. Hannah probably can't even take Emma into the backyard. I don't dare call her again. I can't jeopardize her safety more than I already have.

I turn the TV back on, flip channels until I see myself. It's a local channel, and they have breaking news. The correspondent is standing outside the Dallas Police Department, talking rapid-fire.

"Sources at the police department have indicated that they have leads on the whereabouts of fugitive murderer Casey Cox, and they believe her capture is imminent."

I suck in a breath and dash to the window to peer out through the heavy drapes. There's not much activity in the parking lot below, but I fully expect a convoy of police cars to arrive at any moment.

I limp to the bathroom and check my brown wig, throw all my things and Dylan's into our bags. I have to let him know I'm leaving. It's not safe for him to come back here.

My shoulder and ankle are better, but they still hurt as I walk purposefully to Dylan's car, load the bags into the backseat, and pull out of the parking lot. I call Dylan's burner phone as I drive away.

He answers quickly. "Hey."

"Are you alone?"

"Yeah."

"Dylan," I cut in. "I had to leave the hotel. There was a news alert on the local channel that said they have leads on my whereabouts and expect to capture me today."

"Well . . . I did see some local media out front when we got back from looking at Cole's car, but the detective didn't seem to know anything about a lead. I really think they would have told me, although they were pretty miffed that Keegan and Rollins hadn't looped them in."

"Are you sure your car isn't being tracked? I'm driving it."

"I searched it for a device. If they were tracking it, don't you think they would've come last night?"

"Yeah, I guess. I don't know where to go."

"Stay in Wichita Falls until I get back. I'm looking for the truck. It wasn't at the junkyard."

"Have you found the house?"

"No, not yet. You said Cottonella Street, right? There isn't a Cottonella. Are you sure you're remembering it right?"

"No, not at all."

"Well, can you tell me how to get there?"

"I followed from the Trendalls' house. They got back on that main road, Roosevelt, I think, and there was . . . I think I remember a bank near where they turned left. A green bank. Or maybe it wasn't a bank . . ."

"That's not very helpful. Let me keep trying these streets on the GPS."

Frustration claws at me. "I'm coming back. I know I can find it, Dylan."

"Casey, this is the very last place you should be!"

"It's the place I *have* to be."

"No, you can't—"

I click the phone off. I trust Dylan, but I have to do this.

———

I drive the speed limit back to Dallas, afraid to go one mile over.

When I get to Dallas, I drive to the Trendalls' house, then, as well as I can, retrace the path we took when I followed them that day. I see the bank on the left and turn there, then I come to a stop sign and try to remember if we turned left or right. I look up the road and see a church on the right, and it's familiar so I turn in that direction, hoping there'll be another landmark to remind me where else they turned. When I realize that I haven't seen this area before, I go back to that stop sign and go the opposite way. This time I feel like I'm going in the right direction. The buildings are looking familiar. I remember the dry cleaner on the corner, the park across the street.

And then I get to the neighborhood, and I recognize it because of the house with a goblin in the front yard. I try to remember which way they went, where they turned, and then I see a woman out watering her lawn, and I remember that I saw her before. I turn next to her house. And there it is, the house with the grass grown high and a fence around the front yard and back. I've found it! It's Cattonelle, not Cottonella.

I slow as I come to it. There isn't a white truck in the driveway or the open garage. But I drive around to the side and . . . there it is.

The truck is parked on the back gravel driveway, just within the enclosed back fence. I pick up my phone and turn it back on so I can let Dylan know. But before I can call him, I see something that makes me slam on my brakes.

———

A child is hunched under the truck.

I catch my breath and lean to look out my passenger window. It's little Ava on her hands and knees, hiding at the center of the truck's undercarriage.

Urgency hits me like an electric jolt. I drive around the block and find a house that doesn't have a car anywhere, so I park Dylan's car on the street in front of it. I get out and limp back to the house that backs up to the chain-link fence, my mind racing, trying to make a plan. If I can get to Ava, I can get her out of that yard.

But then what? I can't kidnap her.

I don't cut through the yards. Instead, I keep walking the block as I call Dylan, each step on my ankle shooting pain up my leg.

He answers after half a ring. "Casey, why did you turn off your phone?"

"Because I didn't want to be talked out of coming here," I say in a low voice. "Dylan, I found the truck. It's at that guy's house. It's Cattonelle Avenue, not Cottonella, and the house next door is 233."

"Got it. Where are you?"

"I'm near his house. Dylan, Ava is hiding under the truck! We have to help her."

He lets out a heavy breath. "I'm on my way. Just wait in the car. Please, Casey. I'll be there soon."

I tell him I'll wait, but as I walk back to the car, I cross between yards just to see if Ava is all right. She's still under the truck, but I hear a man's voice from inside the house, thundering out, "Ava!"

I can't leave her. I move closer to the fence and squat down. The truck is between me and the door where the man is standing, so he can't see me. "Ava?" I say as quietly as I can and still be heard.

Startled, she bumps her head as she turns toward me.

"Stay there, honey," I say, moving along the fence. "I have help coming." She's been crying, and she sucks in sobs and doesn't answer. "We're going to get you out of here. It won't be long."

She doesn't answer, but when she hears him yelling her name again, she covers her ears and squeezes her eyes shut.

I can't leave her. She doesn't realize he can see her under here if he comes outside to find her. She won't be able to get away.

I make the decision before I've even had time to formulate a plan. I stay hunched down behind the cover of the truck as I go around the corner of the fence. There's a gate there, and quietly, I open it. I know if I move the two feet to the truck he'll see me, so I wait there, motioning for Ava to come. But she doesn't move.

I'll have to go in. I wait until I hear the screen door bounce shut, then I dash into the yard and move to the side of the truck. I squat down and reach out to her. "Come here, honey. I'll get you away from here."

Opening her eyes, she looks at me, then back toward the house.

"Come on, sweetie. Hurry."

She scoots toward me, but she's still just out of my reach. She's trembling and drenched with sweat.

Suddenly I hear the screen door slam again, and she jerks back and covers her head.

I'm stuck now, unable to move without being seen. I wait for him to see her, and if he sees her, he'll see my feet. I freeze . . . waiting.

My phone rings. I grope for it, trying to silence it . . .

But in a fraction of a second he's there, holding a pistol aimed right at me.

He starts to laugh, revealing a missing front tooth. "Give me that phone."

I have no choice. I stand up slowly and toss him the phone.

He bends to get it. I don't know if he's seen Ava yet. I hope she's seen the open gate by now, and that she runs.

"I . . . I was looking for my dog . . . ," I say.

He laughs out loud then and shoves my phone into his back pocket. Then he pulls out his own. With the pistol still aimed at me, he thumb dials a number, then says, "You won't believe who's trespassing in my yard. I think it's that girl. Casey Cox."

58

CASEY

The man uses the pistol to threaten Ava out of her hiding place, and he takes us both into the house. She stops crying and gets that vacant look in her eyes again. Her nose is running and I wish I could wipe it.

The house is filthy and smells like rotting food and body odor, but the table is covered with yellow pill bottles and a quart-sized Ziploc bag full of pills. There's tinfoil and wrappers, and another bag of white powder.

So this is the thing important enough for the Trendalls to trade their tiny daughter's innocence.

For the first time, I'm glad there's a hell.

He sits down across from me and keeps his gun on me, as he waits for what I assume are the Trendalls to come over and deal with me. His TV is on, and I see my face on the screen again.

"You look different," he says, staring at me, "but I can see that it's you."

I don't say a word. I just sit there and wait, looking around and taking stock of everything in the place that I can use if I'm given an opportunity. He's locked the deadbolt on the back door. I look away, but in my mind I rehearse running to it, clicking the deadbolt to the right, throwing the door open, pushing through the screen door . . .

But what about Ava? I can't leave her here, and I can't just abduct her. But maybe she would follow me out and get away through the open gate.

I look around and see the dusty shelves with things I could throw or swing. There's a chipped vase I could use if I could get close enough to it.

Next to me on the table is a heavy glass ashtray, full of butts and ashes, close enough for me to reach. I could throw that.

He's taken my phone, but he's got it in his front shirt pocket now. Dylan has kept calling, but the man has silenced it. I study his bloodshot eyes. If he's a user and not just a dealer, that could work to my advantage.

Finally, I hear a vehicle outside, and the front door flies open. Nate and Tiffany rush in. "Mama!" Ava cries.

Tiffany and Nate ignore her. "Aw, man, this is perfect," Nate says. "We couldn't a planned this better."

"You killed Cole," I say through my teeth. "You ran him off the road. And you're letting this scum molest your daughter in exchange for drugs."

Defiant, Tiffany bends down in front of me. "You're the one who ran him off the road. That's what we told the cops. It's all over the news. We could shoot you right now and tell them you came after us. The whole world would congratulate us."

I glance at Ava, who's standing silent by the door. "You can't do this in front of your daughter," I say.

"Ava's mature for her age."

The tragedy in that statement almost undoes me.

Nate lights a cigarette and inhales, then reaches for the man's gun. But he won't surrender it. Nate points to me. "You sit still and you don't have to worry. Unless you give us a hard time, he's not gon' kill you."

"What are you going to do?" I ask.

Nate pulls out his phone. "I'm just gon' make a quick phone call." He navigates with his thumb, then clicks Call.

I hold my breath as I hear a man answering. Nate says, "Detective Keegan, Nate Trendall here. You'll never guess who's sitting in front of me."

59

CASEY

Sick, I spring to my feet at the name *Keegan*. I glance toward my phone, vibrating in the dealer's pocket. I take a quick inventory again—the ashtray, the vase, the bottles . . .

Nate clicks off the phone. "He'll be right here. Better clean up this place, Fred. Cops are on their way."

Fred curses and grabs some wadded plastic grocery bags, shakes a couple of them open, and starts awkwardly bagging the drugs and bottles with just one hand, since the other one is holding the gun. It's still pointed to me, but it moves around as he grabs the pills and bottles, shoving them into the bag.

I stand there a moment, rehearsing my choreography. Grab, throw, run . . . turn deadbolt, open door, push through screen door.

It's too many steps. There are three of them, and they'll catch me before I get there. I don't move, and I wait, counting the seconds, imagining how far away Keegan is. Maybe he's at Candace's. How long will it take him to get here?

Fred drops a few pills, and Tiffany goes after them. He moves the gun from me to her. "Back off!" he yells.

I grab the ashtray and lunge for the door, throw the deadbolt. He swings back around with the pistol.

I spin the ashtray like a Frisbee toward Fred's head. It hits him, knocking him back, and I get the door open and throw open the screen. It bounces behind me as I race across the yard toward the open gate.

A gunshot jerks me—pain crashing like lightning—as I reach the gate. I keep going . . . outside the fence, through the neighbor's backyard . . . between the houses on the other side.

I'm bleeding as I run, and the pain is almost paralyzing, but I make myself keep going. I emerge from between the houses on the street where the car is, but there's a family in the front yard near it, so I can't get to it. I race across the street, through some woods and up a side street, until I see a gas station up ahead. There's a bathroom on the outside. I stumble toward it and go in, locking the door. I try to catch my breath. I'm dizzy, nauseated, shivering, and sweating. I look in the smudged mirror.

My shoulder is soaked with blood and I can't move my arm. I press my hand against the wound and turn around to see my back. The back of my shoulder is bloody too. Exit wound, I think. I don't know if that's good or bad.

I sit on the lid of the toilet and hug myself. It's over. Keegan will find me now. I'm too weak to run. Keegan will murder me before I get to the jail, and they'll say my killing spree is over. Little Ava will go on suffering, and no one will stop them.

All I can do is wait for them to come.

60

CASEY

I don't know how much time has passed when I hear banging on the bathroom door. It's time, I think. They're here.

I don't answer. I stay back from the door, sure they'll kick it in. Then they'll throw me to the filthy floor, handcuff me, and drag me out in front of everyone.

But instead of the door crashing open, I hear a voice. "It's Dylan. Open the door!"

Gratitude propels me up and I turn the lock, pull the heavy door open. "Dylan!"

He glances at my bloody shoulder but doesn't miss a beat. "Come on. Into the car."

My new car is a couple feet from the door. He opens the back door and I fall onto the seat. He slams the door shut and runs around to the driver's side.

I lie down, shivering. He doesn't say a word until we're several miles away. Finally, I ask, "How did you find me?"

"The blood trail," he says. "I got to the house right after you got away and saw them running after you. They thought I was Keegan and told me they shot you and you ran away. I told them I'd take it from there."

"They called him. He's coming." I look down at my wound. The blood spot is bigger, and blood covers my hand. "Where are we going? Back to Wichita?"

"No," he says. "I'm taking you to the hospital."

I sit up. "No, you can't. I'm fine. There's an exit wound."

"You're not fine. The bullet could have nicked an artery. I'm not going to let you bleed to death."

"I ran half a mile like this. I'm okay." I don't know why my breath is so short. "Dylan, you can't take me to the hospital. You know what will happen. Just . . . just give me something to compress it. We can stop the bleeding."

"You can't even use your arm."

I'm sweating but freezing. My teeth are chattering.

He takes off his shirt, leaving only his undershirt. He turns down a dirt road off the main road we're on and drives for a mile or so. Then he pulls over and gets into the backseat.

"Sit up," he says, and I pull myself up. He gets a jacket I was lying on and drapes it over my shoulders. "You're going into shock," he says.

He wads his shirt and presses it to my exit wound beneath the jacket. "Lean back on this," he says. "Press against it."

I do what he says, gritting my teeth with the pain.

He presses the front wound with the heel of his hand and slips his arm around me, sliding me against him. "Warm up," he says, and I lean into him, warming.

My teeth stop chattering, and I lean my head against his shoulder. He pulls my wig off and leans his jaw against my head. "I don't think it's as much blood as I thought. I mean, it's bad, but it seems to be slowing. If it were an artery, it would keep bleeding. But you have to go to the hospital, Casey. None of this matters if you don't."

Nothing seems to matter anyway. "I've been praying," I whisper. "Talking to God. I feel him listening."

"He is, Casey. I promise you, he is."

"Your car," I say, following random thoughts. "It's parked on the street behind that house. Keegan will see it when he's looking for me."

"I know," he says. "I saw it when I was looking. I got your stuff out of it. It's in your trunk. We'll worry about getting my car back later. When I was following your blood trail, I called the detective on Cole's case and told her where the truck was, and that the man has been abusing Ava."

"You did?"

"Yes. That'll explain my car being there. They'll just think I'm looking for you on foot."

"He had drugs and pill bottles—white powder and about a gallon of white pills. Tell them that. Tell them he cleaned them up when Trendall called Keegan but I don't know where he hid them. Ava was terrified. He may have abused her since Cole's death—maybe today. They could examine her . . ."

"Ava's probably okay for now as long as they think cops are all over that place." He slides his arm out from behind me and leans up to his cup holder. He grabs a bottle of water, opens it. "Here, drink this."

I gulp the water down, so thirsty. It's like liquid energy.

"I think the bleeding has stopped," he says. "But I need someone to look at you. I have an idea."

He lays me back down, makes sure I'm comfortable. Then he dials a number as he gets back into the driver's seat. "Dex, it's me. Dylan."

I can hear a man's voice on the other end. "Dude, I've been calling you and calling you. Your phone goes straight to voice mail."

"Yeah, that phone is in the belly of an eighteen-wheeler. Where are you, man?"

"I was headed to Dallas. I'm about halfway there. I thought I might need to rescue you."

"You do. Can you meet me in Tyler in about an hour?"

"You bet."

"I have a patient for you," he says. "Your medic skills still sharp?"

"Like riding a bicycle," he says. "What you got?"

"Gunshot wound."

"You?"

"No, her."

I realize he's told a friend about me. I wonder who this guy is, why Dylan trusts him. But if he does, I do too.

61

DYLAN

We get to Tyler in forty-five minutes, and as I enter the city limits, I call Dex back. "You there yet?"

"Yeah, I'm at a drugstore here, getting supplies. You?"

"Just now. Where should we meet?"

"There's a deer camp a friend of mine took me to once. Hit Rio Range and go south about three miles. There's a mile marker sign. Don't remember the number, but right after that is a dirt driveway. Nobody'll be there this time of year."

"Can you get in?"

"Nope. But there's a gazebo on a pond, and I think it's a good place to work. Real private. Not your usual deer camp. How is she?"

"Okay," I say. "The bleeding stopped."

I've been keeping her talking all the way, just to make sure she wasn't losing consciousness. She's told me about when she and Hannah were kids, things they used to do with her mom and dad, where they went for Thanksgivings, what they got each Christmas, where they went on vacations . . . anything I can think of to keep her with me.

I make my way to Rio Range and turn south. I set my mileage to count off three miles, and then I see the marker. The dirt driveway is right past it, and there are fresh tire tracks. I turn in and drive up the dirt road and see Dex getting out of his truck.

"Forgot to tell you," I tell Casey. "Dex is an amputee."

"What did he lose?" she asks.

"Arm and leg."

"And he's going to do surgery on me?"

"I'll help. Don't worry."

"How did it happen?" she asks.

"IED explosion." I don't say more about that. "You can trust him. He's a good guy, and he's been helping me build our case."

I stop the car and get out, bump my fist against Dex's hook, then I open the back door and help Casey out. She's clearly weak, but she's sitting up and I see that there isn't more blood on the seat than there was before. I pull her to her feet and put my arm around her to steady her. "Dex, this is Casey."

He doesn't offer his hook, but extends his left hand instead. "Nice to meet you."

She holds up her hands. "Sorry, I'm kind of bloody. Thank you for coming."

"Yeah, let me take a look at that. Let's get you over here to the picnic table."

"Is this where they gut the deer?" she asks.

He chuckles. "No, they do that over there. This is for eating and performing minor surgery on gunshot victims. So what happened?"

I tell him as he examines her wound.

ᴗᴄ

A little while later, he's cleaned her up and sewn up her wounds with my help, then bandaged them and made her a sling. "I don't think the shoulder is broken, but I can't vouch for the tendons and ligaments."

He puts the sling over her head and helps her put her arm in it. "At least it's your left arm. You're right-handed, right?"

"Yeah," she says. "Were you right-handed?"

"Was. I've learned to do things with my left hand, but I still write like a third grader. They say learning to write with the other hand sharpens your brain, though, so . . . I'm probably up to a 180 IQ by now."

"Were you and Dylan in the same explosion?" she asks.

I'm quiet as Dex answers. "Yeah. If he wasn't there, I'd be dead."

"I remember that differently," I say.

"You got me out of the fire, Pretty Boy. Must have dragged me a block."

I seriously have no memory of that. I just remember his body blocking mine as the bomb went off.

"He saved me too," she says, and she smiles at me. Her face is pale, but I can see that she feels better.

"Well, I don't know what y'all plan to do next, but you're both gonna need new clothes. You can't be seen with blood all over you. Why don't I run to Walmart or somewhere and get you some clothes?"

Casey gives him her size and some cash that she has in her wallet in her jeans pocket. "Can you also get two new burner phones? They took mine, which will lead them to his."

Dex gives me a look.

"I destroyed mine on the way over," I say.

Dex heads off, leaving us here alone.

She's sitting on the picnic table, looking out at the pond, and I go sit beside her.

"I like him," she says.

"Told you. I brought him in when I couldn't be two places

at once. He's been trailing Keegan and Rollins for me. He's been helpful."

I put my arm around her and pull her against me, and she lays her head on my shoulder.

"You remember when we talked on the phone that first time," she asks, "and you told me to look where God is working? To see it?"

"Yeah," I say.

"I have been looking. I've seen. You know how he's been working?"

"How?"

"He brought you to me. He does care."

There's a knot in my throat, but I try to talk around it. "Yes, he does."

She looks up at me and I gaze down at her for a stricken moment, my heart breaking at the paleness of her eyes. Tears fill them as I move closer, fearing she might jerk back. But she moves infinitesimally closer, and as our lips meet, a thousand emotions roil up inside me . . . drowning me . . . breathing life into me. She touches my jaw, her fingertips like feathers. I touch hers, the soft, baby skin of her cheekbone, wet with salty tears. She smells of rubbing alcohol, but it hits me like a perfume that will forevermore remind me of her. When the kiss breaks, she looks at me, keeping her hand where it is. I press my forehead against hers.

She speaks in a whisper. "I have to go, you know. You have to stay."

I pull back. "No, I'll go with you. I'll take you where you want to go, and we'll work on—"

"No, it won't work. If they find out you were with me, that you helped me, you'll go to jail at the very least. Obstruction, accessory, harboring . . . We need more. You're the only one who can get it."

"But I don't want you out there alone."

"I've done it before. I can do it again."

"But you're too identifiable now."

"I'm good with disguises."

My mind races. I try to think it through, her lost again, me here. "You have to tell me where you're going. I can't be in the dark."

"I will when I get there. I still have my Liana Winter ID."

I can't stand the thought of losing her again, now that I've found her. "Casey, I don't want you to. I feel like I've waited my whole life . . ."

"What's the alternative?" she whispers. "I could turn myself in now, take our chances, try to get what we have to the press. But Keegan's too smart. They might be investigated for the money thing, but how can we prove they killed my dad or Brent or Sara Meadows? Their partners at the department will cover it up like they've done for years. They'll make my family suffer. If I ever make it to a cell, I'll wind up hanging from the light fixture, and they'll say it's suicide. We need more."

I know it's true, that she has to go, and I can't go with her.

But I don't want to let her out of my sight again. I kiss her once more, and I taste the salt in her tears. Or maybe they're my own.

When Dex comes back, I've come to terms with how it has to be. She changes clothes in the car, then I change mine, and we clean the blood off my seat.

When it's all done, I give Dex a brotherly hug. "Thanks for your help, man. Listen, I need to ask you one more favor."

"No more favors," he teases.

"This one's not that big. Just . . ." I pull my keys out of my pocket, take a small one off the key chain. "I need to give you this key to a safe deposit box at Regions Bank."

Dex takes it. "What is it for?"

"I have some of our evidence in that safe. We plan to send it to the media, but just in case that never happens . . . I want someone to have what I have."

"So if the earth opens and swallows you or you're beheaded by a lumber truck . . . you want me to take what's inside and give it to the press?"

"Yes. I want you to do it before you shed a tear over me or go to the funeral home or anything."

"Will do, man."

"So . . . she's leaving in the car. I have to get back to Dallas to get mine."

Dex looks at her over my shoulder. "You really letting her go? I was thinking she's a keeper."

"Just temporarily," I assure him. "When this is all over . . ."

He knows where I'm going with that, and he nods but doesn't make a joke out of it. He knows this is serious.

Dex says he'll drive me back to Dallas to get my car. I'll say I've been looking for her if anyone catches me. Casey can drive her car northeast and be out of the state in hours.

I tell her I'll ride with her up the gravel driveway. Casey thanks Dex and hugs him, then we drive toward the road.

"That seemed like the most peaceful place on earth," she whispers as we leave.

"There are lots of peaceful places," I tell her. "We'll find them together when all this is over."

She wipes tears as she stops the car at the end of the gravel road. I lean over and kiss her again, holding her soft face, knowing it might be the last time. A big part of me feels like I'll never see her again.

"What are you gonna do?" she asks.

"Keep playing the part," I say.

"But Keegan knows . . ."

"I've got a story. He may suspect, but he won't be sure, and I'll convince him that I'm still looking." I kiss her again. "It won't be long, Casey. We're going to nail him, and you'll come back and be with your family, and you and I—"

She touches my lips with her fingertips, stopping me. "Don't say it."

"Why?" I whisper.

"Because. It'll hurt more when it all blows up."

"We will," I assure her, but I'm not sure that's a promise I can keep.

I open my door and get out, go around to her side. She rolls the window down. "Thank you for everything, Dylan. I mean it. God . . . life . . . truth . . . everything."

"Call me," I say, and before the words are out of my mouth, she's driving away.

I want to run after her. I want to go with her. I want to scream at the world that she's innocent, that she's a victim of a group of killers who masquerade as our protectors. I want to end this right now.

But instead I walk back to where Dex is waiting.

62

CASEY

As I drive away from him, I wipe my tears on my sleeve. The future looks bleak, but I push that to the back of my mind and try instead to see God. He was there—in that house in Dallas, in the bathroom where I bled, at a deer camp where an amputee did surgery on me.

He was there when I fell in love.

I try to revise the vision I have of my future, to see it with Dylan, when all of this is behind us. It's faint, but it's there. I will cling to it. Wherever I go, if I can talk to him, I can make it through.

I want to call my mom and rest her fears, tell her that I'm going to prove my case, that I need her to hang on and not fall apart.

But I don't want to turn on the TV tonight and see her in a perp walk.

I turn on the radio, find a Dallas station that's giving a news update.

. . . Cole Whittington death. Police found the truck that allegedly ran Whittington off the road to his death. It was owned by Nate Trendall, the father of the little girl Whittington was accused of molesting. Child Protective Services has removed the seven-year-old from her home after an examination concluded that she was abused by Fred Mardeaux, a known drug dealer. Previous reports that fugitive Casey Cox was involved in Whittington's death were false. We'll have more on this story tonight at ten p.m.

My mouth stretches as relief overwhelms me. Ava's safe. Her abuser is in jail, and so is her father. Maybe her mother will be next.

I whisper a prayer for that little girl to be okay, and for Cole's wife and kids. I pray that everyone will know their father didn't leave them on purpose.

Fresh sorrow overcomes me—making it hard to see the road. I fling both my phone and the battery into a field. My new one is still in the Walmart bag Dex brought me.

A few miles up the road, I pull over and blow my nose, wipe my face, and check my wig, finger-combing the bangs. I look in all directions, trying to figure out which way to go. Finally, I take a right and head for Oklahoma or Arkansas, or farther north.

I try to think like a new woman. One I don't even know yet.

A NOTE FROM THE AUTHOR

Any of you who have read my books know that I often have characters who are experiencing terrible crises, and sometimes they're in danger, or some horrible event has changed their lives. I think that's partially because I have so many challenges in my own life. But there are times when I look back on years I complained my way through and realize those were really good years. I just wasn't paying attention. Have you ever spent years thinking you were fat, then twenty years later you see a picture of yourself and think, "I didn't look so bad then. What was I complaining about?" It's kind of that way for me when I think about all the grumbling I did years ago, when in fact, things were pretty good.

I was recently complaining to some friends about some

stresses in my life, and one of them wrote me an email that I will never forget.

The friend who wrote this is another writer—Athol Dickson, author of books like *The Cure* and *River Rising*. Athol suffered intense grief after his mother had a long, terrible struggle with cancer. He had trouble praying or reading the Bible or even thinking about God because he was so crushed. His wife took him on a road trip across the country, hoping to shake him out of his lethargy, and several days in, he says he remembers looking out through the windshield and seeing the most beautiful sunset he's ever seen, and he began to weep. He says he was filled with gratitude at that sunset, and it flipped something in him. From that point on, he looked for God in everything, finding reasons to be thankful.

He told me, "Starting immediately, thank God for every gift He gives, from those as small as a whiff of honeysuckle or jasmine in your backyard, to the realization that you just had a few moments without back pain, to really big things like the fact that [people you love] are in the next room safe and sound.

"I'm talking about the practice of intentional gratitude. 'Intentional,' because it involves an aggressive effort to remain aware of God's gifts as you move through your day, and to actively acknowledge each gift with a simple 'Thank You.'

". . . In a life filled with the practice of intentional gratitude, there can be no 'Yes, but . . .' or 'It's not fair,' or 'Why me?' downward spiraling kinds of thinking. The two attitudes simply do not mix. Also, to focus on life's gifts you must live in the moment. With the practice of intentional gratitude, there is no time for regrets about the past, or worries about the future. There is only thankfulness for the here and now.

"This is the secret to contentment in any circumstance that Paul mentioned. It's also the secret to Paul's apparently impossible commands to pray without ceasing, because every expression of gratitude is a prayer, which means the practice of intentional gratitude leads directly to a life lived in continual worship."

He went on to say that a default setting in life is to take details for granted, when in fact almost every part of every day is a direct gift from God. He admonished me to work at giving thanks for things throughout the day. "It's not easy," he said, "but it's simple and actionable, and if you do take this seriously and work at it until it becomes a routine part of life, I promise unconditionally that you will regain your joy."

I'd love to tell you I knew this already and practiced it hourly, but I didn't. I decided to take his advice and try spinning my thoughts around. Instead of being upset that some crisis in my life has cost me a lot of money, I think, "God provided every penny of what we needed for that." Instead of whining that I had to do something I didn't want to do, I say, "God gave me the strength to get through that."

But it's a real effort for me. The problem is that sometimes I don't want to do it. Sometimes I'd rather cry or yell or complain, because I think I deserve to. But that only hurts me. When I started this, I realized I was going through most of my life ignoring those things that God deserved thanks for. I wasn't *looking* for God, so I kept missing Him.

Once I reviewed times when God quietly worked in my life at times when I was distracted and discouraged, and sometimes when I didn't even notice until years later, I began to see Him in the little things around me. It changed my brain. Dread became anticipation. Complaining turned into praise. As my friend instructed me so eloquently, practicing intentional gratitude for every little thing truly makes those that were unbearable before seem not only tolerable, but sometimes even blessings. But they're not always immediately obvious.

I'm hoping that God will use this lesson He's taken me through in my life to work in my readers' lives, too, and as Casey begins to see God in everyday things in her life—big and little—that my readers will begin looking for Him too.

Philippians 4:8 says, "Finally, brethren, whatever is true, whatever is honorable, whatever is right, whatever is pure, whatever is lovely, whatever is of good repute, if there is any excellence and if anything worthy of praise, dwell on these things."

I can't say it any better than that.

DISCUSSION QUESTIONS

1. Did Casey do the right thing by getting involved in Cole Whittington's life after finding his suicide note?
2. What motivates Casey into risking exposure to help others?
3. If you knew a child was being abused, what would you do to help?
4. What does Casey learn about prayer in this book? Did you learn anything new about prayer?
5. How does Casey's understanding of God move to another level in this book? How does Dylan help with her understanding?
6. Did any scenes shed light on the condition of PTSD?

7. Why do you think suicide is so prevalent among veterans?

8. What is the key thing about this book that will stay with you?

ACKNOWLEDGMENTS

Last year I celebrated my twentieth anniversary writing for Zondervan, which is part of HarperCollins. I've had the opportunity to go elsewhere, but I'm of the school of thought that "if it ain't broke, don't fix it." I enjoyed having my books published by such a professional group of people who loved books and had a common cause.

But several years ago, I got the news that HarperCollins had also purchased Thomas Nelson, another Christian publisher for whom I had written a Women of Faith book and some novellas. It didn't occur to me how drastically that purchase would impact my comfortable situation. Within a few weeks, I was told that Zondervan and Thomas Nelson would be merging under HarperCollins and would become HarperCollins Christian Publishing. All of the fiction would be moved to

Thomas Nelson, though it would still have the Zondervan imprint.

That meant that the entire team who had become like family to me at Zondervan in Grand Rapids, Michigan, was now changing to a team I hadn't worked with before at the Thomas Nelson headquarters in Nashville. As someone who doesn't like change, I was skeptical. I feared that my world was about to change, and I didn't know if I would stay once I fulfilled my contracts.

What happened instead was that the new team, under fiction publisher Daisy Hutton, gave me such a seamless transition that I've returned to my former level of comfort. I know I've thanked them before in other books, but I wanted to take a moment now to thank them again, with the added context I've given you above. My life would be much more stressful without the constant encouragement and can-do attitudes of all of those on my new publishing team. Daisy Hutton (Publisher) has been a true blessing in my life, along with Amanda Bostic (Associate Publisher), Paul Fisher (Senior Marketing Director), Kristen Golden (Marketing Manager), and Kayleigh Hines (Administrative Assistant). I don't know the names of all the sales reps who get my books into stores, but my gratitude for their work is boundless.

I also thank editors David Lambert and Ellen Tarver, who don't work for HCCP but who are still contracted to edit each of my books. HCCP has been wise enough to allow these relationships to continue so that my process is uninterrupted.

For that I am very grateful. And special thanks to my agent, Natasha Kern, who took me on when there wasn't much in it for her for several more years.

Here's to another twenty years with HarperCollins and all of the pros who help me get my books to you!

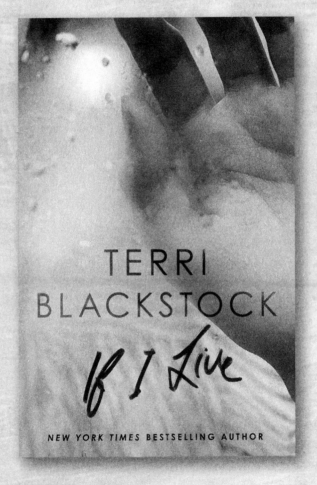

Terri Blackstock loves to hear from readers!
Contact her via social media or snail mail and
be sure to sign up for her newsletter!

www.TerriBlackstock.com
https://www.facebook.com/tblackstock.

THE MOONLIGHTERS SERIES
BY TERRI BLACKSTOCK

Can three sisters—a blogger, a cab driver, and a stay-at-home mom—with only a little courage and no experience, moonlight as private investigators to save the ones they love?

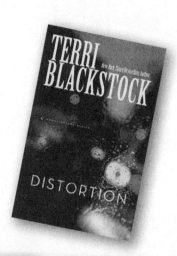

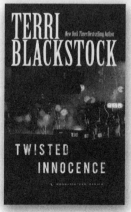

Available in print and e-book

THE RESTORATION SERIES

In the face of a crisis that sweeps an entire high-tech planet back to the age before electricity, the Brannings face a choice. Will they hoard their possessions to survive—or trust God to provide as they offer their resources to others? Terri Blackstock weaves a masterful what-if series in which global catastrophe reveals the darkness in human hearts—and lights the way to restoration for a self-centered world.

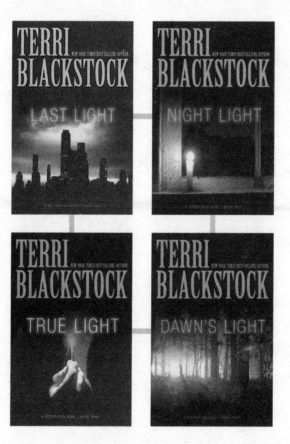

Available in print and e-book

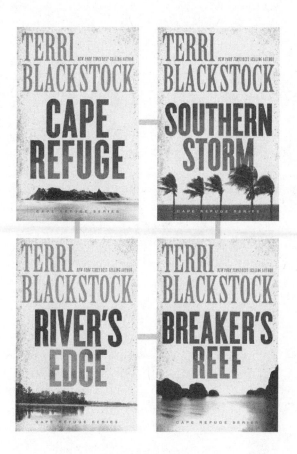

The Intervention Series

Available in print and e-book

ABOUT THE AUTHOR

Photo by Deryll Stegall

Terri Blackstock has sold over seven million books worldwide and is a *New York Times* bestselling author. She is the award-winning author of *Intervention*, *Vicious Cycle*, and *Downfall*, as well as the Moonlighters, Cape Refuge, Newpointe 911, SunCoast Chronicles, and Restoration series.

www.terriblackstock.com
Facebook: tblackstock
Twitter: @terriblackstock